THE PROTOS EXPERIMENT

Also by Simon Clark

BLOOD & GRIT
NAILED BY THE HEART
BLOOD CRAZY
DARKER
ON DEADLY GROUND –
(formerly KING BLOOD)
VAMPYRRHIC
THE FALL
JUDAS TREE
DARKNESS DEMANDS
NIGHT OF THE TRIFFIDS
STRANGER
VAMPYRRHIC RITES
THE DALEK FACTOR
IN THIS SKIN
THE TOWER
LONDON UNDER MIDNIGHT
DEATH'S DOMINION
THIS RAGE OF ECHOES
LUCIFER'S ARK
COLOUR OF ECHOES: A VAN GOGH MYSTERY –
(formerly THE MIDNIGHT MAN)
VENGEANCE CHILD
GHOST MONSTER
WHITBY VAMPYRRHIC
HIS VAMPYRRHIC BRIDE
HER VAMPYRRHIC HEART
INSPECTOR ABBERLINE & THE GODS OF ROME
SECRETS OF THE DEAD
INSPECTOR ABBERLINE & THE JUST KING
RAGE MASTER
SHERLOCK HOLMES: LORD OF DAMNATION
COLD LEGION
SHERLOCK HOLMES: A CASEBOOK
OF NIGHTMARES AND MONSTERS
BLOOD CRAZY: ATEN IN ABSENTIA
CALLISTO: BLOOD MISSION
BLOOD CRAZY: ATEN PRESENT

Praise for Simon Clark's work:

'A master of eerie thrills' – Richard Laymon

'Edgar Allan Poe for the 21st Century.' – *SFX*

'Not since I discovered Clive Barker have I enjoyed horror so much' – *Nightfall*

'His is surely the most outrageous imagination to grace horror since the discovery of Clive Barker' – *Hellnotes*

'The hottest new purveyor of horrific thrills currently working on these shores' – *Big Issue*

'Simon Clark is a wonderful writer. He has what it takes to be another Stephen King.' – Bentley Little

'To say that Simon Clark is the best novelist to emerge this decade is self-evident. Simon has simply outgrown genre restrictions.' – Andrew Darlington

'Simon Clark has been a vibrant stalwart of the British horror scene for the best part of 25 years. His work is, nevertheless, consistently fresh, urgent and powerful, informed by a broad knowledge of and affection for the classic genre touchstones.' – Conrad Williams

'Clark has the ability to keep the reader looking over his shoulder to make sure that sudden noise you hear is just the summer breeze rattling the window' – CNN.com

'The horror in a Simon Clark book is never where you expect it to be; it's subtle and disarming...it'll creep up on you, politely tap you on the shoulder, then grab you by the throat, squeeze tight and won't let go until it's finished with you...A distinctive, respected, uniquely British voice in the horror genre – Simon Clark is a dark master of his art.' – David Moody

Simon Clark's novels include *Blood Crazy* (now an entire series of books), *Vampyrrhic, Darkness Demands, Stranger, Whitby Vampyrrhic, Secrets of the Dead,* and the British Fantasy award-winning *The Night of the Triffids*, which was broadcast as a five-part drama series by BBC radio.

Weird House Press have recently issued Simon's new collection, *Sherlock Holmes: A Casebook of Nightmares and Monsters,* and the novels *Sherlock Holmes: Lord of Damnation* and *Callisto: Blood Mission.*

He has also scripted audio dramas for Big Finish, including for their reboot of the apocalyptic drama, *Survivors* and their multi-platform *Doom's Day*.

The Cannes Film Festival 2024 saw the premiere of *The Protos Experiment*, a dystopian Sci-Fi/Horror feature film, which he co-scripted with Brian Avenet-Bradley.

Simon lives in Yorkshire, England, where he can be seen roaming this legend-haunted landscape with a black and white Border Collie by the name of Mylo

Website: nailedbytheheart.com

Twitter: hotelmidnight

Facebook: SimonClarkAuthor

THE PROTOS EXPERIMENT

A Novel by Simon Clark

Based on a film script by Simon Clark and Brian Avenet-Bradley

Darkness Visible

ACKNOWLEDGEMENTS

Simon Clark would like to thank the following individuals for their role in bringing *The Protos Experiment* to life

As always, it's a conundrum to put a list of wonderful individuals in order. However, I've opted for something as close as I can to chronological order, when everyone in this list began their involvement with *The Protos Experiment*, whether it be the screenplay, film or the novel you now hold in your hands.

Julian Richards, Brian Avenet-Bradley, Laurence Avenet-Bradley, Mike Sharrak, Roger Keen.

Also, my heartfelt thanks to the cast and crew who worked so hard and with such dedication on the film. And a special 'thank you' to Trista Robinson, who so kindly gave her permission to use her likeness on the cover of this book.

INTRODUCTIONS TO THE NOVEL AND THE FILM

CREATING PROTOS

Simon Clark
Writer

'How does a story become a film?'

There must be as many answers to that particular question as there are fish in the ocean.

Though my experience of working in the movie industry is slight, I imagine that in many cases, Film and TV companies will commission drama content as part of their business. Other cases will see a famous actor making the kind of film they want to appear in. Or a director might read a novel that they fall in love with, then move heaven and earth to turn the book into a film.

If I direct the question at me, and change the wording slightly, and ask, 'How did your story become a film?' I can share with you my own personal experiences that took my initial idea from my customary messily scribbled note on a piece of paper, to sitting down one day and watching the completed production.

I'd written a short story, 'Murder in Chains', many years ago. It had one of those plots that continued to prod away at something in the back of my mind, as if the story wasn't finished with me yet. Eventually, the prodding led me to realizing that a story of just seven thousand words could be the foundation for a full-length film.

So, great. I had the idea for a film. One that would be full of twists and turns and drama. A film that would ask how far we can trust one another, and ask how far we can trust ourselves in times of extreme crisis. And, crucially, enquire to what extent do our memories make us into the people we are. However, my first obstacle to turning the idea into an onscreen drama was... 'Where do I begin?' I'd never written a film script before. I had no track record in the movie industry. Yes, okay, I'd written plenty of short stories and novels. The nearest I'd come to writing a screenplay was adapting my novel *The Night of the Triffids* into a Big Finish audio drama. Something, to this day, I'm very proud of. And though the audio script for *Triffids* wasn't a screenplay, I did gain experience writing dialogue for actors. And, just to digress slightly, if John Ainsworth, a producer at Big Finish, hadn't encouraged me to pen the adaptation for the audio, I would never have mustered the confidence to write a film script, and *The Protos Experiment* simply would not exist.

Earlier, I said that *The Protos Experiment* began with an idea. Eventually, that idea would become a massive journey, one full of twists and turns and drama in its own right. However, at my 'this seems a good idea for a film' stage, nobody had commissioned the script. Nobody knew that I even planned to write one. Therefore, that first step of the journey was to switch on the computer, open a new file, and begin typing. This is the first part of the first scene I wrote, back in the Summer of 2020: -

```
INT. WAREHOUSE - DAY


JOHN's unconscious, lying on the floor. John
wakes. Groggy, he turns his head and sees a
chain. Puzzled, he stares at the chain, trying
to process what's happened to him, thinking,
'What is this place? How did I get here?'

John realizes that the chain is padlocked to a
steel collar around his neck. He sits up,
horrified. His eyes lock onto the chain,
following those links as they stretch five
metres along the floor. The other end of the
chain is padlocked to a steel collar that
encircles GOLIATH'S neck. The big man lies
there, unconscious.

Even though Goliath sleeps, he radiates brutal
aggression.

John tugs the chain at his neck; it's padlocked
securely.  Once again, he looks at the
unfamiliar surroundings.

                    JOHN (TO SELF)
               How did I get here?

Goliath's eyes snap open to reveal rage-filled
eyes.
```

There are many reading this who know a heck of a lot more about scriptwriting than I did, back in 2020. Admittedly, my script was unconventional in execution. I wrote it in Word, while most scriptwriters use a dedicated screenplay software. I didn't even own such a program. However, somehow, I got there, with the help of plenty of strong coffee – that, and heading out into the countryside with Mylo, the Border Collie, for plot-mulling walks. After six months of translating the story, which was blazing so impatiently inside my head, into words on a screen, I had a completed script sitting there on my computer.

The next obstacle on the script-to-shooting journey now blocked all forward progress. I didn't have any contacts in the motion picture industry. So, who could I send the script to? Would all the filmmakers' doors remain sealed tightly shut to me? Would I end up with a completed script gathering proverbial cobwebs on my computer, which would never have actors speak its lines? Would one of the key characters forever lie there on the floor with a chain fastened around his neck? Possibly so.

Then I remembered a name. It was the name of someone who did work in the film industry. This would be a long shot because I hadn't emailed him for years and years. However, we follow each other on X. So, I gathered my resolve to send a direct message to him out of the blue, mentioning that I was trying to sell a script, and knowing full well that he might have a hundred writers a week emailing their screenplays to him. Even at the time, I did think that I was being brazenly presumptuous asking for his help to find a producer for my work. Don't you hear countless stories of long-suffering film agents and directors having a script thrust at them by total strangers?

And yet I wrote this DM to Julian Richards, CEO and Head of Production at Jinga Films: 'Hello, we haven't been in touch for a while. However, I've written a script, and I wondered if you would ...' And so on. Very graciously, Julian replied with these wonderful words: 'Yes, Simon. Please send me your script...'

To my surprise, and very happy amazement, the script found its way into the hands of Brian and Laurence Avenet-Bradley. They are L.A. professionals in the Film and TV industry. They are also people who love film, and they have independently produced their own features. These include *Dark Remains, Ghost of the Needle,* and the extremely successful *Echoes of Fear*, starring Trista Robinson.

Then I receive another email from Julian saying that Brian and Laurence would love to produce my script. There follows several moments of heart-pounding excitement as I try to come to grips with the news – that *The Protos Experiment* is poised to be launched into pre-production. For a while, I admit it, I was stunned. All the hitherto daunting obstacles were being overcome; soon the cameras would roll.

Now, we take a leap forward to January, 2021, when Brian, Laurence and I meet via Zoom for the first time. The video call lasts a formidable two hours but we talk so enthusiastically about *The*

Protos Experiment that time flies. I'd swear only ten minutes have gone by – not one hundred and twenty. I learn that Brian and Laurence have lots of ambitious ideas for the story. Initially, I envisaged that *The Protos Experiment* (back then, my working title was *Taste Hell*) would be filmed in one studio with a very minimalist set. Brian and Laurence explained that they wanted to expand the story. To make it bigger. More ambitious. And to make good use of some fantastic locations they had scouted.

After that first meeting, the story grew much, *much* bigger. During numerous Zoom meetings, Laurence, Brian and I brainstormed ideas. Everything from character motivations, to plot, to stunts, to special effects – and much more. And when the three of us agreed that certain characters would be wearing sophisticated electronic headsets, it was Laurence who took on the job of inventing these complex electronic devices, then she sat down with a soldering iron, diodes, wiring, and the latest chip technology, and built fully functional headsets that the actors would wear in demanding locations.

After those epic brainstorming sessions, Brian and I worked on the script to accommodate far more wide-ranging locations, and even more powerful scenes than I had originally created. Brian's visionary input soon made me realize that it would only be right and proper to suggest to him that he be acknowledged as being the co-author of the screenplay. Being the gentleman he is, he never asked for a co-credit; however, I made a strong case that he very much deserved that writer credit – and he accepted. And, yes indeed, I will be the first to admit that Brian's input raised the story to a much higher level.

And so, the journey from penning the script to shooting the film continued. There was a huge amount of work accomplished by Brian and Laurence in pre-production. They found the actors, hunted for the right studio, nailed down breathtaking locations in wilderness places, devised amazing props, eerie costumes, and they figured out how to create unique lighting solutions for scenes that I'd described as being lit in a decidedly unusual way to create an otherworldly, nightmarish environment for the action.

Pre-production was a fascinating time. I loved every moment of it. Though, admittedly, my contribution was from far away. Brian and Laurence live and work in California. I'm based in the English county of Yorkshire. Thankfully, Zoom brought us together at the speed of light, resulting in lots of brainstorming sessions. Also, we passed the script back and forth, each of us enlarging and enriching this story of dystopian evil.

Then, one memorable day, Brian emailed me a private link to a video streaming site with the words: 'For your eyes only, below is a link to the latest cut of the film. It's a fine cut – but very close to lock we hope!'

The journey was almost complete. I could sit down at the computer, headphones on, cup of coffee in hand...There's the title onscreen: *The Protos Experiment*. The character 'John' is lying on the concrete floor. The chain is fastened to his neck. And, ladies and gentlemen, the film begins to tell its story.

This is the perfect point to introduce to you Brian and Laurence Avenet-Bradley, and to invite you to read about their own experiences of *The Protos Experiment* – from when it was purely words on a page, to that exhilarating moment when Brian and Laurence shouted, 'Action', the lights blazed down, the camera started to run, and a group of amazingly talented actors and dedicated crew invoked their own brand of magic and brought the characters alive. The atmospheric score by Benedikt Brydern deserves a special mention, too. The music is as sublime as it is haunting – and, at times, as scary as hell.

Collaborating with Brian and Laurence was one of the best adventures of my career. Their energy, inventiveness, professionalism, and enthusiasm left me in total awe. The film they have created is astonishing. I love it. And I hope you will love it, too.

Therefore, please allow me to hand you over to Brian and Laurence. They have their own fascinating story to tell...

UNLEASHING PROTOS

Brian and Laurence Avenet-Bradley
The Production Team

The year was 2020, deep into lockdown...and little did we know that the Protos were coming.

We had finished our film *Echoes of Fear*, and Julian Richards at Jinga Films was handling its international sales. While discussing future films with him, he highly recommended we read a script by Simon called *Taste Hell*. We were intrigued and said, 'yes'. We're so glad we did.

Simon's script was a page turner, and when the script ended, we wanted the story to continue. Our producing partner, Mike Sharrak, loved it and felt the same. We wanted to know what happened to the characters and who was orchestrating their torment and also 'why'. So, we spoke with Simon via Zoom, and we learned that he had kept the script very contained to gear it towards a low budget projection. He was very receptive to expanding the story further. And thus began a fantastic collaboration, working together on the script for over a year. Through the drafts *The Protos Experiment* came to be, and the answer to the story's mystery revealed itself. We were all excited with how the shooting script ended up.

Now the challenge was to film it – because the carefully engineered low budget story, with only a couple of locations, had evolved to require numerous interior and remote exterior locations, more characters, more costumes, more props...You get the picture. We had really done a number on ourselves. But we rolled up our sleeves and called upon all of our years of indie filmmaking experience to figure out a way to pull it off. We assembled an amazing team— from the actors and the crew, all the way to the composer— who all believed in collaborating in making a film worthy of the story.

It was a tricky, demanding shoot. We had to create outfits that glowed – they kept shorting out due to the actors' sweat in the oppressive heat – and we also had to build unique blinder headsets that needed to remotely change color in synch. Multiple locations required an hour-and-a-half mountain hike carrying our gear. We filmed inside four challenging underground locations with different looks, and we also filmed inside a massive rock tunnel that was carved out by convicts to help an entire city flee a nuclear attack through the mountains. There were remote desert locations – including a hilltop where we were battered by wind so hard that part of an outfit was blown away and Mike had to improvise a replacement on the spot. There were complicated sets to build that needed to be shot in 360-degree views, and from above.

Once, while we were filming, we heard a real Swat team descending outside one of these sets, trying to capture a gunman; we kept rolling inside the studio as choppers thundered overhead.

And there were a fair number of bigger curveballs. But Simon was there in spirit every step of the way, and he continued to help adapt the script to knock those curveballs out of the park. And in the end, we had that rare, marvellous experience where all the production pieces fitted together to create something even beyond our original intentions. That does not happen often in filmmaking.

And now we, and you, have the great thrill of reading *The Protos Experiment* as a novel. Simon has taken the story and expanded it as only he can with his vivid imagination and his years of writing over forty novels and novellas in the horror and science fiction genres. For us, it's like discovering the story anew – because he's cracked open the story further by allowing us to peer into the minds of the characters. So, turn the page – you're in for one crazy and wild ride. Unleash the Protos!

CHAPTER ONE

The man lay in darkness.

This was self-imposed darkness.

Because he was afraid to open his eyes. If he opened his eyes, it would confirm the nagging suspicion that something terrible had happened to him. In fact, the *worst* thing that could happen. The nerves that ran through his flesh, from the back of his head, down his neck, spine, buttocks, to the very ends of his legs, confirmed that he lay on his back upon a hard surface.

Where would you find a hard and very flat surface like that?

The answer seared his mind. *On the steel table in a morgue. The cutting table. The table with drainage furrows and a sluice to wash away all that red stuff that pours out of a human being when the gruesome process of dissection begins.*

The man shuddered. Then asked himself what other kind of hard surface he could find himself lying upon. *Why, none other than the hard flatness of the bottom of a coffin. That's why I can't open my eyes. Because I am dead.*

Terror moved through his entire body, thickening the congealing blood inside his heart. His flesh was as cold as the granite slab of a tombstone. His nerves pulsated with dread. His belly felt like it was filling with liquid. Was that the first stage of physical corruption already taking place? Was his gut becoming bloated with the juices that putrefaction extracted from his intestine and liver and kidneys as the final rot set in?

The man tried to open his eyes. He couldn't.

Fear wouldn't permit him to raise his eyelids. Because he was terrified that he'd find himself looking up from an open casket at the funeral home ceiling. Or his eyes would consume the horrific vision of the mortician's bright lamp...just before the merciless flash of the scalpel blade dazzled him. And then the cutting would begin. To discover the cause of his death.

He thought: *No...you can't be dead...dead people don't think... Something must have happened to you.*

An accident?

But why am I lying on a hard surface? It's as flat as a tabletop. Flat as a mortuary slab...

The man tried to clench his fists and take a deep breath. However, his body didn't respond.

Perhaps I've fallen and I'm lying on the ground?

He recalled climbing the ladder to rescue that loveable rascal Lynxie. The cat had climbed onto the roof and couldn't get down. A scaredy cat...afraid of heights! The man felt an utterly irrational compulsion to laugh. Though he knew it would be screaming laughter – the screaming laughter of a man just before he was plunged into mind-shredding panic. But he couldn't laugh. He couldn't move so much as a finger. Even his tongue was paralyzed. Panic very nearly did overwhelm him, however, as images erupted inside his mind. Images of him lying on the ground after falling from the ladder (if that is what had happened). What if his neck was broken? After all, he couldn't move his arms and legs.

Nevertheless, his thoughts flowed smoothly as he issued this command to himself: *Open your eyes.*

No...I daren't. I don't want to see, because...

Because what? What is it that I don't want to see?

The man's stomach prickled as if some huge insect with pointed feet had crawled over him. Surely, just imagination. Yet the prickling was as intense as it was horrible. Once again, he wanted to scream. However, he couldn't even take in a big gulp of air that he could then vent from his lips in a howl of sheer fucking terror.

Think, he told himself. *Remember what you were doing just before the darkness came.*

He recalled bright flashes of memory. Yet he couldn't be certain that they were memories of what had happened immediately before his accident, or whatever it was that had befallen him. He recalled walking with Lynxie. After a great deal of time, and a massive expenditure of loving patience, he'd taught his cat to walk with a leash attached to her collar. It wasn't a desire to curb Lynxie's freedom, or to prevent her from playfully running around. No, the first house he'd owned was near a canyon that swarmed with rattlesnakes. He'd been afraid for the cat, worrying that one of those venomous serpents would kill her with a single toxic bite. Afterall, that's what had happened to his neighbor's dog. Therefore, being connected to his lovely tortoiseshell with the limpid yellow eyes felt much safer. He could prevent Lynxie from straying into long grass where the rattlers were lurking.

The man struggled to remember more.

One memory that came with shocking clarity was when he was five years old. He'd been staying at his grandmother's house – it was a funny little shack of a place made from yellow boards and had a roof of bright red tiles. His grandmother would gently put her hands on his shoulders, then look into his eyes with such a serious expression on her face that it would put a lump in his throat and a tingle of tears in his eyes. Her face would be so sad – it always moved him. Then she'd say, 'You can play in the yard with your toys but don't go into the forest. There's a lake there. It's so deep it goes down and down for hundreds of feet. The sides of the lake are sheer, like the face of a cliff. Should little boys and girls fall in there, they can't climb out the water. The sides of the lake are too steep and too slippery. There's nothing for children to hold onto to pull themselves out, and they sink all the way to the bottom where nasty creepy-crawlies live. Little children that fall into the lake never see their mommies and daddies again. That's an awful thing to imagine, isn't it, darling boy? Never going back home, and your toys just lying there all dusty in a box. They will never be played with any more...and your mom and dad are crying so hard because they know you will never be with them until you meet in Heaven.'

His grandmother was trying to protect him, of course. She didn't want him to fall into the lake, so she painted a grim picture of drowning to scare him so much that he'd never venture near the water. Yet her words gave him bad dreams at night.

Then, one afternoon, as he played with his toy cars in the yard, he heard shouts for help. The shouts came from the forest where shadows flowed amongst the trees, creating their own lake of darkness. A dry lake, granted, but that darkness was all-engulfing.

The cries for help continued. They were more desperate sounding now. He ran to the house to find his grandmother asleep on the sofa. She always had a nap in the afternoon. He almost woke her – in fact, he very nearly did. He was reaching out with both hands. He was ready to shake her shoulders as she snoozed on the couch, her silver hair fanning out over the big green cushion.

Then a thought occurred to him that took him by surprise. A thought that excited him and made him feel grownup. A moment later, he had darted from the house, pulled open the gate (taking care it didn't clatter shut behind him and so wake his grandmother). Then he ran along the path into the wood, and into the lake of dark shadows. There were no people about. He was all alone. He was a tiny figure flitting through the gloom, as vulnerable as can be. The path, which he followed, moved in elongated S shapes, weaving itself through the trees.

The shouts for help were more desperate now. They were a high sound – the sound was becoming fractured, as if whoever was shouting was too scared or too tired to shout properly. He wondered if a boy or a girl had become lost in the woods. His plan was to find them, then take them back to his grandmother's house. He imagined how surprised his grandmother would be. He pictured how she would laugh with delight and say how clever and brave he'd been.

The man recalled that how he, as a five-year-old, had run through the forest, his ears guiding him to the source of those cries for help. Then he had been struck in the face by a blast of light. He realized he'd run out from beneath the thick canopy of branches into sunlight. The lake was there, right in front of him. A circular expanse of water that was as black as liquid darkness. The same kind of black as the pupil of your eye.

The screams had stopped now.

He approached the edge of the lake. His blood turned to ice in his veins as he recalled his grandmother saying that the lake was hundreds of feet deep. That the sides were too steep to allow anyone to climb out. That anyone who fell in would scrabble and claw and helplessly grasp at the smooth sides of rock that formed the lake edge, and that they wouldn't be able to grab a hold of anything to pull themselves out onto dry land where they would be safe.

He remembered all those dreadful predictions made by his grandmother. How little boys and girls would struggle in vain to escape the water. That their death would be inevitable. That they would never see their parents again.

Gigantic trees grew up around the lake. To his five-year-old self, they looked like monsters. They were big, shaggy things, with branches that stretched out like claws. One tree was dead, all its leaves were gone, and it leaned over the lake. Its branches were jagged, zigzag shapes, so it looked like the branches were frozen lightning bolts that stabbed down into the body of the water.

Then came the dreadful moment when he'd looked down into the lake. Beneath its surface was the clear image of a face. This must have been the person who had been shouting for help. However, they could shout no more because their face had become submerged. They must have been too exhausted to swim. Their arms extended out at either side of their body, and the limbs did not move at all. The fingers were slightly curled inward. The fingernails were pale ovals beneath the surface. A pair of terrified eyes stared back at him. Somehow, they seemed to be eyes that screamed.

The eyes screamed out that the lady knew she was going to die.

Suffocation...even as a young child he knew that word possessed a dreadful meaning...*suffocation*. That meant you could not breathe. That even though your lungs hurt, and you wanted to suck oxygen into your body, you couldn't. He knew that *suffocation* meant just one thing – and that awful thing was **DEATH**.

There she was...in the water. And she was dying before his very eyes. Her long blond hair was all swirly around her head – forming a yellow mist in the murk. Such long hair. Like Rapunzel from a storybook. That's how he recalled her. But then those were the memories of a terrified five-year-old. They were so awful and muddled. After all, that horrific experience had been processed by a mind that was so young and so innocent.

Yet he retained a clear memory of the face that was slowly sinking down through the water. It became an indistinct oval. The eyes remained shockingly bright, though. Like twin lamps that burned up through the dark water as they stared up into his face.

Her mouth opened, allowing a trickle of silver bubbles to rise to the surface. Then the doomed woman sank slowly out of sight. And yet he truly believed he could see her eyes…still staring at him…as she sank deeper and deeper. Until her eyes were like a pair of tiny silver stars that glinted from a night sky.

The man lay there, processing his thoughts, recalling memories. Even though he had no power to move his limbs, or even his tongue, he fully had power over his mind again. And he had no trouble in retrieving the terrible memory of seeing the woman drown in the lake. Back then, he couldn't swim, so he couldn't have even tried to rescue her. What's more, he'd only been five years old. How could a little child rescue an adult from drowning?

Strangely, by the time he'd walked back to his grandmother's house, what he'd witnessed seemed more like a scary dream. And as he began to play with his toy cars again, on the bare patch of dirt in the yard, the woman in the water didn't seem real. When his grandmother had woken up and sang out to her 'lovely boy' to come into the kitchen for warm milk and cookies, he'd realized that the memory was becoming so hazy. And by the next day, when his parents arrived to take him home, he'd forgotten about the woman in the lake completely. Therefore, he never mentioned what he'd seen – or what he thought he'd seen – to anyone.

It was only years later that the memory came prowling out of those secret vaults in the back of his brain – from that place inside our heads where bad memories are consigned to be suppressed.

Memory is a funny thing, he told himself. *Not always funny* ha-ha, *though.*

The man lay there. He remembered how the image of the drowning woman had come back to him on his very first night at university. The shock of recollection had felt like he'd been punched in the face. He'd staggered out of bed, his muscles cramping up painfully tight as the awful memory ripped through his mind. And yet he never told anyone what he'd experienced as a child, because he imagined that people would laugh at him. They'd dismiss it all as a bad dream that he'd had. And they'd insist that he'd never witnessed a woman drowning in the lake. So, he kept his mouth shut. Said nothing. Then got on with life at the university with his new friends.

Suddenly, the man felt a change take place inside his body. He realized he could move his tongue inside his mouth. His fingers flexed, then curled inwards.

That's when he slowly raised his eyelids. And the strange sight that met his eyes was nothing less than terrifying.

CHAPTER TWO

What the man saw instantly dispelled the notion that he was dead. He was very much alive, and he was very much seeing that his surroundings were decidedly strange. No...correction...they weren't merely strange...his first impression was correct: *they were fucking terrifying*.

He was lying on his back in a huge room that may have been used for some industrial purpose in the past, possibly a warehouse, or a disused factory that had all the machinery removed. The floor was littered with shoes, paper cups, scraps of cardboard. Disturbingly, there was even a child's teddy bear just feet away from him. There was no sign of a child.

He glanced to his left. The dark skin of his hand contrasted with the floor of grey concrete. Here and there, he could see pockmarks in the concrete. Had someone fired bullets at the floor, gouging out holes? But who would fire a gun at the floor at close range? Such a dangerous thing to do – the bullet could bounce back with lethal results. Even more disturbingly, the huge space was partitioned by plastic sheets that hung from ropes, thereby creating translucent walls. And that smell? He could catch the faint odor of pine disinfectant on the air.

His eyes followed the soft wall of plastic sheets, toward the room's center where a structure had been placed. Bizarrely, someone had built a wooden pyramid, constructed from pallets. The man wondered if someone had created a weird altar for religious purposes.

His eyes darted back to the bullet holes in the floor. Had people been forced to lie on the concrete then shot at close range? All too easily, he could picture bullets smashing through flesh and bone before emerging from the body to punch holes into the concrete.

Once again, no sooner had the horrific image flashed through his mind when he noticed something even more disturbing.

A chain snaked down his chest. He had remained lying on his back, so he hadn't even noticed the chain at first. And the strangeness of his surroundings had distracted him from the sensation of the metal links resting on his torso.

What the fuck?

His heart began to pound so forcefully that his chest hurt. A chain? Why was he lying on the floor with a chain strung along his body?

The man's hands went to his throat, his fingers searching for the end of the chain. What his fingers did find was a padlock. The padlock was connected to the chain.

And the padlock was fastened to a collar that encircled his neck. How could he have not known it was there before? But he realized that his entire body had been paralyzed when he'd woken up. For a while, he'd been unable to move his limbs. Possibly, parts of his body had been numb, too.

As he sat up, his mind accelerated. He was desperately attempting to process all the data his nose, ears, eyes, and epidermal nerve endings were pouring into his brain. Smell: the sharp odor of pine-scented disinfectant prickled his nose. Hearing: he heard nothing but the thud of his own pulse in his neck. Sight: the strange objects in the room. Feeling: skin tingling, like he was being dipped into cold water – that was a result of his nerves switching into hyper-activity as he experienced a visceral sense of danger.

This isn't a safe place, he told himself. *This isn't a safe place at all*. What's more, because someone had fastened a chain to his neck then, clearly, he was in deep, deep trouble. Anyone who puts another person in chains isn't doing so to be friendly. In fact, their motives must be downright ominous.

The man had no memory of seeing the room before.

*This place looks like...*he realized he was afraid to even put into words what this place reminded him of. The phrase, nonetheless, came blazing into his brain:

TORTURE CHAMBER.

Here he was, a man secured by a chain. Furthermore, he was inside something that looked as if it could be an actual venue for torture. A place where people screamed and suffered...

Panic flared dangerously in his mind. The sort of panic that, if it ran out of control, might tear his sanity apart. He took a deep breath. He was a rational man. He possessed intelligence. The time had come to figure out a solution to this immediate and pressing problem. Then get the hell out of here.

The chain snaked away from where it was fastened to the collar that was clamped around his neck. The chain stretched out across the floor, then it passed under one of the large plastic sheets, which created another discrete zone next to the one he occupied.

He thought: *Okay, find the other end of the chain. Unfasten it. Then leave. And leave fast before whoever put you here gets back.*

Meanwhile, he struggled to process the data which his senses were pouring into his mind. As his gaze followed the course of the chain, he realized he was wearing a blue shirt and cream-colored chino pants. Those were the kind of clothes he'd wear for a casual evening out in a bar. So, had he been heading out for a few beers when whatever happened...well...happened? This was a terrifying thought. Had some weirdo knocked him unconscious, then brought him to the torture chamber and put a chain on him?

He found himself staring at the section of plastic sheet where the chain snaked under the flap. The plastic wasn't wholly transparent. Nevertheless, he could just make out that there was a shape beyond the plastic sheet. The more he stared at the indistinct form beyond the sheet, the more he began to convince himself that it was ominous enough for him not to make any sudden movements. Or to pull at the chain.

Of course, just when you tell yourself not to make even a whisper of a sound, that's when you do the very thing *you did not want to do*. As he gently lowered the chain, that's when its links slipped from his fingers with a surprisingly loud *CLINK...*

The shape behind the plastic had been lying on the floor. Now it sat up. It was an abrupt movement – one that suggested muscular force. Power. Full of menace.

He realized that he was seeing the figure of a human being, yet only in silhouette through the plastic drape. The figure was evidently sitting cross-legged on the floor. A shiver ran down the man's spine, because he feared that what he saw wasn't fully human.

The figure had been little more than a shadow cast onto the far side of the sheet. However, a light seemed to glow in the same place where its skull should be. The radiance appeared almost ghostly – a cold, cold green. The kind of green light that might emanate from the pagan tomb of a warlock. From way back...when people believed thunder was the enraged bellowing of the gods, and that lightning was their brutal weapon of vengeance.

Then something dreadful happened.

The monstrous creature, whatever it was, appeared to sense that it was no longer alone. Abruptly, the light that emanated from the face turned from green to yellow. The figure lurched to its feet. Then it stood there. Swaying slightly.

This suspicion that the creature sensed it was no longer alone erupted into ghastly certainty when it moved forward – into the sheet of plastic, which pulled tight over the body, revealing the impression of a torso, the shoulders, the misshapen head.

Then the creature walked forwards. And the hanging sheet was slowly rising over it, revealing legs, a belly, the bare flesh of a chest. Whatever the brute was, it knew the man was there. And it was clearly intent on finding out who had invaded its lair.

CHAPTER THREE

There was so much happening that the man found it hard to assimilate what he was seeing. First: an enormous figure strode from the area screened off by plastic sheeting. This was a brute of a creature. A big man, aged about fifty, his bare chest covered in tattoos, and wearing torn clothes. His muscular arms terminated in powerful hands that looked strong enough to bend steel bars in two. Or, if the mood took him, crush the skulls of his screaming victims.

And what about that head…the one with a face bathed in an eerie glow?

Then the man understood. The stranger wore a decidedly bizarre device clamped to his skull. The device resembled horse blinders; that is to say, possessing a pair of flaps – one flap projecting forwards from each side of his head. They formed palm-sized shields that extended out from his face, thereby restricting his field of vision to objects that were directly in front of him; not at the sides, unless he fully turned his head to look either left or right. These 'shields' cast a yellow glow into the stranger's eyes.

The sight of this behemoth approaching would be enough to make even the bravest person run away.

However, the man saw that he wouldn't be able to run far. Because the chain that was connected to his neck ran out some fifteen feet or so to the stranger. And, shockingly, the other end of the chain was connected to a leather harness that was strapped to the stranger's torso. Consequently, there would be no way easy way to flee from Goliath, because the truth of the matter was this: they were chained together. Two human beings in shackles. One leashed to the other by tough steel links.

At that instant, the man knew that the name, which had spat into his mind, was an appropriate one. This stranger was a veritable Goliath. A Goliath decorated with tattoos. A Goliath with a pair of viciously blazing eyes. A Goliath who looked ready to kill the first thing that moved.

The man sensed Goliath's aggression. For all the world, rage seemed to radiate from the figure. Goliath's brutal gaze raked the room as if searching for a victim. Someone to hurt. Someone that Goliath could make scream – and scream again and again.

Yet, at that moment, Goliath appeared not to notice the chain fixed to his own body. Nor did he seem to notice the man that he was chained to.

Nevertheless, this did appear to be Goliath's domain. Did that mean that he had brought the man here? But did it seem likely that

Goliath would stride through busy city streets dressed like that? In ragged clothes? With weirdly glowing blinders clamped to his skull? No, that wasn't likely at all. Then was Goliath a victim, too, of some unknown and unseen jailer? Probably so.

Goliath completely ignored the man. He marched forwards and, in doing so, passed so close he almost brushed against him. The chain began to pull tight, all slack vanishing from the links. In the nick of time, the man grabbed hold of the chain to prevent the brute dragging him so forcefully it would have snapped his neck.

At last, the man found his voice. 'Hey! Stop!'

The man stumbled after Goliath. He was trying to ensure that the chain remained slack enough to avoid him being dragged off balance or from suffering a painful wrench to his neck.

Goliath ploughed through soft walls formed from plastic sheeting. The man realized that the 'walls' radiated outwards from the wooden pyramid in the center of the room, like the spokes of a cartwheel. The walls, in turn, formed triangular-shaped cells within the main room.

Goliath suddenly paused, his head tilting to one side in a menacing 'do I hear intruders?' kind of way. Then, *snap!* The chain pulled tight again as Goliath rushed through another set of plastic drapes.

The man yelled out in pain. 'Ouch! Stop! You'll break my neck!'

However, not only did Goliath seem incapable of seeing the man, but he also couldn't hear him either. He simply continued his vicious mission to find the intruder that he clearly believed had invaded his territory.

Goliath abruptly stopped again. He tilted his head, evidently listening hard for any sign of a trespasser.

The man wasn't at all sure how to put an end to this bizarre sequence of events, where a giant tattooed stranger dragged him back and forth through this bleak-looking chamber.

The man spoke as calmly as he could. 'Uh...look...sir. We're chained together.'

Goliath stopped. He appeared to become suddenly frozen there. Not moving a muscle. Not even blinking. Was he listening to instructions being fed through the blinders? The man had no way of knowing what was happening for sure, other than Goliath just stood there. The big guy stared at a wall of plastic sheets in front of him. Maybe now was the time to make Goliath understand that he wasn't alone in this forbidding place? The man began to slowly move closer to the giant. The chain drooped down, going slack. He approached Goliath from behind. Gently, and not without a blood-chilling dose of fear, the man tapped Goliath on the shoulder.

Goliath reacted in a blur of speed. The reaction wasn't what the man expected. Goliath lunged toward the man; however, he did not even glance at him. It was like he was completely invisible to this formidable stranger.

Goliath surged through the plastic sheets, this time slamming his fists into the soft material, and sweeping them aside, as if they had become the enemy. The man had a powerful impression that Goliath craved to inflict pain and suffering with those huge fists of his.

The man had to follow, like a puppy being dragged along on its leash by a cruel owner.

Goliath punched his way through the plastic walls and into one of the distinct screened-off areas.

And – *SLAM!*

A figure was suddenly there. This one was slightly built, with long dark hair and wearing dungarees that were a reddish brown in color.

This was a figure that Goliath absolutely *did* see. There was nothing to mask the young woman from his ferocious gaze.

The woman's eyes were flashing with panic as Goliath surged toward her. And then, clearly, she did the first thing that came to mind – she must have realized that she had to act now or die.

In a voice that was surprisingly calm, considering the circumstances, she hissed these words – not at Goliath but at the man: 'This is my space. Mine...and you're a dead man.' Then she grabbed hold of the man and thrust him toward Goliath, while shouting, 'Take him! Take him! Not me! Look! He's here! Right in front of you. Take him!'

However, Goliath still did not see the man, who swiftly took a step back to put some distance between himself and the frightening brute.

Goliath did see the woman, though. For a second, he paused. Was he thinking about what he should do next? Or was he waiting for instructions from their jailer?

Goliath stared at the woman. The blinders cast their uncanny light from what must have been light-emitting diodes built into the inner surface of the blinders. They made Goliath's face glow yellow.

That's when the light changed.

From yellow.

To red. To murderous red. Blood red.

The woman tried so hard. She must have decided that she would have a chance if she took control of the situation. She began to point at Goliath, as a schoolteacher might point at a naughty child.

'No.' She spoke in a firm voice. 'No. Do not touch me. Take him. I demand that you leave me alone.'

The red light bathed Goliath's face, making it look as if his skin had suddenly been soaked in blood. It was a strange, glistening radiance that somehow appeared to have mysterious properties other than mere light.

The woman repeatedly pointed at Goliath as she uttered the same command: 'No...no...no...'

Goliath's body convulsed as if an electric current had suddenly torn through his muscles. His eyes bulged. His face contorted into absolute fury.

The woman knew what would happen next. And she screamed so hard and so loud that the man was forced to clamp his hands to his ears as the sound drilled right through his brain in a shriek of absolute fucking terror.

The man now saw why the woman didn't run. She was chained by her waist to the wall of the building.

Goliath lunged forwards. His hands sped out to grab the woman by her throat. Then he did a terrible thing. He lifted the woman from the floor by her neck. His huge, muscular paws were clamped tight to the woman's throat. Squeezing and squeezing – harder and harder. The woman's eyes rolled in her head as pain overwhelmed her senses. Her feet were kicking furiously at nothing but air. A shoe flew from her foot.

Two thoughts burned deep into the man's psyche – they were dreadful truths that were inescapable. The first thought: *so many shoes litter the floor*. Now one of the poor woman's shoes had joined the grim assembly of footwear. It didn't take a genius to figure out what that indicated.

The second thought was remembrance of the woman in the lake, when the man was five. He'd looked down into that dying face...and the word which had filled him with dread had oozed into his brain. **SUFFOCATION**.

Now, the word came horribly oozing back to him once again. **SUFFOCATION**. No air was entering the woman's lungs as she hung there, suspended above the floor by Goliath's murderous grip. Her heart would be clamoring. The blood in her veins would be growing thicker, darker, stickier...as oxygen levels depleted, and carbon dioxide increased.

SUFFOCATION.

The man could almost hear the ghost of his long-dead grandmother give a soft sigh of regret as she murmured, *Poor thing. She will never see her mommy and daddy again.*

Goliath shook the woman as his thick fingers crushed her throat.

A moment later, she suddenly hung limp in his hands. Her feet were loosely swishing through the air, eighteen inches above the floor. The lights burned blood red in the blinders – their electrical fire was igniting rage in Goliath's brain. Then, all of sudden, fiery red yielded to a cool blue glow.

Goliath's body relaxed. There was a sense that hard muscles

were becoming slack. Softening. All the rage was swiftly vanishing. And then, as if disposing of nothing more than worthless garbage, he simply dropped the woman's corpse onto the floor. That done, he walked toward the man. The blue light bathed Goliath's face – a face that now possessed relaxed features and dull eyes. Goliath brushed by the man as if he didn't exist.

Despite everything, the man let out a sigh of relief as he realized he was still invisible to that man-monster.

The chain snapped tight, resulting in the man being dragged helplessly behind the giant. As he was hauled through a hanging sheet of plastic, he glanced back in horror at the woman on the floor. Her arms and legs had begun twitching as dying nerves clamored, impossibly, for life to return to the body. The poor woman. She had suffered dreadfully...

The chain snapped tight again as the man was brutally dragged back into the area where he'd woken up, just a few moments ago. There was a wooden pallet lying flat on the floor. This bed-shaped framework of wood was clearly Goliath's intended destination, because he swiftly headed to it, then lay down on the pallet like it was a comfy mattress. He put one huge paw of a hand under his head, then appeared to fall instantly asleep.

For a moment, the man gazed at the face, which was oddly serene in the soft glow of the blinders. Goliath was sleeping peacefully.

The man realized that he'd been granted a merciful opportunity. He immediately tugged the end of the chain that was connected to the metal collar that encircled his neck. If he pulled hard enough...

That's when he heard the soft tones of a woman whispering from the shadows. 'It's no good. You won't break it.'

The man gazed in the direction of where the voice appeared to come from. He realized it emanated from the wooden pyramid – a structure which so much resembled a profane altar where all manner of blood-thirsty gods would be worshipped and appeased with human sacrifice.

He stared into the shadows, his heart beating fast.

'Who's there?' he whispered. 'Show yourself. I want to see your face.'

What he really meant (and he knew it) was: *Show me your head. Prove to me that you don't have one of those demonic light systems fixed to your skull.*

An oval face loomed from a gloomy aperture within the pyramid. The figure wasn't wearing blinders. That was something to be thankful for. However, a pair of frightened eyes fixed on his.

'We must get out of here,' she whispered. 'Or we'll be killed.'

CHAPTER FOUR

The man approached the wooden pyramid. His eyes had locked onto the face that appeared in a gap in the woodwork. Clearly, the woman was just at the other side of the structure. He had the impression, however, that she was partially inside that latticework of wood, like she was leaning into it. Strange. Very strange. For some reason, she made no attempt to join the man in the space he occupied, and where he was chained to the sleeping Goliath.

As he neared the bizarre structure, he was granted a clearer view of what now appeared to be another companion here in the torture chamber. Or nightmare slaughterhouse. Or whatever the hell this place was. The woman was, he guessed, in her twenties. She had a pleasant oval face, smooth skin, which was as fresh as cream, and clear eyes that were as blue as Baltic skies. Her hair was blonde, and it hung in loose waves over her shoulders. As far as he could tell, given the restricted view of her through the gap in the structure, she wore what might have been a military-type jumpsuit in olive-green.

Although she didn't appear to be afraid of him, she was examining his features as if trying to read any evil intent in his expression. What she saw in his face must have reassured her because she remained there, her face close to the opening, clearly wanting to communicate with him.

As carefully as he could, he moved closer. He was trying very hard to avoid any noise that might wake Goliath, who now, fortunately, appeared dead to the world. Perhaps the device he wore on his head induced unconsciousness – just as it appeared to render the man invisible to the that brute's eyes.

The man leaned in close to the aperture, his face just inches from the woman's. He saw that her expression was full of worry. She was scared. Hell, he was scared. Welcome to the terror party.

He whispered, 'What's going on here?'

The woman gave a helpless shrug. 'I don't know.' She raised a hand to reveal that she was manacled to a chain. 'I woke up, trapped here. Like you.'

She looked to a cut on her forearm as if seeing if for the first time. The wound appeared to form a letter 'T'. It clearly puzzled her, but she said nothing more and quickly lowered her hand as if wanting to conceal the mysterious-looking stigmata.

The man had more pressing questions to ask instead of inquiring about the condition of her arm. 'Where are we?'

Again, she could only give a regretful shrug. 'I've no idea. You got a phone?'

'No.'

'Mine's gone, too,'

The man pressed on with the questions, desperate to discover at least some answers. Knowing even the slightest bit of information about what had happened to him would give him a reassuring sense of having some control over events. Because right now he felt like he'd been reduced to a weak and helpless guy that had been chained to a monster. One who committed murder the instant the lights on the blinders turned red.

He asked, 'How did we get here?'

'I don't know. The last thing I remember is jogging with my dog. Then I woke up here, chained to this thing. How about you?

'Playing with my cat.' Considering the circumstances, his answer seemed almost banal, but that was the truth of the matter. He clearly remembered being with Lynxie. Stroking the tortoiseshell's soft fur, being amused by the way she looked at him with those amber eyes that made him half-believe she could read his thoughts. His most recent memory (at least he *thought* it was his most recent memory) supplied a clear image of Lynxie on her leash...then nothing. Nothing, that is, until he awoke to find himself attached to another kind of leash.

His heart began to race. He realized he needed to keep asking the woman questions, otherwise the panic he felt rising up through his belly would overwhelm him.

So, he asked, 'Did you see anyone bring me in?'

'No. When I woke up, you were already here. Asleep.'

There followed an awkward silence. He realized that neither of them knew how they'd been conveyed here. Or *why* they were here. Equally, he knew that both of them understood that they were in danger. His stomach muscles clenched painfully as the image screamed through his skull of Goliath putting his hands around his throat. Gripping tight. Squeezing.

Suffocation...

The ghostly voice of his grandmother whispered through his mind: *You'll never see Lynxie again. You've fallen into a bad place, my darling boy. A bad place that you'll never ever climb out of...*He clenched his fists in such a way that his fingernails dug deep into the soft flesh of his palms. He needed pain to drive away the ghost voice of his dead grandmother. Of course, there was no ghost. He didn't believe in ghosts. Nevertheless, when your imagination turns rogue it gnaws its way into your brain. It oh-so eagerly drives images of your painful death into your mind's eye.

Concentrate on the here and now, he told himself. *Figure out a way to escape. Do not let your own thoughts poison your mind. You're not alone now. This lady with the kind eyes is here with you. You can work as a team. You can survive this.*

Okay. Time to form a bond.

He said, 'I'm John.'

'Kyra.'

'Hi, Kyra.' He found he could even manage a smile. Then the smile died on his lips. 'Kyra...'

He found himself looking at her more closely as he rolled the name around the inside of his mind. She looked at him differently, too, her head angling slightly to one side. He could almost read the questions in her eyes.

Kyra took a deep breath, seemingly dispelling some notion that had made her uneasy. Quickly, she whispered, 'Did he kill that girl back there?'

John grimaced. 'Looks like it.' What more could he say? He had to focus on the survival of the living now, not obsessing about a murder – no matter how tragic it was. He stared back at the man lying on the pallet. 'His clothes...they're like something an inmate would wear. You think he escaped from an asylum?'

'He's crazy alright.'

'He's gotta be messed up in the head. Or on drugs or something. He acts like he doesn't even know he's chained to me. Like I'm invisible. For some reason, he can't even see me.' John's fingers returned to the hard links of the chain. 'Why am I chained to him?'

Kyra could only shrug. 'I don't know. What's that thing on his head?'

However, before he could answer another voice suddenly rang out – a much-too loud voice that startled them both.

'*Kill him.*'

John saw Kyra's frightened eyes dart around the room, searching for whoever had spoken. John did the same. Apart from the sleeping killer, there was no one there.

The voice came again. And it was dangerously loud. This was the kind of tone that could wake a monster from the deepest of sleeps. 'Over here...hey...look. I'm here.'

John realized that Kyra had seen the stranger at the same instant as he did. There he was – the shouter, the stupid loudmouth! A guy with dark eyes and brown hair peered out from a recess formed from those plastic shrouds. A Hispanic guy in his twenties. And he was chained to a formidable stack of wooden pallets. The man had the gentle, soulful eyes of a saint.

But he had the voice of a bullhorn.

John hissed, 'Hey...not so loud, right?'

'Kill him.' The guy had dropped his voice – only by a tad, though. 'And you need to do it before sleeping beauty wakes up.'

Kyra's whispered, 'Who are you?'

'Nev.' He pointed at the sleeping figure on the pallet. 'Kill him. *Now.*'

'With what?' asked John.

'With whatever. Just do it before he's awake.'

For a moment, there was silence. Kyra's expression suggested that she believed John would violently pounce on the sleeping man and choke the life out of him. John tried to picture himself doing just that – and failed.

John shook his head. 'No. We've just got get out of here.'

Kyra shuddered. 'That guy killed a girl back there. He'll do the same to us.'

Nev bared his teeth – something more like a snarl of total savagery rather than a grin. 'Sure, he will. That's why you need to kill him. You understand?'

Again, an awkward silence. John felt the expectation of his two companions lying heavy on his shoulders. They wanted him to murder a sleeping man.

When the silence seemed as if it would turn malignant, Kyra spoke to ease the tension. 'Nev, how did you get here?'

'I was out delivering pizza on my bike. Got a nice tip after delivering a whole heap of pepperoni big boys to a wedding party. I pulled over for a piss behind some bushes. Then – *wham*.'

Kyra's eyes grew wider. 'What? Someone hit you?'

Nev frowned, trying to remember. 'I don't know. Look, it doesn't matter. I'm trapped here now with you two guys. John, you've got to kill *loco* guy before he rips our heads off. You get what I'm saying?'

John felt a prickle of irritation at Nev's persistence. 'How, Nev? How do I kill him?'

'If I was close enough, I'd do it.'

'Huh, I bet you would.'

'Choke him.' Nev pulled the chain up against his own throat. 'Use the chain.' Nev's voice grew louder. 'Stick your fingers in his eyes. Right into the sockets.' He made stabbing actions with his fingers. *'Blind him!'*

Kyra put her finger to her lips. 'Nev. Shush.'

Nev called out, 'Stand on his throat!'

John's own voice began to rise as he snapped back, 'Just shut up, alright? Let me think.'

Nev did shut up. He stood there, panting, while his eyes burned into John. Nev appeared to be using the power of his stare to try and persuade John to land the fatal blow. Kyra's eyes were glistening. Truly, he saw a glimmer of hope in her expression. He had the impression that she really believed he would snuff out the man-monster.

John put his finger to his lips. 'I need absolute silence from you both. Okay? I'm going across to Goliath now.'

'Goliath?' echoed Kyra. 'Is that his name?'

'Seems as good a name as any,' replied John grimly.

Nev gave a double thumbs up. 'Now you've named the guy – go send him to hell.'

Cold shivers trickled down John's spine. He put his finger to his lips again, a renewed plea for silence. Kyra and Nev both gave solemn nods. They then watched his progress as he moved slowly toward the sleeping man, while taking care not to rattle the links of the chain. As he approached, he scanned the figure in front of him. Now was the time to take a closer look at the man. Then he needed to apply his own intelligence to figure out a solution to the problem.

What struck John as a priority was to detach himself from Goliath. While they were shackled together, John was more vulnerable to attack. After all, he simply could not run away. He studied the leather harness that the man wore. The leather straps formed an X across his chest. The leather harness was secured by a buckle; therefore, all that was required was for him to unbuckle the harness, then ease the sleeping man from it. That done, John could stroll away.

Well, to be more accurate – *run!*

Yeah, sure, the thought was an attractive one. However, he would free Kyra and Nev before he began hunting for an exit from Torture Chamber Central here.

John got closer to the man. The sensation of being so near was visceral. He could hear the man's breathing. He saw the tattooed chest rising and falling. He could see the powerful muscles within the man's bare arms. Disturbingly, the muscles began to twitch. The guy actually moved in his sleep, pretty much the same way a dog will scurry its limbs when it's asleep and dreaming about chasing rabbits. John could feel the guy's body heat. It was rising up against his face. The guy also gave off a faint chemical odor. Something that reminded John of the chemistry lab odors back in his high school days.

With the same kind of delicate care that would be exercised by a brain surgeon, John leaned over to take hold of the buckle. Goliath muttered in his sleep, though in truth it almost sounded like the warning growl of a pit-bull.

Nev suddenly called out, 'Hurry! If you don't kill him, and he attacks us, it's your fault.'

John shot Nev a glare of absolute savagery. Was that infuriating guy trying to wake Goliath deliberately?

Nev held up his hands in apology, then he was smiling and nodding as if to say: *It's cool, don't worry, I'll keep shtum.*

Kyra was watching John – she seemed to focus her entire being on him. She was willing him to succeed. She gave a tiny smile, nodded, then gave him a thumbs up.

John turned his attention back to the buckle on the harness. If he unfastened the buckle then he could ease the straps free of the man's huge torso. Dear God in Heaven, this might actually work.

He held his breath, so as to reduce any sound he might make that would disturb the sleeper. Carefully, he took hold of the buckle then began to feed the free end of the leather strap through the metal loop, just like you'd unbuckle a belt around your waist.

The strap jammed.

In his eagerness to get the job done, John pulled harder.

Then he pulled too hard. The harness cinched tight against the bare flesh of Goliath's torso.

That triggered disaster.

The glow emitted by the blinders turned yellow. The big man snapped awake in a heartbeat. Instantly, he sat up on the pallet, swung his legs around, then stood up. His eyes raked the room, searching for fresh victims.

Yet again, inexplicably, that ferocious gaze simply skated across John's face without seeing him. The giant's posture immediately radiated aggression. Beast man was back in the room. And he wanted fresh blood.

John shuffled backwards. He was lowering his shoulders and his head as he did so, trying to maintain whatever it was that made him invisible to the killer. Kyra and Nev had instantly ducked out of sight. Goliath then noticed that the end of the leather strap, which had once slotted snugly and tidily through the restraining loop, was flapping free. That was the moment Goliath appeared to notice for the first time that he was attached to a chain. The silver links suddenly fascinated him. He took hold of the chain and ran his fingers along the glittering metalwork as he stared at it. His gaze settled on the end of the chain, which was fixed to the harness that he wore. John saw that a thoughtful expression was spreading across the man's face. He must have been thinking: *If one end of the chain is attached to me, where does the chain go? What is the other end attached to?*

John clamped his hands over the chain where it was fastened to the collar around his own neck. As if he could conceal the end of the chain from the murderer. That was impossible, of course.

Goliath, quite slowly, quite deliberately, allowed his gaze to follow the route of the chain down his torso, down his legs, to the floor, then across the floor. The tension made John's heart thunder in his chest. Silver sparks danced in his eyes as he began to hyperventilate. Any moment now...

Suffocation.

Agony.

Death.

Because Goliath's eyes slowly tracked along the fifteen-foot length of chain that snaked across the floor toward John.

And John stared in horror at Goliath. Just seconds from now, the killer would realize that he was shackled to John. Any minute now it would begin...the final dance of death. Goliath would find his second victim.

John experienced nothing less than a mind-explosion of terror. He panted for oxygen so furiously that the very air he breathed felt as sharp as broken glass. Pains flared in his throat, chest, and lungs as he sucked in enough oxygen in preparation for what would be a fight to the death. His stomach muscles snapped tight – the tension making his belly hurt so much that he grunted.

Then a fierce yell. This was Nev's voice, rising to a shriek. 'Hey! John! I found a soldering iron!'

The yell startled John so much that his entire body convulsed. His jaws slammed together, his teeth crunching into his tongue, which created a stab of pain that blasted right through to the back of his skull. John spun around to see Nev leaning out between two flaps of plastic sheet. The guy brandished an orange-handled soldering iron, its black power cord dangling.

Instantly, Goliath lost interest in where the chain would lead him. His fierce glare locked onto Nev's face.

Nev was shouting so loudly, it was like he was intoxicated by the excitement of his find. As he waved the soldering iron above his head, he was screaming, 'John! Stab him! Stab his eyes! Kill the bastard!'

Nev tossed the soldering iron toward John. A terrible throw. The soldering iron hit the floor three feet from John. John noticed that Goliath watched, too, as the soldering iron bounced away before skittering through a gap between the planks of the pyramid and the floor. The soldering iron vanished under the structure.

John threw up his hands in despair. Then he awarded Nev such a look of disgust at the guy's absolute inability to throw the thing with any degree of accuracy.

Goliath glared at Nev.

Nev saw that the monster's attention was fully on him now.

Nev let out a groan of sheer horror. 'Oh, no.'

Goliath charged toward Nev, forcing John to grab the chain, lest his own neck be snapped. Nev, meanwhile, retreated behind the drapes of plastic, clearly in search of a place to hide.

Even if that was the frightened man's intention, he couldn't stop the words spurting from his mouth in panic. 'I'm sorry! I'm sorry! No...no!'

Goliath breasted through plastic sheets the way a strong swimmer breasts through surf as they stride through the ocean toward deeper waters. John was dragged along, helpless as a little puppy on a leash. Plastic sheeting painfully slapped his face as he was hauled through into the zone that Nev had occupied. John noticed that the 'walls' formed from plastic sheets all converged on the pyramid structure in the room's center. He glimpsed Kyra's face. It was milk-white with fear. Her terrified eyes were fixed on Nev as he cowered behind the stack of pallets his chain was bolted to.

Then it all happened so quickly.

John's view was obscured by the pallets. However, he saw enough. More than enough.

Vomit rose into the back of his throat – burning, stinging, utterly vile.

Goliath reached down. And that's when John thought he heard the crack of breaking bone.

Nev's feet kicked. They made a desperate churning motion, like he believed he could run through fresh air.

He couldn't of course. Then he lay still.

Goliath's eyes blazed in triumph.

Kyra must have flinched back because John heard the *chink* of steel links on her chain. Goliath heard it, too. He spun around to fix his rage-filled eyes on the woman. Instantly, she shrank back in horror from the giant.

Kyra gasped, 'Shit.'

Goliath bunched his fingers into fists that must have been hard enough to break skulls.

Then he surged toward her.

The killing wasn't over yet. And the greatest terrors were still to come.

CHAPTER FIVE

Kyra did her best to scrunch herself down to invisibility behind the wooden pyramid. However, being chained to the thing meant that the woman's movements were hindered and her ability to hide was compromised.

Goliath knew that Kyra was there. And that's where he was headed. Grunting like a beast, eager to claim another victim.

Kyra's eyes flashed with terror. She knew what was going to happen to her. And she knew that she could do nothing to save her life. Firstly, the girl had been choked, then Nev had been beaten to death – or so it appeared. Now, Kyra faced a violent and painful end to her life, just seconds from now.

John realized that Goliath didn't even know that another human being was shackled to him. He simply dragged John across the concrete floor. John's feet were violently slamming into discarded shoes and children's toys as he struggled to maintain his balance – that and hold on tight to the chain to prevent his head being ripped from his shoulders. Goliath's strength was immense.

John, in full panic mode, yelled at the man: 'No! Leave her alone!'

The brute did not hear.

John, by this time, had managed to find his balance, and he was trying to pull Goliath back by the chain. Trying...and failing.

John shouted again, 'Don't hurt her!'

Goliath dragged John through one of the hanging sheets of plastic. Now the brute was just twenty feet away from Kyra. He was flexing those thick fingers of his – he was getting ready to choke the life out of the terrified woman.

Kyra shouted, 'John! Keep him away from me!'

By a stroke of sheer luck, John succeeded in bracing his feet against the floor. Then he yanked the chain back toward him with all his strength. He'd done it! He'd managed to stop Goliath in his tracks. The big man actually tottered backwards as the chain almost dragged him off-balance.

There was also another first. Goliath spun around. And for the first time he realized that John was there. For a moment, Goliath stared at the chain. Clearly, he was struggling to process the evidence of his own eyes – that he was chained to another person. When understanding finally oozed into that monstrous brain of his, that's when an expression of total fury appeared on his face. His eyes blazed with rage. With an explosive movement, which was full of speed and sheer muscular strength, Goliath grabbed hold of the chain. He pulled it so hard that – *crack!* – sparks flew from the links as they snapped tight.

John's heart lurched with fear. He could hear the blood roaring through the arteries in his neck. His lungs began to burn as he hyperventilated. This is it! This is where he must fight for his life.

Goliath began to reel John in – pulling the chain hand over hand – drawing John closer to the man, and closer to those dangerous hands that could so easily strangle the life out of his victims. John tried to prevent himself from being drawn closer. However, his feet slid across the concrete. There was nothing near enough to grab hold of to prevent himself from being dragged nearer. There was no improvised weapon he could snatch from the floor. John could only watch the man's enraged face that was illuminated by a yellow glow from the device clamped tight to his head. John could hear a pulsating drone emanating from the blinders – an awful sound that felt like it was painfully drilling through John's ears into his head, setting his teeth on edge.

Then everything changed.

Just as Goliath reached out a hand to grab John, the lights in the blinders switched from yellow to blue. The drone instantly vanished. A second later, it was replaced by a gentler sound. Almost the whispery murmur of waves softly washing across a beach. Goliath relaxed. Rage simply bled out of his face. Instead of anger, there was now an expression of drowsy calm. The eyes were becoming dull looking.

John thought: *It's the colored lights in the blinders. They control him. Blue for calm. Red for rage...*

Briefly, John felt a surge of hope. If the blue lights remain, then—

The hope was cruelly short-lived.

Abruptly, the lights switched from blue to yellow. Goliath appeared to mentally reset himself because he reverted to 'hunt' mode. Surprisingly, he could not see John again. That huge head of his swung around as his predatory eyes searched the room.

There was no doubting the target of Goliath's murderous fury now. He instantly locked those blazing eyes onto Kyra. That done, he lumbered toward her, dragging John after him. Such was the power of the man's stride that he easily dragged John along. Once again, John tried to brace his feet against the floor, but this section of concrete might as well have been made of ice for all the traction that it offered. He simply slid along behind the man, while desperately holding onto the chain with both hands.

Kyra tried to make herself as small as possible by scrunching herself up close to the wooden structure. 'Stop him!'

John almost wept with frustration. 'I can't! He's too strong!'

He was brutally dragged through another 'wall' of sheeting, the rough plastic painfully scraped his face. His back muscles felt as if they were close to being torn from their anchor points on his bones. His neck flared with agony as the chain yanked the collar.

Kyra, meanwhile, had no refuge into which she could retreat. In sheer desperation, she climbed up onto the wooden pyramid, perhaps hoping there would be some place that would be beyond Goliath's reach.

No such luck. Goliath grabbed her ankle. Then, with malicious satisfaction, he began to pull her toward him.

Kyra tried to break free of his cruel grasp. She cried out, 'Get him off me!'

John looked more closely at Goliath. He was searching for a weak point in the man, or something – anything! – that he could exploit to save their lives. John spotted a small pack fixed to the harness on Goliath's back. From the pack, electrical wires snaked up to the blinders. John tried to find an opening to the pack, hoping it would reveal controls. However, there was no opening he could see, and definitely no controls of any sort.

John roared, 'How do you make this thing turn blue?'

Suddenly, John had an idea. Reaching forwards, he pulled the blinders from the giant's head. Then he stepped back, to avoid the risk of being punched if the man went berserk. The blinders hung down the man's back, still glowing yellow. Apparently, John's removal of the blinders had broken the system of remote control (if that's what it was) and yet the man's rage didn't diminish at all. In fact, he seemed even more hellbent on venting his homicidal fury on Kyra.

Briefly, she succeeded in yanking her ankle free of Goliath's huge paw of a hand. Quickly, she scrambled further across the pyramid, though she'd almost fully used up the extent of her own chain now. She wouldn't be able to get much further. However, as she glanced down through the aperture, created by this bizarre stack of pallets, she suddenly appeared to notice something of importance.

She whipped her head around, so she could fix her eyes onto John. 'John! Get the soldering iron! It's right under me, but I can't reach it!'

John abandoned all hope of switching the blinders to blue. Instead, he flung himself at the base of the wooden pyramid. Straightaway he saw it. The orange-handled soldering iron, with its sharp metal point, was just four feet from him. Lying on the concrete beneath that mound of woodwork, he thrust his hand through an opening. *If I can just reach...*

He snarled with frustration. The soldering iron was just inches beyond his clutching fingers. What's more, the gap in the wood-work wasn't large enough for him to scramble fully into the pyramid. He tried so hard to reach the soldering iron that the edges of the woodwork dug painfully into his upper arm.

'Damn it!'

Meanwhile, there was another struggle occurring five feet above his head. Goliath had grabbed hold of Kyra's ankles. He used her body to drag himself onto the pyramid – his hands then gripped her arms as he clambered forward. Clearly, he intended to put his hands around her throat at the earliest opportunity.

'John! Don't let him kill me!'

The shriek of terror from the woman was enough to urge John to lunge deeper into the structure. The soldering iron was still beyond reach. However...

...the power cord wasn't.

Gotcha!

John grabbed the cord, then he was pulling the soldering iron toward him.

He let out a howl of triumph. 'Kyra! I got it!' Instantly, he shoved himself backwards to get clear of the pyramid. What he saw when he scrambled to his feet was nothing less than horrific.

Because Kyra was in a world of pain. Tears bled from her eyes as she grabbed hold of the far edge of a pallet. Goliath was trying to drag her toward him. She was like one of those victims of the medieval rack. The rending force on her shoulders, elbows, and wrists must have been horrendous as she hung on desperately as Goliath tried to tear her free.

Despite the agony ripping through her body, her voice still possessed undeniable force. 'Stab him!'

John wrenched at the chain, hard enough to make Goliath halt his brutal torture of Kyra. Goliath's eyes swept toward John.

It's now or never.

John shifted his grasp from the power cord to the handle of the soldering iron. For a moment, the thing fascinated him. It had become a weapon of war. John repositioned the soldering iron so that he held it like a dagger. This was something he could use to stab another human to death.

Kyra panted, 'Do, it, John...do it. Or we're both dead.'

John raised the hand that gripped the weapon. That was the moment he felt a trembling sensation begin in his belly, which swiftly rose through his chest until that tremble rattled his teeth together.

'John, stab him!'

To his horror, he realized he couldn't bring himself to plunge the point of the soldering iron into Goliath's chest.

Goliath had no such scruples. And he wasn't in the least bit squeamish.

With a snarl, he grabbed John by the throat.

John, despite the terror and the pain, thought: *He can see me...Dear God, he can see me. He's going to kill me now.*

Goliath seized John by the collar, to which the chain was attached, and he slowly lifted him from the floor. Goliath looked him in the eyes from a distance of five inches. The giant seemed to derive a lustful satisfaction from gazing into his victim's eyes before the killing began.

The blinders swung from side-to-side as Goliath raised John higher. The movement allowed John to see that the device's lights had turned from yellow to blue. John understood that the blue light would not save him, because that all-important soothing blue glow wasn't reaching Goliath's eyes.

John couldn't breathe now. He recalled how, as a child, he'd seen the woman sink beneath the surface of the lake. She didn't struggle as she drowned. Her body had gone limp underwater. Death had been creeping into her flesh to replace life.

John tried to prevent Goliath choking him. But his own strength was leaking away from his limbs. He could not fight. He could not break free. He could only hang there as Goliath gripped his throat so fiercely that purple flashes streaked across his brain. And the pain...it felt like the sharp teeth of a vicious creature ripping through the muscles of his neck. He dropped the soldering iron.

His heart thudded with a grave rhythm as the oxygen in his bloodstream was depleted ...he glanced across at Kyra. Their eyes met. Her blue eyes were full of despair and regret in equal measure. John tried to communicate what he felt with a glance. *I'm sorry, Kyra. I just couldn't stab him. And now he'll kill us both.*

Goliath's body suddenly convulsed like a lightning bolt had struck him. The jolt that ran through the man's body shook John so fiercely he would have screamed in pain if it wasn't for the fact that the man's hands were asphyxiating him. He couldn't even breathe, let alone scream.

Goliath eyes were watering. He began to cough.

John watched Goliath in astonishment as he hung there in the man's grasp. And his astonishment increased when blood began to ooze out from Goliath's lips. Soon, it formed a wet mass of crimson around his mouth. That's when Goliath dropped John.

John immediately began to suck in huge quantities of life-giving air.

Goliath took a couple of faltering steps backwards. He was feebly clawing at his neck, and shoulders, and chest, as if rats were scur-rying over his body and he was trying to brush them off. The giant had been deprived of all his strength. Slowly, he crumpled to the floor. He was gasping for breath so forcefully that it produced a wet crackling sound in his throat. After convulsing again, he flopped limply onto his side. His eyes were staring blankly. He wasn't moving.

That once formidable powerhouse of a man had become a life-less corpse. John spun around to look at Kyra. She crouched on top of the wooden pyramid. Her eyes were locked onto the dead face of Goliath.

Then he and Kyra were looking at one another as if asking each other: *What just happened?*

John moved toward the pyramid as Kyra climbed off the structure. Both were bruised, aching, exhausted. But their expressions proclaimed their elation. Despite everything, they'd somehow won the battle of their lives. They'd survived. Now they were going to live.

They both sank down to the floor where they sat with their backs to the pyramid. They were side-by-side, and so close to one another that their hips were touching. John realized they'd formed a special bond. A near-death experience had brought two strangers together, closer than the closest of friends.

Kyra smiled at John. John smiled back. She gently patted him on his arm, and somehow her eyes said far more than words ever could.

John had scooped up the soldering iron. As a weapon, it had been useless in his hands. Now, however, it might have some use as he began to pry apart the two halves of the manacle around Kyra's wrist. The lock was beginning to give way. As soon as he broke the catch, he could open the manacle and free her from the chain that was bolted to the structure. After that, they could escape this room of the damned.

Where it came from, they had no way of knowing. Suddenly, a wailing sound burst from an unknown source with enough power to make them clamp their hands over the ears – the sound was loud enough to be agonizing. The lights went out. The darkness against his eyeballs felt like a solid thing. He could see absolutely nothing. Kyra's hand found his and held on tight. Like two children lost in the woods, they were holding hands in a dangerous place.

Out of the darkness loomed strange figures. They appeared to be dressed in flowing garments that approximated surgical gowns. Their faces were masked. And the only reason that John could see them in the darkness was because they were illuminated from within. For all the world, it looked as if their flesh was transparent, and that their skeletons were rendered visible due to the bones being filled with a spectral glow.

The figures were holding strange-looking tubes in their hands. And John knew that those menacing figures were coming for him and Kyra.

But that's all he did know. Because the tubes began to flash with the power to dazzle him. And then there was a different kind of darkness. One that flooded his mind. Sending him deep down into a sleep that was, for now, utterly dreamless.

CHAPTER SIX

They used a cart to wheel the corpse of the giant of a man into a room that was severely clinical in appearance. Harsh lights illuminated the place, revealing figures in protective clothing that might have been a hybrid between hazmat suits and surgical gowns. The masked figures slowly pushed the corpse of the tattooed man toward a table, on which a scalpel, flesh-cutting shears, and a bonesaw had been neatly set out in a row.

One of the figures bent over the corpse to examine the face. Its dead eyes were staring blankly into eternity. The mouth was still smeared with blood that had bubbled from its lips.

As a figure picked up a scalpel, and checked the cutting edge to satisfy themselves that it would cleanly cut through skin, a male voice shimmered from a speaker set into the wall. The voice was unemotional, utterly professional, and as cold as a tombstone at midnight.

The voice addressed the operatives who prepared the cadaver for what would come next. 'It's really quite a shame. He held so much promise, but a high failure rate is only to be expected. Nevertheless, we have learned so much from him.' The voice became sharper as it directed an order at the personnel in surgical garb. 'Very well. Cut him open. Send me the autopsy report. Then incinerate the body.' The man's voice dropped to a murmur, almost as if he was speaking to himself. 'Alright, let's reset – and start again.'

CHAPTER SEVEN

She opened her eyes to utter darkness.

'I'm not in bed.'

This is scary. To wake up. To open your eyes and see nothing but darkness, and to know that you are absolutely not in a bed. *No, this isn't scary, this is terrifying.*

Sharp objects dug into her side. Were those stones? Was she lying in a field? In a parking lot? On a dirt track?

Her heart began to race. Purple flashes that were evidence of her panic cut through her brain with the force of lightning bolts. What had happened to her? Had she been attacked? Then left for dead?

At that moment, she dare not move. She lay still, while trying to hear if her attacker was close by. After all, a movement, or the faintest sound from her might trigger a frenzied assault on her to snuff out her life. She tried to listen carefully for any sign of a potential murderer close by; however, the panic she felt, and which she tried to stifle, had created a kind of tinnitus effect in her ears. And that tinnitus effect conjured phantom jangling chimes that drowned out any sounds nearby. They weren't actual sounds, of course; they were all a product of her frightened mind. At that instant, she craved to let out a huge yell of fear.

But no...

...keep quiet...

...do not move. Do not move a finger. Do not even breathe. The person who attacked you might be standing above you. Though you can't see them.

It's so dark.

A black fog pressed against her eyes.

The sensation was horrible – she had never felt so vulnerable before. She forced herself to regulate her breathing...to inhale slowly, to exhale slowly, so as not to hyperventilate. If she did allow herself to be overwhelmed by panic, she'd become a screaming, mindless creature that would soon become the writhing victim in the hands of whoever had brought her here.

She controlled her breathing. In turn, that meant she could regain control of her mind.

That's when she did what she had always done, when she found herself in a cruel relationship (oh, that had happened so many times), or when life's punishing blows had beaten her down. The woman took a deep breath then, very purposefully, very calmly, she pictured her skull becoming a castle of bone. This castle was the place of safety. A place she could withdraw into when life became too miserable to bear.

As if she really was inside the strong walls of a castle, she moved deeper into her head. Into the fortress of impenetrable bone.

At last, she began to feel more secure. This was a place of safety, deep inside her head. Where drunken lovers couldn't punch her, or drug-dealer neighbors couldn't hurl stones at her, to keep her out of her yard when they were vending coke and weed.

I am safe, she told herself. *Nothing can harm me. Nobody can hurt me. I am protected inside my walls of bone.*

The harsh jangling, caused by tinnitus (if that's what it was), was beginning to fall silent. The purple bolts of lightning that had been the product of her panic, and which had been searing the inside of her brain, were fading away.

Though her eyes were open, she saw only utter blackness. There wasn't even the glimmer of a streetlight or the twinkle of a star above her.

Make light, she told herself. She realized that she could make her own light inside her skull by picturing a bright image.

Violent lights blasting down. A plastic incubator. A tiny figure. A baby. A silent baby. Lying oh-so still as the alarm shrieks a warning of imminent death.

Where that image came from, she didn't know. It wasn't a memory she recognized. It must have been a phantom image generated by the panic she'd experienced just moments ago.

Recall a happy memory. Think about something nice. She forced the disturbing image of the baby from her mind.

Instead, she pictured a day that was sunlit and happy. She was in a park with her dog. There, the ice-cream truck sold pink confections to excited children. A yellow kite looked as if it had been glued to the blue sky. She threw a frisbee for the dog, and the dog ran after it, barking with pure joy.

The image of her dog made her feel much better.

So much so that she realized she dare explore her surroundings now. After all, no fingers had lunged from the darkness to clutch her throat. *Maybe I am alone after all?* If that was the case, she needed to stand up, then go home.

Caution still dictated her movements. First, she carefully listened.

Her own breathing? Yes, she heard that. A whispery sound — quite regular, too, now that she had quelled the inferno of panic. She could hear nothing else.

See anything?

Nope. Zilch. Zero. There was just pure darkness.

She inhaled.

Smell?

Oh, God, yes.

The cold air smelt of water. But rotten water. The kind of water found in a stagnant ditch.

Taking a deep breath, she sat up. One of her feet happened to kick a stone. The sound it made as it rattled away across a hard surface set up a series of echoes that slowly receded before dying far away.

As she sat there, she stomped her foot down. She was trying to form a picture of her surroundings by making a noise. When she'd stomped her foot, a flurry of mad echoes had rushed at her – sounding like a dozen running feet. And then the echoes flew away into the darkness, where they became distorted into a strange chattering sound – a monstrous creature's teeth clacking rapidly together. That's what it sounded like to her.

She thought: *Get the fuck out of here! This is a bad place. If you stay, you die!*

Although she remained sitting, she extended her arms. She could feel cold air moving sluggishly against her reaching fingertips. She lowered her hands. A floor – a stone floor. One that was gritty. Covered with small stones. Then something that might have been a twig – or, come to that, part of a human skeleton. Despite the shocking mental image of a floor littered with bones, she remained calm. Her movements were purposeful, her mind was clear. She leaned to one side where her fingers immediately touched a hard block in the darkness. A concrete wall? No, the block was uneven. Her sense of touch suggested this was a boulder.

Her fingers scuttled through the darkness and up the side of the boulder. The rock flattened out at the top.

Her fingers continued the search on top of the rock, detecting small stones, then – *uh!* The horror of touching something wet. She had touched an object that was soft and moistly squishy. Instantly, her imagination fired an image into her brain of a human face that had been cut from the front of the skull and left on the boulder. *A psychopath has been busy tonight.*

And you're next.

She crushed the frightening image back down into her mind, lest it trigger a screaming bout of panic. Then—

Wow!

Is that what I think it is? Her hand closed over a small cylinder. The object was flattened at both ends, a switch in the center. She hardly dare believe that she'd found a flashlight in the darkness. That had to be a miracle.

Or is it a cruel trick?

Despite the fact that there might be a grinning killer lurking in the darkness, she did not hesitate.

Click!

She pushed the switch forward with her thumb.

A dazzling light spat from the end of the flashlight. What it revealed was nothing less than an onslaught of stimuli on her senses. The light burst over walls of rock, boulders, hunks of rusted metal pipe, lengths of timber that had been crusted with mineral deposits.

A cave. I'm actually in a cave.

She quickly climbed to her feet. Then she was spinning around, sweeping the light this way and that. Thankfully, there was no leering psycho there, eager to rip open her throat. She was alone.

But how did I get into this...this...My God, it's not a cave...it's a mine. These are mine-workings. She stood in a cavern that was big enough to put a whole church inside. The rock ceiling must have been fully sixty feet above her head. The rock was dark green in color with lines of white running through it. Just ten feet from her was an underground pool, consisting of evil-looking water. There was a mining cart upended in the pool, its steel wheels pointing up at the ceiling. It was as if long ago the abandoned cart had rolled over and died.

The face?

She'd felt a face – it had been all wet and soft on the boulder. With a slash of dread running through her, she swung the light back to the boulder.

The face...

No. It wasn't a face. It was just a piece of rotting cardboard that was crumpled and swollen from water dripping down from the ceiling. In the darkness, she'd touched something wet and soft – that's when her imagination had supplied the vile image of a human face that had been torn from bone.

The woman had no way of knowing how long the battery would last in the flashlight, so she decided to quit this damp vault of a place and get back into the sunlight. She began walking past pieces of mining machinery that lay corroding in the vast cavern. There were random streaks of red paint on the walls – at least she thought they were paint. Here and there, mysterious numbers had been written on the rockface, together with phrases like *End of Zone A* and *Assembly Point 3B* and *Triage Station*. And, far more worryingly, the command *DANGER. DO NOT GO BEYOND THIS POINT!* The woman had no choice. She must find an exit.

She moved swiftly, her footsteps echoing ahead of her.

Occasionally, she paused to shine the light into narrow crevices, and into tunnels that came to dead ends. Everywhere, there were the skeletons of mining machinery – these appeared as grotesque forms. Like the skeletons of dinosaurs in the harsh glare of her flashlight.

When the tunnel split into two, she paused, trying to decide which route to take. That's when she heard footsteps. These weren't the echoes created by the movements of her feet. No, not at all. She hadn't moved in the last twenty seconds. No, some furtive creature was scuttling through the tunnels – whether they retreated from her or came closer, she could not tell.

She decided to make contact. 'Hello? Who's there?'

The footsteps appeared to come from the left-hand branch of the tunnel. Maybe someone else was lost down here? She listened hard. The footsteps were becoming fainter.

Then, shockingly, a loud crunch of a sound came from the darkness behind her. She spun around. The light stabbed back into the darkness to reveal…

Nothing but rock walls.

Her heart was beating so hard it actually hurt her. She couldn't stop here, though. She must escape from this place. What if the flashlight died on her? She'd be left alone in the darkness. No food. No clean water to drink. *Get out, while you still have the light.*

She rushed along a tunnel that was so narrow that the stone walls scraped her elbows. At one point she moved past steel roof supports that had been mangled by what must have been an explosion. Metal spars had all been bent in the same direction – just in the same way that long grass stalks all bend in the same direction when blown by a strong breeze. The explosion had bent the spars in such a way that they resembled sharp fangs. The points were lethally sharp. Anyone blundering along this tunnel in the dark would suffer a nasty injury if they ran into those metal teeth.

She continued walking. For a while, there were only pieces of stone on the floor and random pieces of electrical cord, and soggy items of clothing – a shirt, a sock, a hoodie sweatshirt with a long rip up the back. But then she noticed something else.

A little oblong of red candy. She picked it up, hoping it would be a clue that could help her get out of here.

The woman noticed another nugget of red on the floor, ten feet from the first. It was a second piece of candy. She picked that up.

Someone had been here recently. She was sure of it.

The woman shone her light along the tunnel where it widened out. She wondered if she'd find more of the candy. Instead of candy, however, what she did see made her flinch back with shock.

Because there, in pale cream fabric and standing on four spoked wheels, was a baby buggy.

Her heart began to beat faster as she approached the buggy.

The word that echoed within the recesses of her brain was: *Baby.*

Just the manifestation of the word 'baby' sent a whole flurry of shivers across her body, puckering her skin into gooseflesh. This was a real 'someone just walked over my grave moment'.

What kind of person would abandon a baby down here in this dripping, stinking, fucking noxious hell of a place?

Slowly, she approached the baby buggy, while keeping it in the center of the light. And now the dreadful part...the part where she wanted to turn and run away. But she couldn't do that. She had to see for herself. That was the humane thing to do.

There was a softly rounded form in the baby buggy. That rounded form was covered by a blanket of pale-yellow material. The blanket made a gentle pulsating movement. There was something alive in there...

The woman moved closer. As she did so, she reached out with her free hand, ready to ease back the blanket to expose whatever lay beneath it. The shape beneath the blanket moved ever so slightly. Was that a tiny chest rising and falling as it breathed in and out?

Slowly, and ever so gently, the woman took hold of the hem of the blanket between her thumb and forefinger, and she began to ease it back. Her heart was pounding. She was holding her breath. Then she saw what lay beneath the blanket.

'My God.'

At that moment, a fast-moving shadow erupted from the darkness. It flung itself at the woman. She felt what seemed like fierce talons curl around her wrist. They gripped tight. Painfully tight.

Then a stark, white face lunged toward hers. And a red mouth hissed with the ferocity of a serpent: *'Don't touch her!'*

Suddenly, the hands that gripped the woman's wrists began dragging her into the gloom, and away from the glow of the flashlight, which had slipped from her grasp and fallen onto the floor.

CHAPTER EIGHT

The creature that attacked the woman was a wild thing. Hissing. Snarling. Its hair flaring out around its head.

The creature shouted the command again: 'Don't touch her!'

The woman, with a huge effort, broke free of what felt like painfully tight talons around her wrists. The figure had a flashlight of its own and switched it on.

She saw that the wild creature was, in fact, a young woman of around twenty-five. This tempestuous stranger had long hair that was black, and which curled down over her shoulders and back. She wore brown dungarees over a T. The young woman had large, frightened eyes. There was something other-worldly about her delicate features and those big brown eyes. She had the look of an enchanted princess, who'd been brought here from a mysterious, faraway realm.

The young woman snarled, 'Don't touch my kitty!'

The woman ignored the bizarre command and said, 'Who are you?'

The young woman reached into the baby buggy and gently pulled a cat out from beneath the blanket. The cat was extravagantly fluffy. Its fur was as white as snow.

'You hurt my kitty.'

'I did not.'

The young woman cradled the cat against herself as if it was a tiny baby. The cat let out a 'meow' that resulted in ghostly echoes shimmering along the tunnel.

The woman eyed the figure in front of her who embraced the cat so tenderly. She said, 'I'm just looking for a way out.'

The young woman snuggled herself against the cat in her arms.

The woman said, 'How did you get in here?'

The stranger said nothing and lightly kissed the cat on top of its furry head.

The woman persisted in a deliberately calm tone, 'I'm Kyra. What's your name?'

No response.

Kyra tried a different angle. 'What's your kitty's name?'

The young woman's dark eyes suddenly fixed on Kyra's face, and she smiled. 'Her name? Her name is Lilli.'

Kyra realized that there was something seriously amiss with the young woman. After all, who'd bring a cat into a mine?

Quickly, Kyra scooped up the flashlight from the floor. Having possession of her own light might well make the difference between getting out of here and being trapped in this bleak subterranean world forever.

The young woman appeared more relaxed now. Shyly, she turned sideways to show Kyra the cat in her arms.

Kyra flinched back with shock because half of the cat's face lacked fur. If anything, it had the appearance of being burnt off. Clearly, the poor animal must have been caught up in a horrific inferno. The cat gave a loud 'meow'. It moved its head, and there was a distinct whirr of something mechanical. Kyra saw why the face had a melted appearance. It was made from plastic. Its eyes were twinkling glass set into the face. Kyra realized she was looking at a comfort cat – that is to say, one of those reproductions of a cat, which was constructed from plastic and fake fur. Comfort cats were often owned by people who loved cats but were perhaps not in the best of health, meaning that they couldn't take care of the real thing.

Kyra's intention was to get out of here. Certainly, before the flashlight batteries died on her. And before whoever had left her in the tunnel returned. Right now, this individual with the enchanted princess looks, and with her mechanical cat, was the only one who could possibly help her.

Kyra gave the warmest of smiles she could muster. 'Lilli...that's a beautiful name. Do you know how you and Lilli came to be here?'

'No.'

'Can you tell me your name?'

There was a pause, as if the young woman wasn't sure if it was wise to reveal her identity. However, after what appeared to involve a struggle with herself, she whispered, 'Amber.' Then she gave a big, beaming smile.

'Amber. Do you know why we've been brought here?'

Amber's smile abruptly changed to an expression of alarm. She appeared to be afraid to answer the question. Nevertheless, she gave a quick shake of her head by way of reply.

Kyra's tone was firm when she asked, 'Do you know of any way out?'

'There is no way out.' Her expression became wary, like she no longer trusted Kyra. 'I have found a kitchen, though. I need to feed Lilli!'

Amber held the cat in one arm while shining the torch ahead of her. Deliberately, she picked out the trail of red candy, then she began to swiftly follow it. She'd clearly created a route marked out by the candy, so that she wouldn't become lost in this gloomy labyrinth. Her footsteps echoed loudly as she scrambled over a pile of fallen rocks.

Kyra didn't see any option other than to follow. They both had flashlights; therefore, if one did fail at least they would still have light.

Amber led the way into a high chamber, formed from greenish

rock. There were more numbers painted in white on the walls. The numbers meant nothing to Kyra. Possibly they were geolocation coordinates, or even reference numbers that recorded the quality of the rock being mined here. They might even have identified miners who had been killed in this tomb of a place.

To Kyra's surprise, Amber approached what appeared to be a small makeshift kitchen area. This homely facility was so incongruous in an outlandish place such as this. There was a large crate that served as a table. On the crate were bowls, cutlery, and an open bag of the same red candy that had marked out the route here. There was also food in packets and jars.

Amber sang out: 'Bread. Forks. Spoons. No knives though. Not a single knife.' She looked down into the cat's burnt face. 'You want a sandwich Lilli honey-pie? PBJ?'

From a grimy paper bag, she pulled out a sandwich.

Amber smiled fondly at the cat. 'Time to eat, Lilli. Eat it all up.'

Amber held the sandwich to the cat's mouth. The mechanism inside the cat made its mouth move. It 'miaowed' again. Amber seemed to truly believe the cat was feeding on the sandwich. She smiled and moved her own mouth to mimic chewing movements, just as a parent feeding their baby will do.

Cold air stirred around Kyra. She shivered as the draught ran its cold fingers across the bare skin of her neck. From far off, there came an eerie shimmer of echoes. Was that someone talking in one of the tunnels? Kyra's shiver turned into a shudder that went deep into her bones. Whoever, or whatever, roamed these tunnels...she doubted if they would be friendly.

Kyra's gaze swept around the vault, searching for any clue that might suggest an escape route. What she did see immediately grabbed her attention, because painted in large white letters on a boulder were the words: *RMEMBR U KNO JON.*

Kyra read the statement aloud. 'Remember, you know John.' She glanced sharply at Amber. 'You put that there?'

'No.' Amber's focus was on Lilli – she still held the sandwich to the cat's mouth that mechanically whirred as it moved. 'That was here when I found the kitchen.'

'You know a John?'

'No.' She gave Kyra a sly look. 'You?'

Kyra ran her finger over the words painted there, as if the act of touching them would help connect the name to the mental image of a face. 'No...I don't know anyone called John.' She hesitated, thinking hard. Then she shook her head. 'No, I'm sure I don't.'

Amber leaned forwards to stare into her face. 'You don't sound convinced that you don't. Maybe you do. Maybe you're just a bit too teensy-weensy shy to admit it.'

Another flurry of echoes reached Kyra – they were faint and very far away. To Kyra, they sounded like the rattling of chains. She aimed her flashlight in the direction of the sound, but all she saw was the tunnel receding into darkness. At that moment, she felt such a deep and apocalyptic terror. For all the world, it seemed as if the tunnel continued for infinity. Never-ending. A passageway to other dimensions, where the gods of slaughter and death held dominion.

This maze of tunnels harbored a promise of danger that was absolutely visceral. Were there scorpions down here? Venomous snakes? She could detect mushroom odors that were becoming stronger. Did the smell come from fungus that grew on the wet rocks here? Might that fungus spew hazardous spores into the air that would settle inside her lungs and grow and grow within her flesh? And what about the roof above her head? The rock had been fractured. Marks ran across the green stone, revealing fault lines. At any moment, the roof could fall, pounding them to a scarlet-colored mush.

Faraway sounds reached her again. Yes, she was sure of it. The rattle of chains.

Fear of the unknown could be a killer down here. If panic unhinged her and she ran screaming down the tunnel, she might run into a deep pool of water and drown. Or there might be vertical shafts that she might stumble into. They'd surely be deep enough to result in a fall that would snap her bones.

Death was everywhere down here. The promise of a violent death stained the air...

Kyra knew, however, that she could not simply remain there. She must do *something*. Therefore, she took a deep breath, then strode purposefully forwards. She'd find out who was rattling the chains like a fool. *Therefore, grab that fool and make them show me the way out of this fucking hole in the ground.* The anger now heating her veins helped steady her nerves. She moved in a purposeful way. Determined to get out. And absolutely determined to go home.

Kyra walked along the tunnel, while shining the light ahead of her. There were no other sounds now. Amber was silently 'feeding' the fucking machine cat. And what, exactly, was Amber's story? The way she acted – like a frightened little girl one moment, then behaving so strangely, like she was possessed by a demon or an alien or something. Weird. Fucking weird.

Kyra felt stronger now. Using the word 'fucking' was a magic charm in its own right. The filthy expletive was a tried and tested method to empower herself.

'Hey...what...'

Kyra had uttered those words in surprise as a faint clatter of sound reached her. The noise was a close one. She shone the flashlight down at the slimy floor of the cave. There were steel rails here where the mining trucks would have once been hauled to the surface.

Kyra looked at what lay there – it was bathed in the flashlight's silver glow. She saw a black worm-like thing, which she quickly identified as a power cord. There was a small object with an orange handle.

'A soldering iron?' Kyra picked it up. She was convinced it hadn't been there before, when they had walked up the very same tunnel to Amber's 'kitchen' grotto. So, had some unseen individual secretly left it there just moments ago? A worrying thought in itself. Kyra gazed at the soldering iron. Instinct prompted her to hold it as if it was the kind of knife that a killer would use. She stared at the object, there in her hand. Sparks of memory danced in her mind – just out of reach of full recollection. She had seen something like this before…back then, it had much more importance than being a mere tool to melt solder onto electrical wiring. No…the soldering iron had been vital for another reason…

Amber lunged from the darkness. With a burst of savage energy, she hissed, 'Is that a dagger?'

Kyra flinched at the suddenness of the woman's arrival. Even so, she recovered from her shock to utter, 'No…it's just…' The words died on her lips.

'What?' Amber held the cat tightly.

'I remember this…I've seen it before.'

'When?'

'I don't know. *Before*…that's all…just an impression, really. Not even a proper memory.'

Kyra tightened her grip on the handle, and she held it up as if it was a dagger.

Amber's eyes widened – it was like she'd begun to understand some terrible truth. 'It is a weapon. You're wielding it.'

'No. Not me. Some guy. He held it.' Her heartbeat quickened. 'John…I think it was John.' She groaned with frustration. 'Why can't I remember?' She suddenly grabbed Amber by the shoulders. The need for answers threatened to burn holes into her sanity. 'Amber! How did you get here? Think!'

Amber looked scared. 'I…I woke up here. I was just here.'

'What was the very last thing you remember? Before you were *just* here?'

Amber's eyes became dreamy as the uncanny smile returned to her face. 'The last thing I remember, is standing in a beautiful field of flowers.' In a peculiar sing-song voice, she said, 'Flowers are for funerals. That big field of flowers could garnish many, many funerals. Two caskets. A pair of lovebird coffins.' The she sang in a little girl voice, 'Two caskets. Two by two, equals none.'

Kyra's response to that bizarre statement was: *What the fuck!* Though she didn't say the words out loud. Was Amber even human? Kyra realized she couldn't find a shred of empathy with this strange individual who swayed in front of her. Amber was improvising a little side-to-side dance as she gazed vacantly into thin air. Dammit, Kyra felt more empathy with that mechanical moggy.

Kyra knew, however, that she had to press on, in the hope of unlocking a memory inside Amber's head that might just save the pair of them from dying of thirst down here, because that's what would happen if they didn't escape. After all, the water that dripped from the ceiling had a greenish hue to it, so it was possibly toxic.

Kyra, therefore, continued to question the young woman who swayed as she cuddled Lilli. 'Amber. What else do you remember? Before the field of flowers?'

'I'm not sure. I mean it's all foggy.' Suddenly she beamed a girlish smile. 'But I remember lots of things!' Then her expression became cloudy again. 'It's just all...glitchy.'

'Yes.' Kyra sighed with frustration. 'It's all fragmented. Same for me. Like I remember I had a dog named Freedom. Born on the Fourth of July.' Kyra realized that a smile had begun to tug at her lips as she remembered her beautiful dog. 'When she ran off, I stood out in the yard yelling 'Freedom'. My neighbors must have thought I was crazy.'

There it was again. The rattle of a chain reached her ears. It seemed closer this time. Louder. More ominous, too. She directed the flashlight into the tunnel, almost like she was firing a ray gun into the darkness. The light, however, wasn't strong enough. It didn't venture far down that long gullet of rock before everything vanished into darkness.

Kyra gripped the soldering iron tightly. It had become a weapon in her hand. She was ready to strike if a potential attacker came racing out of the shadows. The chain rattled again.

Kyra took five more steps along the tunnel. She was ready to fight for her life.

Suddenly, she heard footsteps – the footsteps were quick, and coming closer. However, she realized that they came from behind her. Kyra spun around to see Amber approaching. She no longer had the cat. What she did have was a knife. A sharp knife with a blade long enough to skewer a human body from their heart to their spine.

Amber hissed, 'I lied. There was one knife.'

Amber raised the knife and plunged the point at Kyra's face. Kyra flung the soldering iron aside so she could grab Amber's wrist in both hands, so preventing the steel blade from punching through the front of her skull.

Amber snarled, 'I'm not going to let you stab Lilli!'

Kyra maintained a tight grip on Amber's wrist. 'Amber! Stop it!'

'Let me!' Amber pushed the blade's point toward Kyra's left eye. 'Let me!'

Kyra knew what Amber meant. She was saying: *Let me stab you.*

Kyra tried to remain calm as she said, 'Drop the knife.'

'Let me!'

The blade's point was now just one inch from Kyra's eyeball.

Amber pushed hard, forcing the blade ever closer. The murderously sharp point even came into contact with Kyra's eyelashes. With a grunt, Kyra suddenly stepped backwards. This caused Amber to stumble. Kyra still gripped Amber's wrist but allowed the woman to fall forwards. A moment later, Amber was lying flat on the tunnel floor. Kyra grabbed the opportunity. She let go of Amber then rushed to the where the cat lay. She quickly picked it up and clamped one hand around the back of its neck.

'Amber, don't move? Or I'll break her neck!'

'Don't hurt Lilli.'

'Why did you attack me?'

Amber wailed with fear. 'You were going to stab us!'

'I wasn't going to stab anyone.'

Amber reached up toward Lilli with one hand. The other hand, however, maintained a tight grip on the knife.

Amber snarled, 'Give me Lilli!'

'You give me the knife.'

Amber lay there panting; her eyes were huge in the gloom. They were utterly otherworldly.

Kyra held out her hand. 'Give me the knife.'

Then Amber nodded. She'd reached a decision. 'I'll put it away.'

As she lay there on the ground, she plunged the knife into her side. Instantly, her savage expression dissolved into one of pain.

Kyra stared at the woman in shock.

Amber's expression became savage again as she focused those unearthly eyes on Kyra. 'You will do as I say.' She pulled the knife out of her side. 'Give me Lilli!'

Kyra's heart pounded – the intensity of the situation almost overwhelmed her. 'Blood...All that blood. Amber, you shouldn't have pulled the knife out. You've left the wound open.'

Kyra acted fast. She thrust the cat into Amber's outstretched hands before dropping down onto her knees to work on the woman. With a swiftness and an accuracy that even astonished her, she pulled up the T-shirt beneath the dungarees to examine the wound that formed an inch-wide slot in her side. The flesh around the wound glistened wetly with the outpouring of hot blood, which began to steam on contact with the cold air. Then resonant words of guidance began to flow through Kyra's mind, hinting that she'd committed them to memory at some point in her forgotten past: *Put pressure on the stab wound. And be sure to keep pressure on the wound until trained medics arrive. It is vital – absolutely vital – that you keep applying pressure. In a situation like this, pack the wound with a clean dressing. In an emergency, if there is no dressing, use anything you can find, such as a piece of clothing or a cloth. Then hold it in place to stop the bleeding.*

Kyra forced her palm against the bloody hole in the woman's side.

Despite this decidedly horrific event, Kyra was surprised by the fact that she appeared to know how to treat a knife injury so efficiently. She had no memory of being taught first aid, yet here she was. Pressing her palm forcefully onto the deep puncture in Amber's flesh. Though Amber would require expert medical attention to be certain that the flow of blood had been stemmed. Kyra then began to think hard as she considered what to employ as an improvised dressing.

Amber's eyes were slipping out of focus. She was growing weaker. Yet she devotedly kissed the cat on its plastic face.

'Amber. Hold on. I am going to save you. I won't let you die. Just hold on.'

When it began, Kyra couldn't really say. However, a blue glow seemed to bleed from the gloom of the tunnel. The glow moved over the walls...as if ghostly forms skated across the rock. Kyra's focus was laser-sharp, and it was entirely fixed on Amber. Therefore, she didn't look back at what was producing the blue light. She thought: *Amber is important now. Stop the bleeding. Do not let her die.*

Kyra's hand was pressed hard to the wound. Hot blood oozed through her fingers. She glanced at Amber's face, searching for any symptoms that might reveal the woman was bleeding out. Amber stared along the tunnel, in the direction of whatever generated the blue glow. Abruptly, her eyes became fixated on the lights. Their radiance turned her face a deathly blue. It only took a second, but the pain vanished from Amber's features. She appeared to slip into a trance. Disturbingly, her eyes stared in a way that was utterly corpse-like. Her eyes did not move. She did not blink. There was simply that dead stare.

Despite all this, some instinct reached out from the depths of Kyra's brain to urge her to not look directly at the blue light. Footsteps were approaching – many pairs of feet. People were hurrying towards her. The walls reflected a dazzling wash of blue, yet Kyra still did not look back toward the source of the light. Instead, she grabbed the knife that Amber had dropped, and then she scrambled a few paces away from the sound of approaching feet. She needed those extra precious seconds. Why she had to do this, she didn't even know for sure. But some vestige of memory dictated her actions.

Kyra crouched down. Her back was to the blue light. Meanwhile, the sound of running feet was getting louder and louder.

With grim determination, she stabbed the tip of the knife blade into her forearm. Then, ignoring the blast of searing agony, she began to gouge, to cut – she was scribing marks there into her flesh.

A pair of hands grabbed her head. And they began turning her head to face the light. However, Kyra continued to carve bloody marks into her arm. She would continue for as long as she could until...

Blue light burned deep into her eyes. The knife fell from her hand. Then she was falling, too...into cold, cold darkness.

CHAPTER NINE

Kyra lay on her back. She stared up at a set of three concentric rings that were suspended twenty inches or so above her face. Cables snaked down from a ceiling of white tiles. The ends of the cables were embedded into that assembly of rings, which appeared to be made from surgical steel. If anything, the ring structure resembled the light that would be positioned by a dentist above the patient as they lay back in the chair.

Kyra's mind had a peculiar floating sensation...*drugs...it must be drugs*. The light in the room was harsh, and it stung her eyes. She closed her eyelids. However, fingers immediately pulled her eyelids open. Someone then began taping her eyelids back, so she could not close them again.

Despite the drugs making her feel woozy, she was still able to appraise her surroundings. She appeared to be in a medical treatment room. There was a sense of austere sterility. White tiles on the walls were glassily clean. Figures moved around her, as busy as honeybees in a hive. They wore surgical gowns of some sort. Heads and faces were covered by tight-fitting plastic hoods, which made these figures look like alien beings from a poisoned world, where the air would melt your lungs and kill you in seconds. For sure, those were strange images, yet that is the impression she had, as she tried to scrutinize the place where she'd been brought after...

After what?

She struggled to remember.

After the mine! Yes, she'd been in a tunnel with a strange woman with the mechanical cat. And then there'd been a blue light. She'd recalled nothing else until she woke up.

Beware the blue light...beware the blue light. The words rattled through her skull, over and over. *Beware the blue light...*

Why have my eyelids been taped back? My arm is sore...the knife. I did that to my arm. I cut myself...why? The thoughts that jangled through her skull were threatening to run out of control. She forced herself to think clearly. *So, where am I now?* She realized she'd been strapped down to a bench of some sort. Her head had been clamped into a metal restraint, meaning she could not move her head to the left or to the right.

Just then, oblongs of light flickered from the far wall. Instantly, she realized she was looking at an array of a dozen TV monitors. One revealed the shocking image of a big man with tattoos. A red light shone onto his face from a device strapped to his head. Most shockingly of all, he had grabbed a young woman by her throat and had lifted her from the floor, so that her feet kicked free. She was in agony. Another screen revealed a forest at night. A man was running through the trees. He was on fire. Orange flames blazed from his head. She saw that his mouth was moving, though she could hear no sound coming from the screen. The burning man couldn't run far, because a long chain was shackled to one of his ankles. The other end of the chain was fixed to a tree. Then he fell, blazing, to the ground.

Why would someone stream footage of a woman being strangled on a screen where Kyra could see it? And that dreadful silent footage of a burning man? Then she understood. This was all about power. Someone was demonstrating their power over her. They (whoever 'they' were) could force her to watch atrocities. Her head was clamped. She couldn't look away. Her eyelids were taped open. She couldn't close her eyes to what was happening on the screen. Someone was telling her: *Look, I can force you to watch whatever horror I want you to watch. I have the power. And I have the power of life and death over you.*

Another screen revealed Amber – that enchanted princess of a woman from the mine. Amber was wheeled, unconscious, on a gurney into something that resembled an operating theatre. Figures in surgical gowns and masks clustered around her. She still clung onto the cat. One of the figures tore the fake animal from her grasp and dropped it onto the gurney by her feet. Was Amber dead? Her eyes stared up at the ceiling, she wasn't moving; her dungarees were drenched with blood.

The footage of Amber vanished, to be replaced by a man's pale face. It loomed gigantically from the center of the screen. He was bearded, aged about forty-five, and wore a business suit that was a severe black. He appeared to be staring directly at Kyra from the screen. When he spoke (in tones that were calmly professional) she realized he could see her, and he was examining her...the very image of a scientist gazing down into the entrails of a dissected rat.

The man said, 'She has introduced a new variable.'

Another voice came from the screen. Yet whoever spoke the words wasn't revealed: 'Know, John.' He appeared to be reading the words. 'How could she remember John?'

The image onscreen changed. The man's white face that ghoulishly stared down at her was replaced by a view of Kyra lying on a gurney. There were leather straps holding her down. Her head was clamped in a steel frame. She was watching a livestream of herself lying there. Helpless. Unable to prevent them doing whatever the hell they wanted to do to her.

As Kyra watched the screen, the camera that filmed her zoomed in on her bare forearm. She saw bloody cuts on her flesh. They oh-so redly spelt out the words *Kno Jon*. As if to confirm that she was seeing a close-up of her forearm, the flesh began to sting again. She recalled the point of the knife gouging marks that spelt out that stark message: *Kno Jon.*

The screen reverted to the looming face that was as white as bone. The man leaned forwards, staring down at her – his eyes were as cold as they were cruel. He nodded, apparently satisfied with whatever brutal decision he'd made.

He murmured, 'I don't know how she overcame the process to remember John. But it will be enlightening to see its effect.'

The steel rings above her turned purple. Instantly, pulsating lights washed over her face. Within the rings, there was a round object – something like a metal ball or orb. The way it glowed…there was something fascinating about it. Fascinating yet frightening, as if the orb contained forces that could be dangerous to her. Slowly, the orb began to descend toward her face. This movement was accompanied by a deep throbbing noise. Initially, the sound was quite soft; however, it quickly grew in its intensity until powerful sound waves punched deep into her ears. The purple light became brighter and brighter. It burned through her eyes, which she could not close. And then the purple light began to burn a pathway into her brain.

That's when Kyra understood.

With all her strength she screamed, '*No…please! I want to remember!*'

CHAPTER TEN

Kyra was woken by a kick. She opened her eyes to find that she was lying next to a man she did not know. Her first thought was: *Why am I in bed with a stranger?* The dark skin of his face and his shaved head shone beneath a bright light from directly over-head.

A flurry of kicks struck her right hip and thigh. *That fucking hurts!* She gasped with pain.

Then a female voice that blazed with fury shouted, 'Get out! Both of ya! Out!'

Another kick – this time in her side – and hard enough to make Kyra's eyes water.

The guy quickly climbed to his feet. Evidently, he'd been kicked, too, because he was rubbing his stomach and grimacing with pain. Kyra scrambled to her feet to be confronted by an angry woman. The stranger was in her thirties, her hair tightly curled. Her eyes were nothing less than savage. The woman raised her right hand – it had been bandaged yet grazes on her knuckles were clearly visible. No doubt she'd been in a vicious fist fight.

And gripped tightly in that same hand was a piece of metal that had been crudely sharpened to form a shiv...this was the kind of weapon that jailbirds secretly make to butcher their enemies in the prison exercise yard. She slashed the homemade knife through the air while her eyes stabbed with absolute ferocity at Kyra and the man beside her.

Then this savagely aggressive woman yelled words that made no sense. 'Find your own light! This is my light! Get out! Go on – get out!'

Kyra and the man immediately backed away, aiming to stay well back from the vicious slashes of the blade.

A woman's voice from behind them, an older voice, rang out with desperate urgency. 'Hey! You three! Stand in the middle of the light!'

The woman with the knife began to move closer. The look in her eye told Kyra that she was hellbent on slaughter. Meanwhile, the guy who'd she woken up beside was holding up his hands, trying to placate the angry woman.

The woman then circled around them, her speed and her anger made her clumsy. She hacked at the air with the blade, trying to intimidate them.

Then Kyra realized that they were standing in a pool of light, which was perhaps fifteen feet in diameter. All around them was darkness. Utter darkness. This was like being on a theatre stage with a spotlight picking them out, illuminating them in a dazzling radiance, while all around them was a black fog of darkness.

The woman shouted, 'Get out of my light!' Then she took a step backwards.

Slash!

The movement didn't come from the woman. Instead, a pair of hands that bristled with hairs, and possessing torn fingernails, and had flesh ripped from the knuckles, suddenly appeared from out of the darkness. The brutalized hands grabbed hold of the knife woman from behind. After that, she was violently plucked from the circle of light.

The woman screamed in absolute despair as she vanished into the darkness. Kyra sensed there were people moving all around the light pool. They moved fast – they were predatory shapes that flitted through utter darkness...the kind of darkness found on dead worlds that have been deprived of their sun. To Kyra, those barely-seen shapes reminded her of sharks that glided through dark waters in search of prey.

The knife woman screamed – a sound that pulsated with terror. She screamed so loudly that the force of the yell must have painfully torn the delicate membranes of her throat. There were the sounds of chains rattling. Then a red glow appeared to Kyra's right, which quickly died away to nothing.

The knife woman gave a shriek of agony. And that died away to nothing, too.

After that, there was silence.

The man's eyes were wide with alarm. 'Shit.'

Kyra stared into the gloom. Her eyes were watering with the effort to see through the murk. 'What the hell was that?'

The older woman cried out again, 'Them! They're out there!'

A man's voice suddenly thundered. It was rough, aggressive. Kyra didn't see who was shouting, though his words were perfectly clear. 'Come on out! Show yourselves!'

Kyra now had a moment to catch her breath and take stock of her surroundings. Firstly, she saw that they appeared to be in a cavernous place, though, in truth, she could see neither walls nor ceiling in the gloom. Secondly, there were three pools of light. She and the male stranger occupied one light pool. Another light pool, perhaps fifty feet away, accommodated a woman in a wheelchair. She must have injured her ankle or her leg because the bottom half of her leg was encased in a blue cast. Even further away was another pool of light. Three people occupied that one. There was a young guy in a striped T-shirt. Standing next to him was a young woman with what appeared to be a cat in her arms. The third occupant was a guy of around forty. He wore a colorful shirt that sang out, 'this is my Hawaiian beach party look', while the look on his surly face might as well have been snarling, 'give me your purse, or I'll break your fucking nose'.

The three people in the furthest light pool moved restlessly. Like caged animals. Pacing around their little zone of radiance that was no more than five yards in diameter. Strangely, they were afraid to get too close to the edge of the light. As if they feared that the edge of the light might burn them or electrocute them. They kept trying to get into the center of the light pool, even though that meant jostling against their companions.

The dark-haired young woman with the cat repeatedly flinched when her companions brushed against her. Her large eyes revealed that she was scared.

The man in the Hawaiian shirt kept bellowing threats. Those threats seemingly directed at someone he hated but could not see. The younger man was reacting to noises in the darkness. He was jittery. He appeared to be terrified that a monster would lunge from the shadows to attack him. In fact, his next words bore this out.

'They're all around us!'

The woman in the wheelchair was endeavoring to be motherly and protect her new companions. 'Whatever you do,' she told them, 'stay in the light. Do not leave the light. Do you understand?'

Hawaiian shirt guy got cocky. 'Come on, let's fight 'em. Let's all gang up and march out there! Rip 'em to shit!'

The woman in the wheelchair shrugged with exasperation. 'You're an idiot. I know how to survive. I've been here the longest.' She raised her arm as if calling out to God. Or the Devil. 'Hear me! I'm queen of my light pool!'

The guy standing beside Kyra called out to the woman, 'Where are we? How did we get here?'

The woman gave an expressive shrug. 'No one knows.'

The guy appeared to be trying to figure out what was happening here. And, clearly, he'd decided to gather more information, because he called out to everyone there. 'We should know each other's names.'

The woman in the wheelchair sang out in a surprisingly bright voice, 'I am Rosa.'

The three in the light pool furthest away gave their names.

Hawaiian shirt thug: 'Tanner.'

Young woman with cat: 'Amber.'

Young guy in striped T: 'Nev.'

Kyra spoke up, 'Kyra...my name is Kyra.'

Her companion nodded. 'Okay. So, none of you know how we got here?'

Nev called back, 'Nope. A light suddenly appears, and folks are – *whoosh* – there. Like you two.'

Rosa spoke in gentle, motherly tones. 'Just stay in the light and stay alive.' She smiled. A very odd smile in the circumstances, Kyra decided.

Nev's voice rang out with absolute certainty, 'We're trapped. Prisoners.'

Kyra heard her light pool buddy mutter to himself, 'Lab rats...' His eyes seemed like they'd turned inward to stare at some horrific image inside his brain. Yet, a moment later, he shook his head, then frowned, as if he struggled to remember something that was vitally important.

That's when he glanced at Kyra. His attention immediately fixed on her bare forearm. His eyes widened in surprise, and his expression was so intense that she looked at what he was staring at on her arm. She saw cuts there in her skin – they were still raw-looking. Still seeping blood. The cuts formed words gouged from flesh.

KNO JON. That's what the words spelt out.

The man looked her in the face. He almost seemed scared of her. 'I'm John. Different spelling of my name...though it could be me.'

Kyra's heart was racing as she held out her arm for the man to inspect more closely – this was an electric moment. As if she was revealing a secret part of herself. His brown eyes were grave and utterly serious as he met her gaze. A thrill ran down her backbone. Their glances communicated an instant mutual trust. They had formed a bond. Their eye-contact was undeniably intimate.

She whispered, 'I think we know each other.'

The sound of feet scuffing quickly against the concrete floor made her glance at the three in the furthest light pool. They moved restlessly in the little puddle of light while looking out into the darkness. Their agitation revealed that they believed they'd be attacked at any moment.

Out there in the darkness, chains rattled. Not a loud sound, yet deeply ominous.

John took hold of her forearm, his fingers gently curling around her arm. She felt a shivery sensation run across the soft skin of her belly.

John stared at his name that was bloodily carved there. 'What happened?'

'I...I think I did it.'

'When?'

'From before. There must be a *before* this. These cuts must be to remember.' She felt a surge of frustration. 'We have to remember what happened to us.'

'Why don't we?'

Kyra sighed. 'I don't know. It must be part of what's occurring here...they're messing with us.'

John digested what she'd told him. 'A sick game?' he asked.

'Maybe.' Then an idea occurred to her. 'Maybe some kind of test? Can you remember doing anything like this before?'

John thought hard. 'I'm pretty sure I remember...'

She looked at him with a renewed hope.

He whispered, 'I'm pretty sure I remember *not* remembering many times before. That sounds pretty crazy.'

'It's not crazy. I feel the same thing. Kind of remembering that I *can't* remember something that is hugely important.'

'In fact,' he murmured, 'whatever did happen, my gut feeling tells me you were there, Kyra. I'm sure we faced some...some weird, dangerous thing together.'

'Yes. We were together. I feel that.'

'But you can't actually recall how many times we've met?'

Kyra shook her head.

John released his gentle hold of her forearm. 'And you don't remember how we got here?'

'No.'

John noticed something else that had been hidden by her sleeve. Carefully, he eased her sleeve back to reveal more letters cut into the skin. They spelt *Blk lite*.

He frowned. 'Black light? What does that mean?'

'I don't know.'

Abruptly, a light shot down from the ceiling. It resembled a pillar of fire against the blackness. Kyra shielded her eyes against the dazzling glare as a light pool formed there, just ten feet away from the one they stood in.

There, in the center of the disk was a baby buggy. It was pink in color. The metal spokes of the wheels glinted brightly enough to dazzle the eye in that column of harsh brilliance.

A moment later, a cry came from the buggy. A baby's cry – one that was threaded with fear. Chains rattled in the darkness. Predatory shapes moved out there, circling like hungry sharks.

The baby's cry grew louder.

Kyra did not hesitate. There was a baby in danger. She would allow no harm to come to a child. Kyra ran toward the edge of her light pool. She was ready to plunge into the evil shroud of darkness that surrounded her.

CHAPTER ELEVEN

Kyra sprinted toward the baby buggy as an unseen infant began to wail in terror. However, a hand gripped her arm before yanking her back so fiercely that her teeth clacked together, and the tendons in her shoulder were so overstretched that they sent a jag of pain up through her neck to detonate inside her head. The jolt hurt so much she cried out.

John had pulled her back from the darkness – and only just in time, because the silhouette of a figure lunged at her. Its hands were briefly visible as they neared the edge of the light pool. Then the figure moved backwards, away from the light, as if afraid the intense radiance would cause their hands to burst into flame. Kyra realized that the figure had tried to attack her at the same time as she heard a whirring noise, followed by the clatter of chain links. Was her attacker chained? Had it been hauled back by a motor attached to the chain? She had no way of knowing, yet the noise she heard suggested exactly that. That, in turn, inserted disturbing images into her mind of savage people out there in the darkness...people who were shackled to chains that controlled their movements. Savage beasts on steel leashes – that was the troubling image that came to mind. Sometimes the leash was lengthened, sometimes shortened.

John kept hold of her. He was clearly frightened for her, thinking she'd rush to the baby buggy. There was no sign of a baby, however. Was there a sadist out there? Toying with their minds?

She watched John track the red glow that was moving through the darkness with his steady gaze. He was in a state of catlike readiness. The red glow turned briefly yellow as it slowly moved away. A moment later, however, it began to burn blood red. The glow moved with sudden speed toward Nev. A movement full of menace. Nev noticed the approach of the red light. Yelling, he lurched back to the center of the light pool. By accident, he knocked against Tanner as he did so.

Tanner thundered at Nev. 'Watch it!' He grabbed hold of Nev's hair in his thug fist. 'Or I'll throw you out!'

Nev grimaced as his hair was pulled. 'Stop.'

Tanner didn't stop. He shook Nev, as a bully would shake a child. The violent shaking resulted in Nev colliding with Amber. She'd been staring into the darkness as if hypnotized. Now she snapped – snapped big time. Wildly, she began waving the cat. A toy cat, Kyra realized.

Amber screeched so loudly it set Kyra's teeth on edge the same way it would when a knife blade *scraa-aaws* against a plate. An awful sound.

Amber brandished the cat at the two men. 'Get back. I'll burn it down. I'll burn it all down. You're not my family...you can't just take me in!'

John murmured in astonishment, 'Just look at her. She's waving the toy like it's a burning torch. Like she's going to set those guys on fire.'

Amber's voice dropped to whisper. 'You don't know me. You can't feel my pain.'

Tanner stared at Amber in disbelief. Then he viciously pointed at her. 'You! You're fucking crazy!'

Tanner was clearly showing everyone that he was the number one boss man here, because he aggressively pushed Nev. The shove sent Nev reeling to the very edge of the light, just an inch from the killing darkness.

Nev screamed in panic. 'Stop that!'

John called out, 'Tanner. Leave him alone.'

Tanner grinned. *A downright, fucking evil grin,* thought Kyra. *Tanner's a bully.* She'd met plenty of guys like that before. Hell, she'd dated guys like that before. Nice at first, then they bad mouth you, then they dish out a stinging slap when you don't immediately give them what they want.

Tanner got a sweaty excitement on. He clearly loved to see Nev's expression of panic. It got worse...Tanner pushed Nev toward the edge of the light. Nev almost lost his balance. He had to frantically windmill his arms to prevent himself from falling out into the darkness.

Tanner was getting ready to push again when Nev abruptly glanced down. His expression turned to one of shock as he understood a terrifying fact.

Nev gasped in horror. 'Hey! Look...*look.*' He pointed down at the line where light became darkness.

Amber and Tanner recognized something in Nev's tone that prompted them to step closer to Nev and look down at what he pointed at.

Nev whispered, 'The light. It's shrinking.'

Both Tanner and Amber flinched back. Both were alarmed by what they saw.

Rosa called out, 'You three. Get in tight to the center. As close to each other as you can!'

Amber and Nev rapidly obeyed. They hurried to the center of the white disk. Tanner, however, swaggered toward the edge of the light. He was cocky. He was the Big Man. He was in control. He glared down at the edge of the light pool, like he was daring the darkness to approach him.

The light pool began to ever so slowly shrink. At the same time, the sound of dragging chains grew louder. Little buds of yellow floated in the gloom. To Kyra, they looked like weird planets floating in the blackness of space. But no…she realized she was looking at human faces illuminated by a device clamped to their heads. The devices resembled horse blinders. Strange things, they were. And absolutely frightening. She was tempted to run away, but she feared attack if she left the apparent safety of the light.

The faces were all damaged in some way. Either heavily scarred or possessing facial wounds that had been crudely stitched shut. Some of the faces were smeared with blood. Their blood? Or the blood of—

A pulsating drone began. An evil sound that sent shivers cascading down Kyra's spine. Fear amplified every sensation in her body. She could feel the pressure of her taut skin that overlaid her muscles. The muscles clenched as tension twisted her flesh up tight. She could feel the frightened spasm of her heart, pushing blood through her veins. The cuts on her arm were singing their own pain melody. Her belly was so tight with fear that her lungs felt compressed to the point where breathing became difficult. She tried to suck in a lungful of air, but the air felt as sharp as broken glass in her throat.

And all around them, the 'sharks' were circling the pools of light. That's the impression she had. The figures out there were like vicious predators. Soon they would attack. What would happen then? Could they successfully fight back? Or were their opponents stronger? Fiercer? Were they killers?

Nev and Amber clustered tight into the center of the light pool. Tanner appeared to have lost some of his alpha male bravado. The faces that circled them in the dark were frightening. Tanner evidently felt that fear now. He retreated to the center of the light until his back thumped into Amber and Nev. By unlucky chance, the collision knocked Amber to the very edge of the light. She reacted like she'd been zapped with an electric cattle prod. Instantly, she leapt back, into the center of the light. Like a frightened child, she put her arms around Tanner and Nev and pulled herself tight to them.

Kyra shouted encouragement. 'That's it!'

Rosa called out, 'Hold onto one another!'

'Keep in the middle!' That was John, his expressive eyes were fixed on the three. He was willing them to keep safe.

Amber held the cat in front of her and pressed herself and the cat into Tanner's back, as if to shield the toy animal. Tanner's eyes bulged, his face turned red, then he cruelly shoved the young woman. Clearly, he was attempting to oust her from the light. Amber retaliated by hurling herself at Tanner. She tried to push him into the darkness. However, she was slightly built, and Tanner began to manhandle her from the center. The expression of sadistic glee on his face told everyone that he was going to evict her from the place of safety. And this bully was going to bloody-well enjoy himself as he did so.

Instead of waiting to be hurled into the arms of the prowling figures, Amber suddenly ran from the light. She dashed across to Rosa's light pool. A moment later, she entered the unearthly glow occupied by Rosa in her wheelchair. Rosa looked up and smiled with relief at Amber.

'You made it, child.' Rosa beamed with happiness. 'You stay here with me.'

Amber evidently had a plan. She grabbed hold of the wheelchair's handles then shoved hard. The wheelchair rolled to the edge of the light, with Rosa hanging on tight, her eyes going huge with shock.

Rosa let out a howl of terror. 'No!'

Amber's gaze locked onto Rosa as the wheelchair glided into the darkness.

Kyra yelled, 'Rosa! Come to us!'

John beckoned frantically. 'Hurry! You can make it!'

Rosa began to work the wheels of the chair. Soon she was gliding across the concrete floor. Quickly, she vanished into the fog of gloom, instantly becoming invisible to everyone in the light pools.

That's when the circling 'sharks' began to move. The yellow gleam, which emanated from devices fixed to the heads of the people, revealed strangely impassive faces – a zombie look. All the more chilling due to the way the eyes stared blankly, as if they belonged to corpses.

Rosa must have been desperately wheeling the chair closer to Kyra's light pool. Kyra could not see her, though she could hear the squeak of the wheels. What she could see was the predatory way the yellow lights moved toward the sound of the unseen wheelchair that was slowly approaching the light.

Kyra thought: *Let Rosa make it – please, let her make it.*

CHAPTER TWELVE

Kyra and John ran to the point nearest where Rosa should emerge from the darkness in her wheelchair. The squeak of the wheels was the only sign that she still moved toward them.

They both began shouting encouragement, as did Nev. Tanner had resumed his belligerent demeanor. Evidently, the act of shouting for the woman to save herself was beneath his dignity. Amber merely stared up in the direction of the ceiling. There was a sweetly innocent expression on her face, like she'd done nothing wrong.

Kyra yelled, 'Rosa! Hurry!

The rattle of chains grew louder. The yellow lights that illuminated the faces of those disturbing individuals were converging on where the wheelchair should be. Out there in the dark.

Then it all happened at once.

Rosa materialized like a ghost from the shadows. The woman desperately turned the wheels with her hands, driving the chair forward at a considerable speed. Kyra took a chance. She leaned out over the boundary where light ended and darkness began, her hands reaching out into the inky gloom. Chains rattled louder. There was a swirl of yellow lights behind Rosa, as if the menacing figures were doing some kind of crazy dance.

Kyra yelled, 'Grab hold! Grab my hands! I'll pull you in!'

Rosa's eyes blazed with terror. 'Save me, child! Don't let them take me!'

Rosa did grab tight to Kyra's hands, but instead of Kyra pulling the woman in, the woman inadvertently pulled her out, such was her panic. Kyra's feet skittered over the smooth floor. Rosa possessed a formidable strength and dragged Kyra into the darkness – out where those dangerous figures moved like hungry sharks.

The lights had been yellow...now they changed.

Red. Blood red. A blazing red that pulsated with an angry violence all of its own.

John put his arms around Kyra's waist. He pulled so hard she heard her elbow joints make crackling sounds. Pains shot from her wrists to her shoulders. She grunted at the hurt, but she hung on. She wasn't going to let go. *No fucking way.*

Kyra and John were pulling together. Drawing Rosa toward them. Kyra was now fully back in the light again. Rosa's feet on the wheelchair footrest inched forwards from darkness into light.

Just a few more seconds. That's all it would take to bring Rosa fully into the safety of the light pool.

Rosa panted, 'That's it, pull me...pull me in.'

Then Rosa screamed. A blood-soaked hand had clutched her throat. More arms wrapped themselves around her upper body. Chains rattled. Red lights blazed. They revealed rage-filled eyes. And they illuminated faces that had been devastated by appalling injuries. Then Rosa's attackers dragged her wheelchair – and Rosa with it – back into the void where no light fell.

Rosa screamed. She screamed again. Then the scream petered out into a croaking sound that was full of pain.

Chains rattled loudly – a sudden cacophony of sound. After that... silence.

Kyra screamed across the bleak void to Amber, 'Why did you push Rosa out of the light?'

John voiced his own disbelief at Amber's cruel actions: 'Why? In God's name, why?'

Amber clutched the toy cat to her chest. 'For Lilli.'

Now that Amber was closer, Kyra had a better view of the cat. She saw that it was a mechanical comfort cat. The fur had been burnt from its plastic face. Nevertheless, the cat still emitted little 'miaow' sounds, while its tail slowly moved, and it tilted its head from one side to the other. To Kyra, the toy cat seemed so familiar. Supposedly a cute thing, but now rendered hideous because part of its plastic face had melted. Kyra looked at Amber more closely. The young woman was familiar, too. That pretty face, which looked as if it could belong to an enchanted princess. What's more, the young woman's bizarre demeanor rang a bell.

Amber stood in the center of the light, where she cuddled the toy animal to her chest. She smiled as if pleased to be there, and that she'd be safe.

Amber now smiled up at the ceiling. It was as if she saw a familiar face gazing down from above.

Then Amber called out in a peculiar sing-song voice, 'Hello, forever.'

That's when the light pool she occupied began to shrink. It shrank fast, the light becoming brighter, more concentrated on the floor. Amber looked down in shock. She moved her feet as she searched for an area where the light would not die completely.

She was out of luck.

The light disappeared. Amber vanished into the darkness.

Her voice rang out, 'No!'

After that, there were no more sounds. Once again, silence had put a deathly hand on the place. Kyra saw that John was staring in shock at where Amber had been standing, though the darkness made it impossible to see anything.

That's when Tanner lost it. He brutally grabbed hold of Nev, then the thug began to rant as if panic had destroyed his mind.

Tanner yelled into the otherwise silent emptiness: 'Take this piece of shit! Just leave me alone. Take him!'

Tanner attempted to throw Nev from the light pool. However, Nev dropped to the floor in the center of the light, balling himself up tight, attempting to protect his own neck and head with his hands.

Tanner started to drag Nev across the floor.

Nev cried out, 'Don't!'

Kyra yelled, 'Tanner! Leave him alone!'

Tanner roared, 'This is my light! I'm going to have it for myself! I'm going to have it all!' Then he yelled these words at the unseen figures in the darkness: 'Here, take Nev. He's yours. Do what the fuck you want with him. Rip off his head and shit in the hole if you want to. He's yours!'

Nev howled, 'No, leave me alone. Please, Tanner. They'll kill me!'

Tanner began kicking Nev in the ribs. By this time, Tanner was howling with deranged ecstasy while Nev howled in pain.

Nev, still lying on the floor, tried to squirm away from Tanner, yet there was no place to go. Their refuge was a smudge of illumination that was, by this time, little more than five feet in diameter, having diminished from a width of fifteen feet.

Tanner kicked again. Then he drew his foot back, aiming to deliver a kick so forceful that it would shatter ribs.

Tanner had already swung his foot back – and then he moved it further back. He didn't realize his foot had left the light. Instantly, a hand grabbed hold of his ankle.

A split-second later, the hand had pulled Tanner's ankle with such vicious power that the big man fell flat on his face. The hand then dragged Tanner away. Instantly, he began screaming. Though Kyra could see nothing, due to the darkness, the snarls she heard coming from those menacing individuals (together with Tanner's screams of agony) made her wonder if they were eating him alive.

Nev, meanwhile, had managed to push himself up into a sitting position. He flinched back as Tanner made an explosive reappearance. Tanner moved on all fours, back into the light. Blood drenched his face. Clumps of hair had been ripped from his scalp, leaving pink areas of bald skin. The man screamed in terror.

'Save me!'

Nev merely shrank back from the bloody figure.

Tanner had nearly got himself back into the light and safety. Not fully, however. Hands grabbed his ankles, which were still out in the sea of shadow. Once again, he was dragged away into the murk. This time, his screams were cut short the same moment that Kyra heard a loud *crunch!* A vile sound that could have been the man's skull being crushed.

Nev climbed to his feet. He was holding his side where Tanner's boots had pounded his flesh.

Nev gazed down at the edge of the light. Despite the pain etched onto his face, he suddenly looked hopeful. 'Hey, my light's stopped shrinking.'

John had other matters on his mind. 'Those...things...like crazy people. The way they ripped into Tanner. I couldn't see properly, but...but I'm sure they were biting...biting pieces of his face away.'

Kyra nodded. 'They're somehow familiar, aren't they? The chains. That thing on their heads. The lights. Yellow. Blue. Red. I feel like I've seen them before. But...' She shrugged. 'I don't know.'

'Why can't you remember?' John sighed with frustration. *Why can't I remember?*

Kyra spoke with sudden desperation. 'But we all remember the past, don't we? Before we got trapped here?' She dug deep into her mind. 'But do we *really* remember our lives before this? All my memories are hazy. I vaguely remember what I was doing. So... what do you remember?'

John frowned. 'What's here, inside my head, it's just flashes of things. Brief images of people and events...but what's in the gaps?'

Kyra struggled to make her mind work like it should. 'Yes...same here. But I can't recall events in any meaningful way. Big chunks of my past are missing. I don't remember my time at school. I don't even know if I was single or in a relationship. What if *we* are married to each other and just can't remember our wedding day?'

'Us? Married?' He shook his head. 'My God, I don't know if we are, or we aren't. So, what is happening to us?

Kyra suddenly spoke with conviction. 'Somehow, they're suppressing our memories...slowly rubbing them out. If we don't escape this place, we won't even know who we are anymore.'

'That's it. We're lab rats.'

Nev called out again. 'My light's definitely not shrinking any-more. It's still the same.'

Kyra and John turned to look at Nev.

He pointed into the darkness as a chain rattled nearby. 'He wore a chain, too.' Nev frowned for a second then appeared to remember something important. 'A big guy in chains. Yeah, I remember! He hit me.' He stared at them in surprise. 'You were there! Both of you! Don't you remember? It happened a few days ago. Think...think hard.'

Kyra could only shake her head. 'I don't remember you.'

Nev spoke louder. 'The soldering iron! I remember now. John, I threw the soldering iron to you.'

John echoed the words, 'Soldering iron.' He seemed to be close to remembering *something*.

Nev's eyes were gleaming like he was getting excited by what he'd recalled. 'Yeah, John, you went completely crazy. You stabbed the guy to death like a pinata. You skewered him through the fucking heart.'

Kyra took a step back from John. Was she standing next to a killer? John began to shake his head like he disagreed with Nev. However, worryingly, there was something in John's expression that hinted he didn't know for sure whether Nev told the truth or not.

Nev pressed on. 'You don't remember me at all? I'm Nev, yeah? The pizza delivery guy? I remember telling you that...just before the big dude, with lights on his head and the tattoos, tried to kill me.'

John frowned as he continued to shake his head, clearly not remembering despite Nev's prompting. Then he happened to glance down. Kyra noticed the way John flinched. He'd seen something that he did not like at all.

Kyra whispered, 'What is it? What's wrong?'

'The light – it's getting smaller. It's shrinking.'

Nev had noticed, too. 'Get into the middle of the light pool! Do it now!

John and Kyra swiftly moved into the center of the light. Kyra's blood turned to ice in her veins. Because the darkness was creeping toward them as the light pool began to contract.

Kyra looked John in the eye. She knew at that moment what he was thinking. Would they end up fighting for the light, just as Nev, Tanner and Amber had done when their light had begun to shrink?

Nev called out, 'Don't let the darkness touch you. If it does, the monster guys will get you. Think of something! You've gotta save your lives!'

Kyra and John shuffled closer together. Kyra realized that, come what may, they'd stay in the light pool even if it shrank down to the size of a dime.

Nev shouted, 'It's no good! You can't both fit in there! One of you has to take the whole light for themselves. If you don't, both of you will die!'

The darkness was an ocean of blackness. And it was slowly engulfing their little patch of illuminated floor.

Nev hollered again, 'One of you – you gotta shove the other out! You don't have a choice. Don't think about it! Do it! Now! Just grab hold of the other guy then throw them to the fucking wolves!'

Kyra realized that the danger she and John faced excited Nev. His face turned bright pink. His eyes were flashing. He could have been a teenage kid who'd found his older brother's stash of porn pix.

John spoke calmly: 'Kyra. Whatever happens, we stick together.'

Kyra gave a grave nod. 'Whatever happens.'

That's when John put his arms around her. For one terrifying moment, she thought he was going to fling her out into the darkness. Out to where the figures shuffled across the concrete floor, their watchful eyes illuminated by yellow lights that were fixed to the headsets. However, John embraced her with a tender strength. Clearly, he was going to hold her to him. They were going to be together. Right to the very end.

Nev shrieked, 'No! No! No! What the fuck are you doing, guys? You must take the light for yourselves. Throw the other out! Take the light for you, and only you, otherwise the bad guys are gonna get you and smash you to pieces. Remember what happened to Tanner. They ripped his ears off. They tore open his face!'

One of the figures lunged toward the light pool. The blaze of light from their blinders had turned to red. The creature was there in the light pool with them! Even though Kyra's heart threatened to explode with terror, she realized that the creature had broken the rules. Because even as it tried to grasp hold of her, there was the loud whirr of a motor. The chain links snapped tight with such force sparks flew from them. A split-second later, the man was dragged back by the chain. She vividly recalled that a cut on his right cheek had been sewn shut with a series of crude stitches like XXXX. And his teeth were red with blood. Maybe Tanner's blood.

She clung tighter to John, and he clung tighter to her. If they were taken by those figures, then they would be taken together. They'd fight together. They'd die together. Better that way, than to be mutilated in the darkness by whatever those monstrosities were.

The light continued to shrink, until they were standing in a little puddle of light that was no bigger than a dinner plate. She saw the furious faces of their would-be attackers all around her. Those faces were bathed in a red glow, which clearly triggered their fury.

Blue for calm. Red for murder.

And all the lights were red.

The figures lunged at Kyra and John. Hands with grazed fingers and bruised knuckles grabbed hold of Kyra's arms. A bloody hand that lacked fingernails gripped John's shirt.

John yelled, 'Kyra, hold onto me! Never let go!'

Then – *WHOOSH!*

All the red lights that illuminated the murderous faces suddenly turned blue. Instantly, the figures sagged like they were exhausted. Their arms dropped by their sides. The mechanism whirred again, chain links snapped tight, the figures were hauled backwards, away from the light pool.

John stared in amazement. 'They took them away.'

Kyra glanced at him – she wondered how much he knew. 'They?'

'They. Them. Whoever is doing this to us.'

Kyra watched as the chains dragged the figures until they

vanished into the darkness. 'Why did they pull them away? They were just moments from butchering us.'

'Maybe it's over? We passed the test.'

The light pool abruptly expanded, returning to its full size of fifteen feet in diameter. Kyra saw the shiv that the woman had dropped when she was plucked from the light. Kyra quickly scooped the makeshift weapon up into her right hand.

Nev sang out, 'We made it. We're going to live. They took away the Protos!'

'Protos?' John repeated the word as if it seemed to hold some significance. 'How do you know those things that were trying to kill us are called Protos?'

'As good a name as any. Like Goliath.'

'Goliath? Who the hell is Goliath?' John shook his head. He appeared angry with himself as though he half-remembered but could not quite join all the dots.

Nev called out, 'Looks like we really did pass the test.'

Kyra dug the point of the blade into her arm. She'd decided to carve the word *test* into her flesh, close to where she must have carved *U Kno John*. But something made her pause. She noticed that there was a partially healed 'T' scratched into her skin. 'T'? Had she begun to etch *test* there at some point in the past, but couldn't remember doing so?

The silence was annihilated by a wailing sound that blasted from an unseen source. This time, different figures came rushing out of the darkness. They wore masks and strange clothes – almost like flowing robes that were made from transparent plastic. The figures appeared to have lines of lights fixed to their bodies. This gave the uncanny impression that their skeletons glowed so brightly that the light shone through muscle and skin, thus rendering the bones visible to other people around them. The lights beneath the plastic robes blazed an intense blue.

Kyra shouted, 'Light!'

John glanced at her in shock. 'What?'

Kyra pointed at the words cut into her arm. *BLK LTE*. 'It doesn't say 'black light', it says 'block light'!' She closed her eyes. 'John. Close your eyes. As tight as you can. Keep them closed. Trust me!'

John grasped hold of her hand while putting his other arm around her shoulders and pulling her toward him, so that they were pressed tightly together. She felt the side of his face touching the side of hers.

Kyra whispered, 'John, don't look at those people. Don't look at the light. Never open your eyes!' Kyra pressed a hand to her eyes and held it there as forcefully as she could. Then fingers were trying to pull her hand away from her face. Through her eyelids she saw the flicker of blue light.

At that moment, she realized that the figures in the plastic robes were striving to pull her and John away from each other. However, another siren blared. Straight away, the hands were taken away. She remained standing there, holding onto John, her eyes still closed.

She heard John murmur, 'What's happening?'

'I don't know. Just keep your eyes shut.'

'I am.'

'Don't look into the light. Please don't look.'

It seemed to come from nowhere. She convulsed with surprise, rather than pain.

That's when she realized someone had just driven a hypodermic needle into her arm.

A cold sensation oozed through her veins. That tingling coldness quickly spread through her body. When the narcotic hit her brain, the light of awareness fled to be replaced by darkness...

CHAPTER THIRTEEN

Amber screamed. Images of burning filled her mind. And the sounds – the remembered, awful sounds of screaming – they filled her head to the point where she believed her skull would burst open with a loud bang. She wondered (if her skull did burst) would she live long enough to see her brain and blood being flung out in gobs of red that would be shiny and wet? Terror twisted her heart so painfully that she screamed again. Amber would have jumped to her feet and run away if it wasn't for the fact that she was held down onto a gurney by brutally tight straps. What's more, she couldn't even move her head. She sensed that her skull had been fixed into a steel framework. Above her, were concentric rings that glowed with a yellow light.

The harsh scream tore from her throat again with such force that her vocal cords burned like they were on fire.

Fire...stench of burning. Sounds of screaming. Fire engulfing rooms. Fire exploding through the roof to paint the sky yellow, red, orange and gold.

Amber fought to break free of the restraints. No good. They held her there. She was lying on her back, looking up at the device above her head that glowed softly.

Once again, she yelled out in pain and terror, 'Let me go! I'll burn you all!'

Instantly, a purple light flooded from the device above her head. She tried to close her eyes against the light that flooded through her pupils, deep into her brain. However, her eyes had been taped open. She could not lower her eyelids.

The purple radiance glowed, brighter and brighter. Amber stopped screaming. She stopped moving. She couldn't even move her fingers.

The voice of a man reached her through the purple glow that gently pulsated. 'You heard? Amber is starting to remember?'

Another voice – this one deeper. It possessed tones of calm authority. 'Only fragments. Nothing of consequence. I detected no sign that she has a clear memory of her foster parents being burned alive. She only recalls fragmentary images associated with burning and flames.'

The man who had spoken first didn't sound convinced. 'Amber is too erratic. She's going to need your color blinders if she continues to behave in such an unpredictable and, frankly, dangerous fashion.'

'No. She's still far more stable than the prototypes. She's no John or Kyra, but she's more useful untethered...for now.'

Amber wanted to yell, she wanted to scream. She wanted to attack the owners of those frightening voices that discussed her as if she was a lab specimen. However, she could only stare up at the purple light and listen to the strange sounds that now pulsed from the walls. The lights were sweeping away recent memories...her mind was becoming blank.

She tried to whisper her name. 'I am called...'

She could not remember what she was called. There was only the purple light now. The purple light had become her entire universe.

CHAPTER FOURTEEN

Kyra's mind rose from the darkness to the light of full consciousness.

I'm a brain without a body, she thought. *I cannot feel my body. My heart isn't beating. I am entirely numb.*

All at once, she pictured herself at the center of a grotesque medical experiment. Her brain being removed – a brain that was thoroughly alive. Then her brain being placed in a vat of blood that was oxygenated by machines. She saw herself as a brain that was being kept alive for centuries in a laboratory. Despite such bizarre images flowing through her head, she remained calm. *I am still a human being,* she told herself. *I will remain sane. My mind will become the world that I live in...*

Kyra dug deep into her memories. At first...nothing. Then images began to flash inside her head with such a vivid power she wanted to retreat from them. The first memory was of a wild beast of man in chains. He was reaching out for her as she scrambled over a wooden structure. Then she was in a cave with a young woman who carried a toy cat. That image exploded into glittering fragments. It was replaced by a young man with flawless dark skin. They stood in a pool of light. Danger was all around. She fought to remember the man's name because she understood it was of vital importance.

As she struggled to remember, it seemed like her senses were being switched on one-by-one. *Click!* She could hear her own breathing; a slow, throaty sound. *Click!* Feeling returned. She could feel the expansion and contraction of her heart. Her left arm felt sore, like an animal had clawed the flesh from wrist to elbow. *Click!* Taste had been switched on. When she licked her lips, her mouth was flooded with a bitter flavor – like touching your lips just after applying sanitizer to your hands. It was such a powerfully bitter taste that it made her screw up her face.

Instinct told her to keep her eyes shut.

But why would instinct tell me that? What is there to fear?

Click! She smelled the air. A strong odor of cleaning chemicals that reminded her of hospitals. Especially emergency rooms, where the scent of disinfectant mingled with the tang of blood. And all the while she struggled to remember the name of the young man who had stood with her in a pool of brilliant light. His name was important. His name was vital. His name was...

'John.'

She had kept her eyes shut when she spoke his name aloud.

A male voice came from close by. A familiar voice. 'Kyra?'

The voice belonged to John. She was certain.

'Yes. I'm here, John. Whatever happens keep your eyes closed.'

'They are closed. I remember the light. The blue light.'

'The light does something to our brains.'

Kyra lay there, panting with fear. She recalled the shambling figures with lights clamped to their heads. Were they close now? Were they going to attack?

Just then, she heard another male voice. It sounded calm, authoritative – the distinctive tone of a Big Man in charge. The man said: 'Kyra. John. You may open your eyes now. The trial is finished.'

Kyra firmly kept her eyelids closed.

The man spoke again. 'You cannot close your eyes to the world forever.'

She recognized that sinister purr. Yes, she'd encountered him before. She recalled how his face had loomed from a giant TV screen on the wall as he'd spoken to her.

Warily, Kyra opened her eyes. She still expected to see those things – what did Nev call them? Protos? That's it. He called them Protos.

Whatever 'Protos' are. But the name suggested something part-formed, or even primeval.

There were no Protos. However, she saw that John, like her, was strapped down onto a trolley. Restraints around their ankles and wrists. John opened his eyes.

Meanwhile, the 'Man' gazed down at them from a massive TV screen on the wall. He leaned forward, staring at John and herself as they lay there. She realized that they were in a sterile room – the kind that might be used for medical procedures. There were electrical devices set upon telescopic poles, though she could not identify what those devices were.

John sounded angry, rather than scared. 'Why are we here?'

Kyra added sharply, 'Why did you do this to us?'

The Man gave such a self-satisfied smile it looked as if he was gloatingly preening himself. 'I must congratulate you both for your behavior. I am very pleased to see two volunteers succeed so splendidly.'

Kyra stared at the Man in astonishment. 'Volunteers? I didn't volunteer for anything.'

'Nor me,' added John.

The Man smirked. 'Oh, but you did.'

Suddenly, the screen split into two separate screens. Both halves of the TV screen revealing CCTV footage with timer numerals scrolling in the corner. There was a man and a woman – one in each screen. Each wore a red coverall of the kind that prisoners wear. The two people were shackled to metal tables in front of them.

Kyra's heart lurched with shock. She realized she was looking at a woman that resembled herself, while the man in the second screen looked like John. The two figures stared at someone, or something, that wasn't in shot.

A voice came from CCTV footage. Kyra could not see who spoke, yet she recognized the speaker instantly – it was the Man.

He spoke in a coldly professional voice: 'Daniel Hawkins, do you freely volunteer to serve as a research subject during the course of this study?'

The man referred to as Daniel, but who looked like John, spoke in a sullen damn-you-to-hell voice. 'Yeah.'

The Man was speaking again: 'Sarah Lott, do you freely volunteer to serve as a research subject during the course of this study?'

The woman that uncannily resembled Kyra answered with an unemotional, 'Yes.'

The Man's voice purred from the CCTV video. 'Now...please sign the form in front of you.'

The two people onscreen each picked up a document and began to read the words printed there.

John reacted with anger. 'Daniel?'

Kyra shouted, 'Those aren't our names. And why would we volunteer for this? This torture!'

Meanwhile, in the CCTV footage, the Man continued to address the people he had referred to as Sarah and Daniel. 'The document that you will sign states that you consent, of your own free will, to be a research subject. And upon successful completion of the study, your death sentence will be commuted to life in prison.'

Kyra gasped. 'Death sentence?

John stared at the screen in horror. 'What the fuck?'

Kyra couldn't believe what she'd just heard. 'Why would we have a death sentence?'

The Man's face replaced the CCTV footage. Clearly, he could see, via a screen in his office, John and herself lying in the room that smelt of hospitals.

A secretive smile played on his lips as he murmured, 'Daniel Hawkins. He fractured a girl's skull with a hammer and disposed of her body in a river. Sarah Lott, nurse, killed six babies at the hospital where she ministered...' His lips twitched. '...care.'

The Man's face vanished to be replaced by prison mugshots of the two people that resembled Kyra and John. Kyra couldn't take her eyes off the image of the 'Sarah' individual. Yes, she resembled Kyra, yet her face was so hard looking. She had the face of a brutal executioner.

The Man's voice overlaid the images onscreen. 'You, John, are Daniel Hawkins. You, Kyra, are Sarah Lott. That is who you are.'

John shook his head. 'You're wrong.'

Kyra's snarled, 'You've confused us with someone else. I'm Kyra. I'm a—'

'A grocery worker.' The Man spoke in soft tones. 'Who formerly had a sweet dog called Freedom.

'I am not Sarah.'

John called out, 'I'm not Daniel!'

The Man continued in that smooth voice, which suggested he was someone who possessed a first-rate education – together with an evil heart of pure granite. 'You prove that both the memory suppression and the new memory implants are one hundred percent effective. Both of you freely volunteered to be test subjects in this, the first ORIGIN study, to determine if nature or nurture has been the cause of your violent, antisocial behavior. At the beginning of the experiment, all memory of your former lives – and the crimes you committed – were suppressed. They were overlaid with memories that I created. And which were completely absent of trauma. Different memories. Different nurture. Yet the same physical bodies. Same nature. Yet you were not inherently violent.' He laughed softly. 'I transformed you into exceedingly *nice* people. No sign of you being born killers. And, believe me, you have given us extremely valuable data to study.'

John was clearly bewildered. 'What are you talking about?'

'I'd never volunteer for this.' She began to pull at her restraints. If only one would snap...

The Man's voice echoed around the room. 'All will become clear...when your true memories resurface.'

A humming sound reached them as a device activated.

Kyra shouted, 'John, close your eyes!'

Kyra scrunched her eyelids as tightly shut as she could. Even so, a purple glow filtered through those flaps of skin that formed her eyelids. Hopefully, the glow's power would be diminished by that tender veil of flesh that covered her eyeballs.

She heard John cry out, 'Shut it off!'

The Man's voice purred. 'This is what you want. I'm bringing Sarah and Daniel back. You will be the people you once were.'

'I'm not Sarah. I'm Kyra!'

'You haven't been listening. Kyra and John do not exist.'

Kyra yelled, 'We do!'

The Man's tone suggested he was smirking. 'Those are not your memories. Those are constructs. Soon you will have no memory of this. Or of me. Or of each other.'

'No!' Kyra's voice echoed back at her. 'You can't do this to us.'

'Kyra. John. There is no "us". You are not you. You are fiction. I created you. Soon you will be back in jail where you belong. And you will have no recollection of your time in this place.'

John bellowed, 'We're getting out of here!'

Kyra strained against the straps that bound her to the gurney, trying to break them.

The Man spoke forcefully. 'Open your eyes. You will gain nothing by doing this. Lie still. Do not hurt yourselves. It is time to look into the light...and to reveal your old selves once more.'

When John spoke, it was directly into her ear. 'Keep your eyes shut.'

She felt hands unbuckling the restraints.

'John?'

'They might be clever at lots of things, but they aren't good with buckles. I managed to free one of my hands. Keep your eyes closed. I've got mine shut. There! You're free. Come on!'

She swung her feet off the trolley. John gripped her hand in his, then they were moving across the room as fast as they dared. Her eyes were shut – she held her free hand out in front of her as she navigated the room by touch alone.

John hissed, 'Come hell or high water, we are getting out of here!'

CHAPTER FIFTEEN

Kyra's eyelids were scrunched shut as John pulled her along by the hand. She saw nothing.

That is, she saw nothing with her eyes.

However, because she could not see with her eyes, her imagination tortured her with images of them being murdered in the next five minutes. Terror screamed through her brain – that terror manifested itself as jagged lines of crimson lightning that seared the inside of her skull. She told herself it was only imagination and that her terror wasn't a hell-storm of crimson fire, yet she still saw it inside herself.

Kyra was certain that brutal fists would soon smack into her face, because she remembered the Protos in the room full of darkness. She almost screamed at the memory of Tanner. With his face torn open, blood gushing everywhere. *That's going to happen to me.* Fear of that dreadful fate blasted more salvos of crimson lightning bolts through her brain. Her senses were cranked up to impossibly high levels of sensitivity. She could feel the weight of her tongue in her mouth. The hospital odor of the room was so powerfully obnoxious she wanted to vomit. The inside of her clothes seemed so rough and so abrasive that they scraped against the sensitive skin of her stomach and her back. Also, her arm stung so much. It felt as if claws had ripped open her flesh.

John was gripping her hand so tightly that she grimaced with pain, yet she did not try to break free. Meanwhile, her free hand swung out to one side, trying to feel for any objects that might hurt her if she blundered into them.

Then Kyra felt a wall. There were tiles as cold as tombstones beneath her fingers. She kept her eyes closed. The feel of the tiles suggested to her that this was, indeed, a clinical treatment room in a hospital. Or a morgue.

Yet, within seconds, a complete change of material pressed against her fingers.

'Plastic sheeting,' she muttered. 'Soft plastic. What happened to the wall?'

Half-stumbling, the panic tightening her throat muscles to the point where she could hardly breathe, she suddenly found herself blundering through a plastic drape that must have hung from ceiling to floor. What kind of hospital was this? Everything was so strange.

John hauled her through the sheets into what seemed a smaller space. Sounds didn't make an echo here. It was much colder. So cold, in fact, that the freezing air stung the inside of her throat. Also gloomy, because she couldn't see even a glimmer of light passing through her eyelids.

She thought: *Don't let panic overwhelm you. Determine your location. Use the information you can glean from your hearing and sense of touch to form an image of your surroundings. And then gauge if you are in a safer place.*

Or a more dangerous place.

John pulled her through what appeared to be a gloomy void. It was as cold as death in there. The sound of her feet didn't generate any echoes. The strange lights she'd encountered earlier, when strapped to the bench, didn't appear to be present here. That meant she could – if she dared – take a look at her surroundings.

She let out a fierce shout. 'Fuck this. I'm opening my eyes!'

Kyra opened them to find herself being pulled along a corridor that was so gloomy she could barely see anything, other than John and sheets of grubby plastic hanging down at either side of her.

John opened his eyes, too. He began looking around in astonishment.

'A moment ago,' she said, 'it was like we were in a hospital. This is like a construction site.'

'Construction site? No. This place looks derelict. Like some old prison that's gone rotten...rotten to the fucking core.' John appeared angry rather than scared.

Kyra felt the same way. She wasn't going to let the Man torture her anymore. She wasn't going to listen to his lies. What was that he told her? That she was a prisoner on Death Row? He absolutely was a total, damn liar. Now she was getting out of his shit hole.

Kyra took the lead. She ran ahead of John, though she still gripped his hand. 'Come on! But keep your eyes down! The light that burns your brain to fuck might come back!'

They both kept their gaze down at their feet as they ran through one plastic sheet after another. They were bursting through from one gloomy space to the next. All those distinct spaces had been created by sheets that hung down from the ceiling to create flimsy walls.

'Damn it,' panted John. 'This place is a maze. How do we get out of here without getting lost forever!'

'Focus, John. There is a way...we must use logic. Do you see any signs on the walls?'

'I don't see any walls. Period. Just these sheets of plastic. They're everywhere. What is this place?'

'Don't allow yourself to panic.'

Don't panic? Easier said than done.

Kyra ran hand in hand with John along corridors formed by soft walls of white plastic. When they flipped the next sheet aside, they found themselves in an eerie passageway. It seemed to go on forever and ever without end. Various lights of different hues – green, orange, pink – dimly glowed through yet more sheets of Polythene. Kyra was instantly on high-alert, in case these lights suddenly invaded her brain like the other lights had done. Therefore, she kept her fingers close to her eyes, should she need to blot out the lights if they suddenly blazed into mind-shredding intensity.

They moved fast. Panting. Feet slithering on smooth concrete. The air smelt dusty now. There was dirt smearing the floor. This place was unwholesome. Like the old killing floor of a slaughter-house, where pigs were hauled to have clamps pressed to their pallid heads...before a jolt of high voltage electricity fried their brains.

'Shit,' hissed John. 'Dead end. We have to go back.'

Kyra saw that they'd entered a corridor, which had strange walls that were formed from tightly woven steel bars that ended in a slab of concrete. There were two iron loops fixed to the concrete, chains trailed down from the loops to the floor. The chains were rusty. The ends of the chains dangled in what looked like pools of congealing blood.

They retraced their steps until the steel walls were replaced by polythene drapes. At any moment, Kyra expected to see figures bursting through the plastic sheets to attack them. Instinct told her that this was a place where she could so easily die. John suddenly yanked her to the right. They crashed through veils of hanging plastic. The next corridor was different. She instantly saw that the wall had been clad with wooden frames.

'This looks like the outer wall of the building,' she whispered. 'Follow it, John. It's bound to lead to a door.'

Colored lights still pulsated beyond the plastic hangings to her right – cloudy smears of yellow, pink, blue, orange.

Both she and John touched the wall clad in wood, feeling the substantial nature of it. At that moment, she was still ready to close her eyes, if need be, then allow the solid wall to be their wonderful guide to a door and freedom.

John, meanwhile, studied the wall more closely. His expression was one of someone finally remembering something dreadful.

He murmured, 'I think I've been here before...there was the pyramid made from wood. Goliath? Yeah, the big guy. Tattoos. Evil eyes. Goliath. That was him...'

'Nev said you killed him. That's not true though, is it?'

'No.' John shook his head. 'Goliath just collapsed and died. A heart attack, maybe...hey, it's starting to come back to me now. You were chained to the pyramid.'

'I cut my own arm. Messages to me.' She'd begun to remember, too. She looked at her arm. It was bandaged from wrist to elbow, though blood had seeped through the fabric.

They continued moving. She was feeling more hopeful of escape. A moment later, they turned a corner of the wall. Kyra had kept her eyes down at the floor, just in case those mind-zap lights suddenly returned. What she did see made her pause so abruptly that she pulled John to a stop by his hand.

Kyra realized she was seeing a boot that was spotted with drops of blood. Her heart sank as a deluge of icy shivers cascaded down her back.

The boot wasn't just an empty boot. There was a foot inside. Warily, she raised her hitherto downcast eyes. She saw a leg clad in a grey coverall. She looked up fully the same instant as John did.

The shock of what they saw made them both gasp. There were four people lined up in the corridor. She almost heard Nev's voice in her ear whispering the word, *Protos*.

She and John flinched until their backs slammed into the plastic sheets that hung down from the ceiling at this side of the corridor. Because four very disturbing men and women stood there in the corridor. They wore harnesses that formed X shapes of leather strapping across their chests. Chains were connected to the harnesses; the other end of the chains being fixed to a steel rail above their heads. The men and women were all different ages. They wore raggedy clothes. Their bare hands were stained with dried blood. Some of those horror people had terrible facial wounds that had been crudely stitched shut. This made them look like a bunch of Frankenstein monsters.

They all had the blinder apparatus clamped to their heads.

John gasped, 'They're standing there...but are they actually alive?'

Kyra knew what he meant. The Protos didn't move. Their eyes did not blink at all. The men and women simply stared at the plastic wall with blank eyes that resembled those of a corpse.

John began to move through the plastic sheets into the next section, away from the four Protos. However, Kyra grabbed his arm to stop him.

'Look,' she whispered. 'There's more, through there.'

John saw them, too. There were yet more figures on the other side of the translucent sheeting. If she and John moved into the next corridor, they'd find themselves face-to-face with another cohort of Protos.

Kyra recalled seeing guard dogs chained to a wall in a prison. She hadn't actually been there, surely? She decided she must have seen the prison on TV. In any event, she'd seen vicious guard dogs chained to the wall. The chains were long enough for them to roam outward by a few feet. The prisoners, if they kept their backs to a wall on the opposite side of the yard, could edge by them without being bitten because the chains weren't long enough to allow the pit bulls to launch a ferocious attack on the inmates. Something similar was happening here. However, human had replaced canine.

Kyra whispered, 'We can do this. Just keep your back to the plastic sheets and move slowly along. Then we can get by them.'

The chains (with them being attached to the overhead rail) would allow the Protos to follow the corridor, but the chains were too short to allow them to venture too far to their left or to their right. Kyra thought: *With luck, with a whole fucking big tubful of luck, the chains won't be long enough to reach us if those monsters decide to attack.*

Kyra and John quietly moved along the corridor, keeping well back from the chained figures. Thankfully, the Protos didn't appear to know that there were intruders in their awful domain. The Protos didn't move. They just stared blankly.

Kyra glanced behind her. Even though the sheets of plastic weren't fully transparent – in fact, it was like trying to peer through thick fog – she could just make out figures moving back and forth some way off, like they were searching for someone. Kyra knew *exactly* who they were searching for.

She hissed, 'John, we've got to move faster, or we'll get caught.'

That's when everything changed.

For the worse.

The blinders attached to the Protos heads began to glow yellow. The Protos' eyes gleamed in the light that was the color of egg yolk.

Now they came alive. They moved slowly, like they were dancers doing slow-motion warmup exercises before a performance. A guy with one eye tilted his head down to his left shoulder, then down to the right one. He turned on his feet a little, his gaze locking onto John and Kyra...yet he didn't attack.

The others were moving, too. Some raised their arms above their heads, stretching stiff muscle that hadn't been used for a while. A young woman with a fresh scar on her cheek, and with wide, staring eyes, suddenly began to make snatching movements, as if trying to grab invisible butterflies from the air around her head.

Kyra shivered. *This is weird. This is scary.*

So far, none of the Protos had tried to make any kind of move toward them. She gestured to John to keep walking. Now, they'd reached the last Proto in the line. He was a huge guy with dreadlocks. He was bigger than Goliath. Hell, he was a big, murderous Frankenstein monster of a figure. He had muscular hands that could, she was certain, snap neck bone as easily as she could snap a popsicle stick.

Then, finally, they were walking away from the Protos – beyond their reach.

The young woman began to sway. She rubbed her own arms as

she did so, as if attempting to comfort herself. She moaned softly –
a sound of utter despair. Tears began to trickle from her eyes.

The yellow glow in the blinders began to pulse – bright, then
dim, then much brighter.

The lights appeared to provoke the figures into moving more.
The young woman who had begun to weep abruptly gasped,
'Water...water...' She muttered the word over and over.

Kyra realized that the lights beyond the plastic sheets were
brighter now. Were these the lights that could somehow hypnotize
them?

'John,' she whispered. 'Eyes down. Watch out for the lights.'

That's when the Protos began to move.

They were attached to the overhead rail by their chains, meaning
that their movements were restricted. Yet, like a living train, they
all began to move along the corridor, in slow pursuit of Kyra and
John. The metal loop at the end of the restraint chains, which connected them to the rail, slid along, making a loud scraping sound
as it did so.

Then the attack came. The Protos lunged at Kyra and John. The
weeping woman grabbed hold of John by his arm. Her eyes were
still dead-looking, like she was a zombie, yet she knew he was there.
She dragged him toward her with astonishing strength.

Kyra, meanwhile, used all her strength to tug John free. She
pulled him toward her until she had her arms around him protec-
tively.

'We can't fight them,' he panted. 'There are too many.'

Kyra shouted, 'Keep back against the plastic sheets at this side.
The chains aren't at all long. We can keep out of their reach!'

She was right. Even so, that didn't stop the Protos trying to rip
their heads off. They reached out, clawing the air.

The lights in the blinders turned blood red. That's when they
went fucking apeshit. They lunged as far as their chains would
allow. Links clattered. The monsters slashed their hands through
the gloom, trying to reach the pair. The Protos were snarling, their
eyes blazed with fury.

Kyra knew that if they stumbled into their grasp, the creatures
would tear her and John apart.

Kyra and John moved faster. They had to shuffle crabwise –
going sideways, their backs to the sheets. Then the wall in front of
them suddenly turned a sharp right. At the same time, she saw that
the steel rail fixed to the ceiling had come to an end. A metal disc
had been welded to the end of the rail, which was clearly intended
to act as a stopper or a buffer. Thank goodness. That meant the
Protos could not follow them. They were free of those monsters.

Kyra and John now ran as fast as they could. They turned the
corner. What happened next was all a blur. However, Kyra saw a

hand gripping a stun-gun. It fired. John let out a scream of pain as the jolt of electricity blasted through him. His body went stiff, and he toppled forwards to the floor. He lay there hurting, yet unable to even move so much as a finger. Kyra was on her own now.

And that's when she saw a guy dressed in a black uniform, complete with a black helmet and black visor that concealed his eyes. He grinned a very mean grin as he pulled out a baton. Then he raised it, clearly intending to beat Kyra to a bloody mess of screaming humanity.

CHAPTER SIXTEEN

The guard hurled himself at her. The strange thing was, even though she fully expected a savage beating, he did not try and strike her with the baton. Instead, he thumbed a switch on its side, which activated a blue light that strobed in her face. The intensity of the light dazzled her. She pictured photons darting through her eyes, then scorching the entire length of her optic nerve, before slamming into her brain.

'Block the light!'

Kyra realized that the instinct to survive had prompted her to shout those words – she needed to prevent the light from sizzling through the grey mush of her cerebral cortex, where it would have shut her down, both in body and mind, as it had so done before. Then all the guard need do was drag her limp body away.

Therefore, Kyra closed her eyes. In fact, she scrunched them so tight shut that the muscles of her face ached like fury. Meanwhile, the guard wrestled her back against the wall. He was as strong as a demon. The sharp scent of disinfectant soap, which he must have lathered himself with before duty beckoned, made her nose prickle. She could see blue daubs of light through her eyelids, yet she kept her eyes shut, dimming the light just enough to rob it of its power to hypnotize her, or whatever the hell it did.

She guessed where the guy's hand was that held the stun-gun. She grabbed hold, but he still gripped on tight to the extent she couldn't wrench it from his grasp. He was trying to pull her head back by her hair. He fully expected that the pain would cause her to open her eyes, to admit a blast of that mind-shredding glare.

Kyra felt the guy's hot breath on her face. She could smell peppermint. She even heard the click of the wad of gum in his mouth as he tussled with what he must have thought was a weakling. She imagined him thinking, *I'll zap the bitch. Pop in a fresh stick of gum. Then do some chewin', as I wait for the guys to come and haul her back to the cage.*

Because there had to be a cage, hadn't there? Or would she end up chained to the rail in the corridor? All these thoughts exploded in her mind as she fought the guard. He played dirty now. Kicking her knees. Attempting to knock her off balance.

Then she heard a loud, 'Uph!'

That came from the guard. Someone must have grabbed his throat, or his balls. Either way, they'd hurt him. She risked opening one eye. She saw dark skin. A pair of bright eyes. They were behind the guard's shoulder.

'John!'

She gasped with relief as John began to drag the guard away from her. The light on the baton went out. The guard tried to deploy the stun-gun again.

Those metal prongs fixed to the gun's muzzle would act like a cattle prod. They would give someone a hell of a jolt. Kyra struggled to get the weapon out of the guy's hand. The guard was in trouble now. Even though he still held on tight to the gun, John had managed to put the baton across the guy's throat and was pulling hard – very hard. The guard snarled but John had got him good now. The edge of the baton dug into the guy's Adam's apple. He started to flail in panic as the air was cut off from his lungs.

This time Kyra was the one to play dirty. She managed to boost a massive kick into the guard's shin. He yelled out in pain, then lost his balance. Kyra and John planted him hard – right down onto the deck.

Instantly, both Kyra and John were on the guy. Kyra squatted on his chest while trying to force the stun-gun from his hand. John knelt on the floor to one side. He was leaning forwards, his hands gripping each end of the baton. This enabled him to force the baton down onto the guy's throat, choking him. Kyra glanced into John's face. That's when she saw the anguish in those dark, grave eyes of his. She realized then that John possessed a gentle soul. Choking a human being wasn't his thing. John's expression was turning to one of alarm as the guard convulsed with pain as the baton dug deep.

John eased back, releasing pressure on the man's windpipe. John wasn't going to kill him. He didn't even want to inflict excessive pain if he could help it. Kyra tugged the gun out of the man's hand. She had no inhibition in hurting the fucker. Afterall, he'd hurt her. Quickly, she aimed at the guard's chest, pulled the trigger.

Nothing.

She pulled the trigger again, expecting to hear the ominous buzz of voltage within the device. The thing, however, had become dead plastic in her hand.

Not that the gun's failure to discharge electricity mattered one little bit, because he'd had enough. The man lay there on the floor, no longer fighting back – he waved his hand from side to side. A gesture that clearly said: *enough*.

John looked at the guard's face – or at least as much as he could see, because the upper half was covered by a black visor. John appeared to be reassuring himself that he hadn't caused serious harm to his adversary.

Kyra wasted no time. After tossing the now useless gun aside, she rolled the guard onto his belly, then went through pouches in his utility belt. 'Ah ha.' She grinned in triumph as her fingers hooked out a plastic keycard attached to a lanyard. After that, she pulled out long strips of flexible plastic. She realized that these were restraints used by guards to tie up prisoners if no manacles were available. Strangely, though she did not consciously know how to use them, it seemed like the knowledge of how to apply the plastic restraints was lodged somewhere deep down in her memory. Before she even realized fully what she was doing, she'd bound his wrists together. John stood up, holding on tight to the baton. That was their only weapon. Fortunately, the guard made no attempt to break free. He lay there, just content to be catching his breath again.

Kyra brandished the keycard at John. 'Now we find the door.' Even though they weren't out of Nightmare Central yet, she realized she was giving John a mile-wide smile. John nodded back at her, even managing a small grin of his own.

Kyra ran along the corridor. John was just behind her. They followed the wall to a steel door (a prison-like steel door, at that). A sensor in the wall glowed red. Kyra efficiently zapped the card against the sensor. Red turned green. A *click* of a mechanism within the door. A steel bolt rolled back. Kyra pushed the door. Immediately, it swung open. And, instantly, they were both struck by such an intense blast of white light that they staggered backwards.

Then Krya understood...

Sunlight.

Seizing John by the hand, she pulled him out through the doorway after her. Then they were running away from the huge building, through sunshine, through warm air that smelt so fresh after that bleak tomb of a place.

Kyra let out a yell of absolute joy: 'Freedom!'

They ran hand in hand, away from a complex of buildings that appeared to be industrial rather than a hospital or a correctional facility. Some of the buildings had holes in their roofs. Those forbidding structures possessed an air of abandonment. There were no vehicles in sight. No people, either. No fences to keep anyone in.

There was only desert. And mountains. And vast, vast wilderness.

CHAPTER SEVENTEEN

Deep in his electronic lair, the Man watched an array of screens that covered an entire wall in front of him. In one screen, Nev paced back and forth in a prison cell. Nev ran his fingers through his hair. His mouth opened and shut as he yelled at people that were invisible to him. There was no sound. The Man heard nothing. Nev was shouting at concrete walls and nothing else.

Another screen presented the disturbing image of four figures standing in a corridor. Chains connected them to a steel rail above their heads. The woman with the scar on her cheek was weeping. Poor wretch – she was grieving for a dead lover. She could remember the grief well enough, but not the actual lover. Was the lover funny or always serious? Was the lover kind or cruel? The Man knew that the weeping woman could not remember her lover's face. All she could recall was a sadness so awful that it was eating into her very soul. The Man's hand hovered over a control that would trigger a blue light that would ease away the woman's grief, and which would leave her standing there, mute and corpse-like. Then she wouldn't recall the sadness that resulted from the death of the human being that she'd loved with all her heart.

The Man decided against administering the analgesic calm of the blue glow. Instead, he left her to sob for the lover she could not remember. Her grief might produce an interesting effect on her mental processes that he could evaluate later.

For many years, he had labored to understand how the brain worked. Initially, he'd been inspired by the nineteenth century neuropathologist Theodor Meynert, who believed that the cerebral cortex segment of the brain was at war with the sub-cortical regions – a war which so often triggered strife within an individual's psyche. Most inspirational of all, was Timothy Leary's Eight-Circuit Model of Consciousness, which the Man had woven into his own ground-breaking techniques that enabled him to implant memory constructs in his test subjects. This, in effect, reprogrammed the men and women who had volunteered to participate in his experimental program (these volunteers had been prisoners on Death Row; therefore, it was either volunteer for extreme reconfiguration of their minds, or take the last walk to the room of no return). Despite expanding his own knowledge of psychology to a remarkable degree, he knew that the human mind was a largely unexplored terrain. Yes, he was making progress in understanding the ebb and flow of human thought. All of it mixed with undercurrents of emotion – and, yes, he was beginning to chart the dangerous reefs of love that claimed the unwary traveler as they moved through the oceans of life. And, just like the vast oceans of the Earth, the mind had great depths, too. Where all kinds of monsters of the psyche roamed. He smiled to himself. He liked to compare the human mind to the ocean. In fact, the comparison was remarkably accurate. Most psychologists would admit that though they could see the surface of the mind, very few would claim they knew what happened in the great depths of our psychology.

The screens in front of him shone their illuminated images into his eyes. He saw Nev protesting at his confinement in the cell. He saw the weeping woman. Another screen revealed people in chains in a basement. They were terrified because they thought poison gas flooded the streets outside (all a carefully constructed test, of course, there was no actual poison gas). Another screen revealed a satellite image of a desert. The few trees that could survive there were just little blobs of green. And even smaller...there were two tiny, tiny figures.

Those tiny figures...they were running for their lives.

CHAPTER EIGHTEEN

Kyra realized they'd have no problem heading away from the stark-looking buildings and into the open expanse that was the desert. Above them, blue sky. A blazing sun. She glimpsed a scorpion standing on a boulder just ten feet away from her. It seemed to be watching her with its cold-blooded arachnid eyes. She and John hurried past it. She heard the click of the scorpion's hard body as it turned to watch them go by.

They continued across sand and between clumps of shrub that were armed with sharp thorns. Maybe the horrors she'd experienced in the last few hours had agitated her imagination to the point of irrationality. Every time she walked by a shrub, she feared she'd lose her balance, then fall into it – and the thorns would rip her throat, face, and eyes. Without a shadow of doubt, the desert did feel like a place that was absolutely bloated with danger.

Thorn bushes. Scorpions. Rattlesnakes. All kinds of venomous creatures wriggled or scurried through this arid terrain. In the distance, the howl of a hungry coyote. Vultures whirled in the sky above her head. They looked like black crosses. Vultures are carrion eaters. Did they believe that John and Kyra weren't long for this world, and that soon they would be pecking at the humans' dead eyes?

Ahead, high on a hill, was a peculiar wooden structure. For all the world, it looked like the wreck of an old wooden ship. She found herself recalling the Ark from the Bible. What if the Flood had retreated and left that Biblical vessel high and dry on a hill in this desert?

Is that my imagination going rogue again? Perhaps so. Because this forbidding domain that she found herself in was such an evil place.

At last, John grabbed her elbow. 'I need to rest...just for a while... I'm beat.'

She nodded. 'Then we must plan where we go next, because they're sure to send more guards after us.'

'Or those damned monsters with lights on their heads and the chains.'

'Protos.'

John looked at her oddly. 'Is that what they call them? Protos?'

'Don't you remember? When we were in the room with the bright lights shining down onto the floor? Nev called them Protos.'

'My memories are still a tad scrambled, to say the least. But sure...' John nodded. There was a bitter expression on his face. 'Protos. Yeah, why not.' He suddenly looked cold and vulnerable. Like a child lost in the wilderness. 'Kyra, are we Protos?'

'No. I am Kyra. You are John.'

'You're right. Sorry. My head is – *whoosh*. Like I've had my brain scraped out of my skull then thrown against a wall, before being scooped up and shoved back in between my ears again.' He laughed like he was joking, but she realized that his recent experiences had left him emotionally shaken.

'John.' She spoke firmly. 'We'll sit here in the shade for a spell. We can see the buildings, should anyone come out to look for us. Then, when we're certain that no one's following us, we will pick a route and walk out of the desert.'

'Walk out of the desert?' He wasn't smiling now. 'You are a machine, aren't you? You don't get tired. You're unstoppable.'

'I'm human.'

'You're Kyra, the cyborg. You gotta be made from steel. Let me check.'

John grabbed her left hand in both of his hands, then he stared at the back of her wrist so closely she feared he might bite it. Perhaps – in a fit of crazy desperation – he wanted to rip her skin away. To check for steel components that had been woven into the flesh. Finally, his eyes softened. Then, for one tantalizing moment, she thought he would kiss her hand.

'I'm sorry.' He looked emotional.

'Don't worry about it.'

'No, you're not a robot.' He let go of her hand. 'You are human. Like me. It's just…it's just I get this feeling…this powerful, powerful feeling that evil people have been doing something bad to my brain. You know? Manipulating how I think. For a moment back there, I couldn't remember that Nev guy. I can remember him now, and him using the word 'Protos' to describe the people with the lights fixed to their heads. But I can't remember how we got out of that building over there.'

'There was a guard. You held him down, while—'

'Yes.' He slapped his forehead, like he was angry with himself, yet also feeling a surge of relief. 'The guard in the helmet. He zapped me. You found the keycard, then – *ffftt…*' He mimed a person running, using two of his fingers to imitate scurrying legs. He took a deep breath. 'If we're experiencing sudden memory lapses, we've got to be careful.'

'Just to confirm. I'm Kyra.'

'I'm John.'

'Pleased to meet you.'

She solemnly held out her hand. He gave a little smile that seemed such a sweet and sensitive one. He gently shook her hand. His skin was pleasantly dry and just a little warmer than hers. Her backbone went a little shivery. And, despite all the horror, all the madness, she found herself smiling warmly at him.

After that, they sat side by side on a rock (though only after she'd checked it for scorpions and rattlesnakes). For a while, they talked about what had happened to them. Or at least as much as they could remember. They both agreed on one thing: That the Man had been lying to them. They both agreed, moreover, that they weren't convicted criminals. And they had never been on Death Row. The Man had been messing with their minds. Attempting to destabilize them. Perhaps even trying to undermine their sanity to make them feel even more vulnerable. Even more frightened. With what aim, though? To control them? To coerce them into committing some kind of atrocity?

For a long while they fell silent, then John spoke softly. 'Kyra?'

'Hmm?'

'I saw wind turbines in the distance.'

'Oh.' She felt a twinge of disappointment. Had she been anticipating he'd say something more personal? Something in the vein of: *Kyra, I like you*?

But no...he'd mentioned wind turbines. Just stupid wind turbines.

'If there are wind turbines,' he said. 'That means there will be access tracks for maintenance vehicles. If we reach the turbines, we can follow the tracks to the highway. Then we hike to the nearest town.'

'Yeah. That sounds like a plan.'

'Kyra?'

'Yes?'

'You're nice.'

'Oh? Thank you.'

'I'm glad that it's you who's with me now. You've got...'

'Got what?'

His smile was a shy one as he looked at her. 'Presence.'

'I've got presence?' *Not nice hair? Not a bright smile? Not lovely eyes?*

'Sorry, Kyra. I said the wrong thing.'

'No, you didn't...it's just I don't know what you mean by presence.'

'Look, we've all got some degree of presence, due to us being in the world. Right? When we sit in a room, or walk through a hotel lobby, or perch on a rock in the desert. Yeah?'

'I guess so.'

'But you, Kyra, have a more significant presence. You do not hint that you are in a room. You make a bold statement that *you* are in *the* room, just by being there. You instantly become an important part of the room. Like you are now a vital part of this desert. If there were other people here, they would turn their heads to look at you. They would know that you are important.'

Smiling, she took her hand in his. 'Thank you.'

For the next hour, nothing more needed to be said. She felt comfortable being with him.

And, yeah...this good-looking guy had *presence*, too.

CHAPTER NINETEEN

The sixty minutes went by quickly. And they had absolutely needed that opportunity to rest up. In the meantime, there had been no indication that they were being pursued. Nobody, as far as Kyra could tell, had left the building that she and John had escaped from. Admittedly, the building was some way off, but she would have seen figures if they had come streaming out to catch the runaways. There were no vehicles in sight, either. Perhaps their captors were confident that the desert would kill anyone who ventured into it. Either a snake would bite them, or a scorpion would sting them, or escapees would simply die of thirst – perhaps that's what the guards believed. Kyra was determined to prove them wrong. She would survive. And so would John.

At last, John stood up from the boulder while extending a hand to help Kyra to her feet. She realized that the act of having to fight for their lives during the last few hours, whether that be tackling Goliath or overpowering the guard, had left their skin bruised and their muscles stiff.

Nevertheless, they began walking through a landscape that consisted of shades of yellow. There was yellow desert sand. Dry shrubs were a dullish yellow. The strange-looking rounded domes of the hills were as yellow as old bones you see in museums. Come to that, the huge rocks that formed the hills resembled human skulls, part buried in the sand. The terrain appeared to be so alien-looking. The complex of buildings they'd escaped from were constructed from silvery metal. They appeared to be largely derelict. The concrete roadways that ran up to the melancholy structures were broken up, and partly covered by desert sand. All in all, she was struck by the notion that this was a place where bad things happened. How many dead men and women lay out here, buried in the desert?

Kyra shook her head as she walked. *Those are the kind of thoughts that trigger panic,* she told herself. *Concentrate on getting out of here. Keep focused. We're going to make it to safety. But what comes after? I mean, what happens between John and me?* She watched John as he walked by her side. His stride was purposeful. He looked focused now. Utterly determined to get out of this place.

Kyra said, 'You think this is the best route?'

'Doesn't matter. We just keep going. The wind turbines are over that way. We'll pick up a maintenance road then follow it to the highway.'

He glanced at her, his dark eyes locking onto her face.

'Okay, I trust you, John. We keep walking. And we're a team, right?'

'Yeah.' He smiled. 'Team Kyra-John.'

John suddenly grunted. His eyes bulged, then his face tightened into a grimace.

'John!'

Kyra grabbed him as he staggered. Straight away, she saw what had struck him.

There, in his back, sticking out from between his shoulder blades was a dart. The same kind of tranquilizer dart that's used to knock out wild animals. The drug acted fast. John's knees gave way, dropping him face down onto the ground. Kyra managed to keep hold. She slowed his fall so that he didn't hurt himself.

She yanked the dart from his back, while hoping that not all of the drug had flowed through the needle into his flesh. A hundred yards away, further up the slope of the hill, was the derelict wooden structure she'd noticed before. Now a figure in black stood there. They were dressed the same as the guard that had attacked them earlier – same kind of uniform, same helmet and visor. The guard gripped a rifle in their hands. Clearly, this was the individual who had fired the dart at John.

Kyra knelt in the sand. She was panting with fear as she shook John by the shoulder. Already, his eyes were slipping out of focus. The muscles of his face had gone slack. He appeared dazed. The drug must already be flooding his brain.

Kyra managed to haul him to his feet. 'John...come on.'

John made a huge effort to begin moving again. Soon, he was managing a shuffle, albeit a slow one. Kyra glanced up at the wooden structure on the hill. She saw three guards walking down the slope toward them. The guards didn't run. They seemed supremely confident that they'd capture the runaways soon.

Then Kyra realized why. The drug was shutting John's body down. He found it hard to balance and his eyes were glazed. The guards were getting closer. Two of them pulled stun-guns from their belts. The third was reloading the rifle with a tranquilizer dart.

Kyra panted hard. 'John, keep moving, we must get away.'

John shook his head. 'Go on. Leave me.'

'No, keep moving.'

That's when John stumbled. Though she tried to help him to his feet, his legs simply weren't working. He sagged down to the ground.

He patted her on the arm. It was a gesture of such profound affection that she let out a cry of something like grief.

John fixed his gaze on her. 'Kyra. You have to go...for both of us.'

The guards were fifty yards away. They weren't rushing. They knew they'd soon have their prey.

'Here,' he whispered. 'Take this.'

He pulled a baton from his belt. It was the same one he'd taken from the guard earlier.

'I'm staying with you,' she told him.

'No...you go...one of us has to survive.'

Kyra hesitated. She'd only known John for a few hours, yet right at that moment she felt as if she'd known him for a lifetime.

He was close to losing consciousness now. No way could he stand up and run. And no way could she carry him. Even though it felt as if grief was shredding her heart, she made a decision. She took the baton from John. Then she looked him in the eyes for one last time, and then she began to run.

Only now did the guards begin to hurry. The one with the rifle fired a dart, though she was weaving from side-to-side by this time, in order to make herself a difficult target to hit. It worked, because the dart hissed by her head a full six feet away before it slammed into a thorn tree, where the knockout drug harmlessly discharged into the tree's trunk.

She glanced back at John. He lay on his side in the yellow dust. When one of the guards walked past him, he grabbed the guy's ankle, while yelling, 'Leave her alone.'

John must have been losing consciousness; however, he didn't release his grip on the guard's ankle. The guard merely stared impassively down at John. The other two guards, however, got busy. They knelt beside John, pulled his hand free of the guard's ankle, and then began tying his wrists together with restraints.

Kyra didn't look back again. She kept running. She was going to escape. And she was going to do this for John.

CHAPTER TWENTY

Kyra's tears had dried on her face. She hated leaving John. She felt guilty as hell for abandoning him.

But what could she do?

The guards would have caught her. Now at least she could escape from here, and she could reveal to the world that some vile organization was experimenting on innocent men and women in a desert hideaway. She began to feel a little more upbeat as she realized that what she told the outside world would result in John gaining his freedom.

Kyra jogged along a dirt track, then down into a valley that consisted of dust and rocks and thorn bushes. More than once, she heard the sound of rattlers lurking in the shadows beneath boulders. As she ran, she thought she heard someone singing. It was a strange dirge of a song. When the track rose over a mound, she saw the singer of that eerily mournful elegy in the distance. A young woman in pale brown dungarees. The woman was carrying a cat.

The astonished words shot from Kyra's mouth. 'Amber! How the hell did she escape?'

Even though Amber was over a hundred yards away, Kyra heard the woman scream with pain. Amber clutched the back of her leg before toppling sideways to the ground. The way she writhed suggested all too clearly that she was in agony. Kyra's first thought was not to get involved with Amber again. But her instinct to help someone in pain overrode that, and Kyra dashed along the track to where Amber lay screaming.

Straight away, she noticed the dart in Amber's leg – perhaps the same kind of dart that had brought John down. Kyra looked around for the person who had fired the dart. There was nobody to seen. With luck, the drug might not have left the dart yet to enter her bloodstream. If that was the case, there was a chance that she could save Amber from being captured.

Kyra dragged Amber across the sand toward a pair of large boulders that would offer protection from more darts, should any be fired at them. Amber was screaming. Tears gushed from her eyes to make her cheeks all shiny and wet. Nevertheless, she still clung to the toy cat, which was the size of a real moggy. The thing, with its overlarge eyes and fluffy white fur, still automatically meowed and moved its head in imitation of a real cat.

Kyra touched the dart embedded in Amber's leg – this hurt the woman so much that she hissed like an angry cat herself. Amber writhed with pain, causing the T beneath the dungaree's torso panel to rise up, revealing a large surgical dressing fixed to her side.

Kyra remembered. 'Knife,' she whispered. Amber had stabbed herself.

Amber yanked her T down to conceal the dressing from Kyra's gaze. Then she buried her face in the cat's fur.

Kyra smiled at Amber. 'It's going to be okay.' She took a deep breath. 'Listen. I'm going to take out the dart.'

Amber moaned. 'It hurts. It really hurts.'

'I'll be as gentle as I can.' Kyra grasped the dart's flight. 'Alright. Brace yourself, sweetie. I'm going to count to three. One.'

Kyra ripped the dart out, which provoked an ear-shredding scream from Amber. Blood instantly oozed from the wound, soaking the leg of her dungarees where the point of the vicious little missile had penetrated her skin.

Kyra examined the dart's tip, which was wet with blood. This, however, was a proper arrowhead, possessing a razor-sharp blade fixed to a wooden shaft. She figured that it must have been fired from a crossbow, rather than from the kind of dart gun that had brought John down; therefore, this dangerous missile could be described as an arrow designed to kill, rather than a dart designed to inject tranquilizer into its victim's bloodstream. So, yes, she realized this was most emphatically an arrow, not a dart. If this had struck Amber in the back it would have killed her. As far as she could tell, however, there was no aperture in the arrow point that could inject a drug into the victim's body. What's more, Amber appeared totally awake. Yes, she was strange, she was weird, even unequivocally crazed, but she revealed no symptoms of being doped with a narcotic from the arrow. In fact, Amber recovered quickly enough from the pain of having the missile ripped from her leg.

Amber hissed, 'Where's Lilli?'

The cat was behind her. As soon as she saw it, she snatched it up, then hugged the fake moggy tightly, while kissing its plastic face. The grotesque face had been burnt at some point – most of the fur had been singed away. The cat gave a mechanical 'miaow'.

Kyra patted Amber on the shoulder. 'Your cat's fine.' She looked into Amber's face. A face that was so undeniably pretty, and possessing big, expressive eyes. 'I remember you. Though I was sure you were dead. You know? From before?'

'Before what?'

'You don't remember? They came at you. Guys with lights fixed to their heads.'

Kyra noticed that blood still flowed from the woman's leg wound. Quickly, she used the purple ribbon from the keycard's lanyard to improvise a tourniquet. Amber didn't even seem to notice that a cord was being tied very tightly around her thigh.

Kyra asked, 'How did you escape?'

'I...I was just walking...here...with Lilli.'

Kyra was satisfied that the wound had stopped bleeding. 'You're going to be fine.' Kyra used a handful of grass to wipe blood from the arrowhead, then she slipped it into her pocket. 'Okay, Amber. We need to keep moving.'

Amber didn't question Kyra's statement. She merely hugged Lilli to herself as Kyra helped her up. They began to walk along the dirt road that led through the valley. There was no sign of human life. Thankfully, that included no sign of guards in their ominous black uniforms, either.

Kyra pictured John's face. Tears prickled her eyes again and she promised herself she'd find a way to free him.

A voice brought her back to the here and now. *'Help! Somebody!'*

A male voice – one that sounded desperately afraid.

'Help!'

Kyra's gaze raked the top of the hill, zeroing in on the sound of the voice. She saw a man chained to what appeared to be a concrete platform at the top of the hill. It was raised above the ground by about three feet. Bizarrely, the platform resembled the combat ring where wrestlers fought one another. The man wore a black hood, which served as a blindfold as it fully covered his head and face. The man struggled to free himself from his shackles. That's when she realized the truth.

'They're tests...the Man is still testing me.'

Amber smiled blandly. 'Tests?'

'To see if I'd help you – or him. To discover whether I'd leave you both to die.' Kyra became angry. 'That's why it was so damn easy to escape from the building. *He* let me. *He* orchestrated all this – the arrow, the guy up there in chains.' Her voice dropped to a whisper as she realized the full horror of it all. 'We are still his lab rats.'

Amber gazed up at Kyra in such a bemused way it was clear that she didn't understand what Kyra was saying.

The man hollered, 'Anyone! Help me!'

Amber leaned close to Kyra and whispered like she was revealing a profound secret, 'Never take in a stray.'

Kyra, however, knew she had to do the right thing. 'Come on.'

She gently took hold of Amber's arm and helped her walk uphill toward the man, who continued to yank at the chain while yelling for help. He whipped his head about, too, desperately trying to shake off the black hood that robbed him of his sight. He soon heard their footsteps.

In a suspicious voice he shouted, 'Who is it? Who's there?'

A powerful instinct for self-preservation prevented Kyra from answering. Instead, she warily looked around her to make sure that there weren't any guards lurking behind boulders. Amber, meanwhile, silently glided toward the platform, the cat held tightly in her arms. Amber climbed onto the platform and lay down on it as if she'd sleep there. Kyra saw that the top of the platform consisted of a steel grill. Evidently, this was a ventilation shaft connected to a subterranean complex of some sort. A breeze flowed up from the depths of the shaft to flutter Amber's long hair. Amber closed her eyes, and cuddled the cat. She reminded Kyra of the beautiful princess from 'Sleeping Beauty' – the victim of the evil witch's spell.

The man clearly realized that people were close – perhaps individuals who would hurt him – so his head twitched this way and that as he tried to figure out where they were by the sound of their footsteps.

'Tell me who you are,' he begged.

Kyra leaned forwards, then she snatched off the black hood. Instantly, she recognized the young man.

Nev stood there blinking, the bright sunlight almost blinding him. Nevertheless, he let out a whoop of relief. 'Thank God. Get me free!'

Kyra quickly examined the chain that ran from a padlock, which was fixed to the steel grill, up to Nev's neck where it was secured to a leather collar. Kyra eased the arrow from her pocket before beginning the arduous process of cutting through the leather with that oh-so dangerously sharp arrowhead.

Kyra said, 'Do you remember me?'

Nev gave a massive nod. 'Oh, I remember you.' He glanced at Amber lying on the grill. 'And crazy lady.'

Amber had opened her eyes now. She lay face down, her hair fluttering in the updraft from the pit. The woman stared down through gaps in the steelwork, down into the darkness that seemed to go on forever. As soon as Nev was free of the collar, the chain fell away. That's when he began swearing softly to himself as he rubbed the sore-looking groove on his neck that the tight collar had inflicted. As he did so, he noticed the way that Kyra was carefully looking around at the landscape.

Nev asked sharply, 'What're you looking for?'

'Arrows.'

'What?'

'Be very aware of your surroundings. It's not safe out there.'

'What arrows?'

'Ask her.' She nodded in Amber's direction.

Nev immediately noticed the tourniquet on Amber's leg. That and the bloodstained fabric just above her knee.

Amber, meanwhile, appeared fascinated by the shaft that extended downwards beneath where she lay. She was muttering in that dreamy 'I'm-not-of-this-world' voice of hers, 'A mine...all mine...a good place to hide...deep inside...'

'Fucking crazy.' He turned away from Amber in disgust. 'Okay,' he said to Kyra. 'We gotta skedaddle before they get here.'

'Do you know which way to go?'

'Away.' With that, Nev began to run downhill.

Kyra let out a fierce shout. 'Nev! Wait! Help me!'

Nev did pause and he glanced back to see her helping Amber down the hill. The young woman was limping badly. It was all too obvious that Nev didn't want to help Kyra with Amber. Nevertheless, he shrugged, then he walked back up the slope to take one of Amber's arms. Kyra took the other. Amber kept a firm and very possessive grip on Lilli.

Together, all three walked down the hillside.

And two hundred miles above them, a satellite gazed down at the three with a cold electronic eye.

CHAPTER TWENTY-ONE

The Man radiated authority. His body language growled, *I'm in charge. Do as I say.*

Filling the wall in front of him were TV screens that revealed his test subjects. They were like juicy flies caught in a spiderweb. They squirmed helplessly – most of them not even knowing they were trapped. And the Man sat in the center of the web – the all-powerful spider that enjoyed the squirming of its entangled victims.

One of the monitors pulsed with a green light. An incoming call. The man let his caller wait.

On the screens were images of test subjects fighting for their very survival. He enjoyed reviewing the footage from past experiments. One screen played archived video of one of the most interesting Test Beds. A title at the top of the screen read, *IRON GALLOWS TEST*. Out in the desert stood a metal frame that resembled a gallows that was a hundred feet high. A woman with long red hair swung on a chain that was ninety feet long. Her foot was resting in a big steel hook at the bottom. She used every muscle in her body to desperately keep the chain swinging, so that she became a kind of living pendulum, whooshing back and forth across the sand. Below her, twenty Protos jumped up, trying to catch hold of the hook. Then they would stop her swinging away from their grasp. Then they would attack.

Simultaneously, another screen revealed more archive footage. This was of a concrete platform at the top of the hill. The metal grid that had once sealed the deep pit beneath it had been removed. A man fought a female Proto near the mouth of the shaft. The female Proto was immensely strong. Gradually, she was forcing her opponent closer and closer to the top of the shaft that pierced the bedrock way, way down into the depths. A most interesting battle that utilized physical strength, mental acumen, and visceral strategy.

The green 'caller waiting' light pulsed onscreen. Nevertheless, he activated yet more archive footage. A man and woman had escaped from the gurneys where they had been strapped down. They moved along passageways, formed from sensor implanted plastic membranes. The Man sighed, knowing he must, albeit reluctantly, postpone watching the outcome of the couple's escape. He touched a switch and his caller appeared onscreen. The caller was a man wearing a white shirt. And he was wearing a decidedly worried frown.

The Man, who sat at the center of his web, began speaking without offering any greeting whatsoever: 'The threat of John and Kyra's memories being erased was all the prodding necessary. They fought to free themselves. As you can see, they were determined to remain together.' The footage onscreen revealed the man and woman wrestling with the guard. The Man continued speaking with absolute confidence in his own genius. 'John was attacked, then had a golden opportunity to kill the officer, but he did not. John let him live despite the provocation. *Perfectum exemplum.* Therefore, I have judged him to have passed the test, and I have ordered that he be removed from the program.'

The caller nodded. 'Kyra, however, would have shocked that guard if your people hadn't disabled the stun-gun. Shocked him to death for all we know.'

The Man allowed himself a wry smile. 'True. But Kyra still has a chance to redeem herself. In fact, I'm pleased to report that after risking her life to save Amber, when she was struck by the arrow, she once again halted her own escape to assist Nev.'

'I'm still not comfortable with them being outside.'

'With careful monitoring, there is no risk.'

The caller on the monitor clearly wasn't convinced by what he'd just heard. 'I don't see how you can keep your test subjects in check out there with your audio and light show.'

'Sensory programming – I prefer that phrase to 'audio and light show'. In any event, we don't need to rely on that.' The man gazed up at the monitors covering the walls – in some monitors, test subjects slept in their cages, while other test subjects had been plunged into nothing less than a torture zone. There was no sound, therefore no screams of terror and pain could be heard. The Man continued, 'No, we don't need to rely on sensory programming at all. Also, if need be, there is always the failsafe. But that won't be necessary. I have complete control.'

One of the monitors switched to the point of view of a drone flying above the desert. It revealed a pin-sharp image of Kyra and Nev helping Amber walk along a dirt road.

The caller saw the same surveillance feed on his monitor. When he spoke, he sounded decidedly nervous. 'I still say we stop while we're ahead. Pull Kyra out, as you did with John. Get her safely caged before she truly breaks free again. That would be our worst nightmare.'

The Man glared at the caller. 'I am the one to decide when it's over. That is, if you want me to sign off on the report...' With that, the Man tapped a button. The caller vanished from the screen before he had time to respond.

The Man, so arrogantly content in the center of his virtual web, turned his attention back to Kyra, Nev, and Amber as they struggled through the desert, toward what they hoped was freedom. The Man smiled. Things were just about to get very interesting for those three people. And the best was yet to come.

CHAPTER TWENTY-TWO

Kyra walked with Amber, supporting the young woman the best she could. The pale brown material of Amber's dungarees was smeared red where the arrow had penetrated her leg, yet the blood was drying, suggesting that no more blood was oozing from the wound. The tourniquet Kyra had tied around Amber's upper thigh had stemmed the flow. Nev walked on the other side of Amber. He helped support her, too. His eyes constantly darted everywhere. The guy was looking for those guards that were armed with cross-bows, and with rifles that fired tranquilizer darts. There might be some with guns that fired real bullets, too.

A wind had begun to blow. It raised swirling dust devils, which drifted in ghostly forms along the canyon. There were no proper blacktop roads here, no houses, no people. Kyra's nose prickled as she inhaled the bone-dry dust from the desert. The dust smelt of creosote. Perhaps the heat was making the shrubs bleed resin, which then trickled down into the sand.

Nev was as twitchy as hell – this place scared him, yet he wanted answers. 'Kyra? What did that doctor guy tell ya?'

'Doctor guy? You mean the Man?'

'Uh? The Man?'

'That's what I call him.'

'The Man. Overlord. Boss guy. Yeah, I get it.' Nev gave a sharp nod. 'I always thought he looked like a ghoul. I wouldn't be surprised if he opened up graves and ate the cadavers. *Munch, crunch, slurp.*'

Kyra gave Nev a hard stare, wondering if he'd become mentally unbalanced by the horror of what he'd experienced.

He gave a twitchy grin. 'No, I'm not crazy. According to legend, ghouls dragged corpses out of their tombs then – *nom, nom, nom...*' He pretended to eat a handful of food.

As she limped along between them, Amber muttered, 'You should never feed strays. They always bite the hand that feeds them.'

Nev rolled his eyes at her bizarre statement. He whispered to Kyra's over Amber's head, 'She's mentally ruptured. Kaput. Fritzed. Psychologically non-functional.'

Amber must have heard what he said about her. She didn't react, however. Instead, she lifted the cat to her lips and tenderly kissed its burnt face.

'So, Kyra,' said Nev, 'what did the Man tell ya?'

Kyra shrugged. 'Doesn't matter. All he did was lie.'

'Come on, you actually saw the big boss man – the fucking puppet-master – what did he say?'

'He told John and I that we aren't who we think we are.'

'Who did he say you were?'

'He called us Daniel and Sarah. He said we were killers.'

Nev burst out laughing. 'Killers? You two? That's a good one. The Man's messing with you.'

Then from nowhere! A metallic squawk. *SCRAWW!!!* The way Nev reacted, jumping back, flinging out his arms, his expression turning to one of horror...anyone would think that he'd been electrocuted. Amber looked at Nev in shock. She held up the cat as if to direct its eyes at Nev.

'See, Lilli?' she whispered. *'It's on him.'*

There came the loud electronic squawk again. This time, followed by the distinctive sound of static. As Nev backed away, he clumsily fumbled a walkie-talkie from his back pocket.

A distorted voice barked from the radio. 'Have you made contact?'

Kyra snatched the radio from Nev. More static came sizzling from the speaker – the sound of frying eggs.

Kyra held the radio up in front of his eyes. She was so angry her hand trembled. 'How'd you get this?'

'That bastard set the thing off. The Man's yanking our puppet strings again. Right? This is another damn test to see what you're gonna do to me.'

Kyra released her grip on Amber who stood there swaying. The young woman's shoulders were hunched, and her head dipped down in a way that suggested she was as wary as she was frightened. Kyra then took a step toward Nev. She was furious with the guy. She bunched her hands into fists. Ready to start punching his traitor face.

Nev was faster. He whipped a pistol from his pocket. He jabbed the muzzle in Kyra's direction. At the same time, he curled a finger around the trigger. 'Kyra. Back the fuck up.' He pointed the gun at Amber's head. 'Both of ya'!'

Kyra noticed that a powerful transformation had taken place in Nev. No longer was he the easy-come-easy-go pizza delivery boy. Maturity hardened his face. He suddenly had an air of authority.

The question was. *Will he shoot?*

Kyra was filled with a sense of dread as she pictured a bullet speeding from the pistol to smash into her chest. And yet...

And yet...anger blazed inside of her. It gave her the courage to make the accusation that had formed inside her head: 'You've been in on this the whole time. You're working for the Man. What did they do to John?'

'Nothing. You and John are all they care about.'

'Why?'

Nev kept the gun on her as he spoke. 'Because you are a success.'

He gave Amber a contemptuous glance. 'Unlike you, nut-roast. Your memory implants didn't fully take in your brain, did they? You're not as crazy as those first Protos – but you're damn close.'

Kyra felt like ripping the guy's balls off and sticking them down his throat. 'It's all clear now. You're lying. You've been lying the whole time. You're one of them!'

'Nah, sweet pie. I'm just a poor bloody volunteer plucked from Death Row. Just like you.'

'I'm not a murderer!'

'You are.' Nev's smile was a nasty one. 'You just don't know that you're a killer. They subjected you to neural programming. Brain-washing. They pumped false memories galore into your brain.'

Kyra noticed that Amber, who stood behind Nev, was stooping to pick up a rock that was the size of a tennis ball. The look in her eyes revealed her intention.

Kyra spoke quickly, to keep Nev looking into her face, so he wouldn't glance at Amber and see that she was getting ready to clout him. 'Nev. There aren't any fake memories.'

Nev was more relaxed now. He even used the muzzle of the gun to scratch away an itch on the side of his head. 'You are so full of shit. I know! I still have the memories of who I really am. What I did. My trial. I can remember as plain as day walking through the door into my cell for the first time, and smelling jailbird poop, which had accumulated in toilets that would not flush. The boss guy, the one who you call the Man, permitted me to remember everything about my old life. *I am the Control.* Don't you get it? I egged you on. I tried to get you to attack other people, and to attack each other.' Nev became exasperated. 'But you and John never did, even in self-defense. No matter how much stress they put on you – even from those chained Protos – you never cracked and went back to being your old killer selves. Hey! You never even remembered that Daniel and Sarah existed.'

Kyra watched Amber holding the stone. The woman was testing its weight in her hand. Evaluating it as a weapon. Thankfully, Nev still hadn't noticed. He was too focused on ranting at Kyra. She decided to hold his focus on her, even if it meant goading him into shooting her.

'You are a fool,' she told him. 'There is no Sarah! There is no Daniel! We're not them!'

He shook his head in astonishment. 'No wonder they think you and John are the poster children that's going to make all their sick dreams come true.'

That's when Amber attacked. She rushed forward, aiming to crack the rock down against his skull. She never even reached him. Nev whirled around, aiming the pistol as he did so. Strangely, even though he didn't fire, Amber suddenly let out a high-pitched shriek. She immediately dropped the rock before clutching the side of her neck with her left hand. Her eyes were suddenly massive in her head as her eyelids slid back. A moment later, she toppled backwards. Lilli fell from her grasp and raised a splash of dust as it hit the ground. Amber lay there. She was making choking sounds. Her lips were drawn back to reveal teeth that were now starting to turn a sticky red as blood oozed up from her throat.

Kyra screamed in fury. She charged at Nev with so much force it knocked him off balance. She instantly plucked the gun from his fingers. Though something wasn't right. The gun...it had very little weight to it.

She stared at the pistol in her hand. 'It's wood.'

He was nervously twitchy again. 'I carved it. You think they'd give me a real gun?'

After tossing the fake weapon aside, she ran to Amber where she crouched beside her. Amber was barely conscious. Every time she coughed, blood surged from her mouth.

Kyra yelled at Nev, 'What did you do to her?'

'I didn't do anything. They did! *They triggered it!*'

'Triggered what?'

By this time, Nev's gaze anxiously swept the surrounding terrain. He was terrified of...of something. But what was it that had scared him? Then he pointed in terror at a black speck that moved along a hilltop. He'd seen a guard in the distance.

Nev shouted, 'Fuck this shit! I'm done with this!'

Nev began to run toward a cliff face. There in the rock, there was a dozen or more square-shaped openings to tunnels – they looked like the entrances to ancient tombs.

Kyra's focus was now on Amber. She lay there with her eyes closed, not moving so much as a finger. Kyra pumped her chest; she felt the woman's slender ribs spring inward beneath the heel of her hand as she pushed in an attempt to keep the heart beating.

'Breathe, Amber. Breathe!'

Kyra abruptly paused the CPR. This seemed so uncannily familiar – and familiar in a way that frightened her. Kyra shut her eyes. A powerful memory suddenly blazed inside her head. She saw herself standing over a baby in a gloomy chamber. Kyra was using her fingertips to give tiny compressions to the child. Then there was a strange spinning sensation inside Kyra's brain, and the vivid image of the baby abruptly vanished.

Once again, Kyra pumped Amber's chest. The ribs must have been bending halfway to her spine, the pressure compressing the heart, squeezing blood through the arteries.

Amber convulsed. Her head and torso jerked upwards from the ground. She opened her eyes wide, then coughed. More blood was ejected from her lips, to leave drops that were sticky and red and wet in the dust. Yet the return to life was only temporary. Amber sagged back to the ground. Blood was streaming from her mouth. Her eyes became dull. Her breathing was a throaty crackle.

Kyra thought: *Amber's dying. You can't save her.*

Kyra glanced across the canyon. Nev was still running hard. Kyra did hesitate, knowing it was horrid to leave Amber. But, clearly, there was very little life remaining in the woman. Her eyes were bloodshot. The skin on her hands had turned a deathly blue as her heart began to fail.

Kyra stood up. Then she began to back away, her eyes still fixed on Amber.

Amber managed to lift her head so she could look at Lilli.

Amber whispered, 'I'm so sorry.'

The cat still moved its head in a mechanical way. Its plastic eyes appeared to gaze back into Amber's face.

Another convulsion tore through Amber. Her head jerked back as her spine arched – she must have been in agony. A second later, it was over. Her body sagged...and she lay there, limp and lifeless, on the desert sand.

Kyra felt like she'd been released as well. She raced after Nev and, within moments, she'd caught up with him as he veered off across an expanse of dry earth that led to massive boulders the size of houses.

Kyra shouted to Nev, 'Where are we going?'

He pointed at the boulders. 'We must get behind those. They'll block the signal.'

On a monitor, the perfectly clear image of two people from above. Data scrolled along the bottom of the screen. Coordinates. Altitude of spy satellite. Speed and direction of targets. The two figures moved through narrow passageways that had been naturally formed by the accumulation of boulders. As the boulders became larger, the shadows became darker. A moment later, the two fugitives vanished from view.

CHAPTER TWENTY-THREE

John couldn't see much. What he did see was enough to freeze his blood.

He'd woken up to find himself strapped to a bench. There were restraints around his ankles, wrists, and throat. His head appeared to be clamped into a steel frame. He could feel the coldness of metal rods pressing against his face. He even saw the cold glint of the metal head restraints from the corner of his eyes. Was he going to be tortured? Or was this a gas chamber? Or something like an electric chair? Were these bastards going to execute him?

The stench of disinfectant was so strong he grimaced – the fumes felt like they were cutting into the sensitive tissue inside his nostrils. The light that illuminated the room was harsh enough to hurt his eyes. A figure appeared in a hazmat suit of bright orange plastic material. A flexible hose snaked away from the mask, indicating that they weren't breathing the same air as him. The individual in the mask said nothing. They merely worked in a me-thodical way at some task. Though what that task was he couldn't tell, due to his restricted view. Hands wearing latex gloves moved toward his face. They began taping back his eyelids with strips of thick paper that had a wet, gluey substance smeared on one side. The glue was so pungent he tried to flinch away, but the steel framework clamped to his skull did not allow him to move.

John recoiled at the unpleasant sensation of wet strips being applied to his eyelids. Which were then pulled back, as the medic, or whatever the hell they were, fixed the other end of the strip to John's forehead.

The process was revolting. He hated the wet feeling as the strips were gummed to his flesh.

He squirmed. 'No...'

The figure didn't react to his voice. John began to try and snap the restraints that secured his wrists. At the same moment, a huge screen that was fully ten feet wide blazed to life on the wall in front of him. The screen was filled with the image of a face. And that face belonged to the individual that Kyra had named 'the Man.' There must have been a camera fixed to the wall in front of John because the Man could clearly see him.

He gazed at John with a cold, clinical stare, like a scientist looking down at the lab rat he was about to dissect. John continued to struggle.

'Please don't hurt yourself.' The Man's voice was icily professional. 'The restraints are not designed for you to break free this time.'

John sagged back onto the bench, panting. 'Let me go.'

'I will, John. You performed admirably. It is time for you to leave.'

Instantly, the overhead light switched from a silvery glare to a purple glow that began to pulsate as if it was the visual representation of a heartbeat. The light had some power beyond actual radiance. There was an energy there that flooded through John's eyes and engulfed his brain. He tried to close his eyes – of course, he couldn't. The glue on the strips of paper had set. They didn't allow him to use his eyelids to protect his eyes from the purple light. A throbbing sound began – so deep. Deeper than hell. The sound made the bones of his skull vibrate until they hurt. And, most cruelly of all, the purple light sank into his brain. It was penetrating cerebral matter to ignite memories that lay hidden, deep down beyond the normal reach of recollection.

He pictured himself looking into a mirror. It was his face looking back at him, yet it was not his face. It was a hard face with the eyes of a hater.

The Man's voice boomed out at him: 'For the record. What is your full name?'

John answered in a such a cold voice that he couldn't believe it had come from his own lips. He said, 'Daniel. Daniel Hawkins.'

The man asked, 'What is the last thing you remember?'

John had no intention of answering, yet the words spilled from his lips anyway. 'Lying here,' he murmured. 'How long has it been? Did I fall asleep?'

The voice shimmered from the TV monitor: 'Yes. You have been asleep.'

John looked up at the purple light. At that moment, it seemed more like purple fire. A fire that had the power to transmute human beings. And now his mind began travelling through time. Back years and years, back to when he was a little boy who'd walked to the edge of a deep lake and looked down, to see a woman drowning there, her hair all floating around her head, her eyes staring up at him in absolute fear. However, some force drew him swiftly to a more recent memory. He now recalled seeing a young woman, lying on her back in a shallow river. She'd been carried downstream to a point where a pair of boulders had caught her, preventing her from floating away. Everything was so vivid. The splash of water rushing over stones. The green branches casting dancing shadows. A golden butterfly warming its wings as it stood on a rock.

The river was only a foot deep, the pebbles at the bottom were so clearly visible. As was the woman. The laces of her shoes rippled in the current. Her dark hair fanned out. There was no expression on her face. She stared upwards into the bluest of skies. She did not blink. She did not breathe...

The memory of the woman faded out. He felt so calm now. The purple lights above his face formed undulating shapes. Beguiling. Enchanting. Hypnotic. He found himself becoming increasingly drowsy.

He thought: *Strange...I had a dream where I was someone called John.*

Finally, the dream of being John slowly evaporated to nothing.

He was Daniel.

He was Daniel through and through.

A drone hung in the desert sky. Its surveillance camera detected two figures running along a dusty valley toward the entrance of tunnel. The figures were tiny from this altitude...but the way they moved suggested they were desperate. And afraid.

CHAPTER TWENTY-FOUR

Kyra ran with a speed that left Nev lagging behind. He panted hard, struggling to suck enough oxygen into his lungs to keep going.

At that moment, however, he pointed and managed to gasp out the words, 'In there. Hurry.'

Kyra realized that he pointed at the square entrance to a massive tunnel that led into the mountain. Nev managed to gather enough energy to sprint along the desert path and into the tunnel. Kyra followed – all the time she was glancing back, hunting for any sign that they were being followed by those sinister guards. They looked like were employed by Satan himself.

Kyra followed Nev for a hundred yards or so into the tunnel. The thing looked as if it had been carved from bedrock to accommodate a railroad or a major highway that had never been built. The entrance was so big that it allowed sunlight to flood in. The floor consisted of a mixture of stones and dust, together with the skeletons of rats that had crawled in here to die. Their white skulls resembled seashells scattered on a beach. Kyra felt uneasy. Why had rats died here in such large numbers? What if the air was toxic in here?

Nev, however, was noisily drawing that air into his nostrils as he caught his breath. His forehead gleamed with perspiration. With a smile of satisfaction on his face, he reached out to slap the tunnel's wall of solid rock.

'This should do it. Hard-as-fuck granite. That will keep the radio signals out. We're safe.' Then he spoke in a way that was strangely casual, considering the circumstances. 'Kyra. Give me the arrow.'

Why does he need a weapon? Kyra took a step back from him.

'Kyra, we need to cut it out now, or we'll never escape.'

'Cut what out?'

'The thing they stuck inside of us,' Nev told her. 'The boss man triggers it when things get out of hand. Like with Amber, yeah? It's in the back of the neck.'

Kyra was suspicious. 'How do you know?'

'Because I get to remember. Remember? I've seen it happen – again and again. I saw the Man take down a big guy within seconds. *Zap!* The victims always grab their neck. Same spot. So, I felt here...' He touched the back of his neck. 'You can feel a small bump under your skin.' He glared at her. 'Do it.'

She kept a wary eye on him as she slid her hand under her long hair to feel her neck. Her heart lurched with shock. She'd found the hard bump under her skin.

Nev's voice rose in triumph as he realized that her expression revealed that she believed him. 'See?' he said. 'Now give me the arrow.'

She hesitated. The blade of the arrow was sharp enough to cut throats – her throat, come to that.

He snarled with frustration when she didn't hand over the arrow. 'Come on! They've never let me outside before. But here I am. Listen to me, Kyra. There's no way they can trigger the thing that's in your neck through rock. The granite blocks the radio signal. Now, this is the only chance I've got.' His tone became viciously eager: 'I'll cut yours out!'

'No. You don't get to practice on me.'

He took a deep breath as he came to a compromise. 'Fine. You do me first. Just get the little fucker out of my body!'

Kyra's mind became unusually calm and clear. 'Take off your shirt.'

He immediately slipped off the long-sleeve shirt before handing it to her. Quickly, she used the arrowhead's sharp tip to cut away one of the sleeves.

As she cut the fabric she said, 'I need to make bandages. Okay, take the knee.'

He immediately knelt on one knee. She moved around behind him where she lifted his hair from the back of his neck to expose the skin. Although it was faint, she could make out a small scar there, shaped like a letter C. A surgery scar. She gently ran her finger over it, and she felt something hard move beneath the skin. There was something implanted in the flesh that was perhaps the size of her little fingernail. She couldn't see it, but she felt it alright.

Nev hissed, 'Go on. Cut the damn thing out.'

'Yes, I can do it. Just keep still.'

The arrowhead felt so right in her hand. Kyra was wielding it as if it was a scalpel. She immediately understood what to do – how hard to press the blade. How she must draw the cutting edge with confidence. The importance of avoiding spinal cord and major arteries.

Nev braced himself. Kyra didn't hesitate and made a neat incision with the confidence of a surgeon. Nev cursed through clenched teeth. Blood began flow – a lot of blood – it dripped onto the dusty floor of the tunnel. Nev trembled with pain. Without anesthetic that deep cut inflicted by the arrowhead must have been excruciating. Nevertheless, he didn't pull away from her, even when she used her fingers to pull open the wound, so she could see inside what had become a pocket of raw flesh. Gently, she probed with the tip of the arrow. Almost immediately, she heard the click of the metal arrowhead against some hard substance. Nev groaned – the pain was getting worse.

'Hold on,' she whispered, 'nearly there.'

As she loosened the hard object, which was initially masked by the flow of crimson, she eventually began to make out a small silvery device that was being lifted out by the tip of the arrow. The device was perhaps half an inch long, with the same circumference as a pen. It appeared to be, as far as she could determine, a small glass cylinder. Deftly, she nipped it from the wound between her finger and thumb.

She said, 'It's okay. I've got it out,'

Nev climbed to his feet. He held out his hand, palm upwards, and she carefully deposited the device there so he could examine it. As he did so, she expertly tied the shirt sleeve around his neck to stem the flow of blood.

Nev was so fascinated by the device that had been pulled from his neck he didn't even appear to notice the pain. He held it up to the light.

He let out a whistle of astonishment at what he saw. 'Some kind of liquid inside. Gotta be poison.' Nev then ran his finger over the neatly tied makeshift bandage. 'Nice.' He gave a wry smile. 'You're a good nurse.'

Kyra glared at him. Deep down inside herself, she knew there was so much wrong with that bland statement he'd just uttered. *You're a good nurse.* She forced herself to focus on what needed to be done now. She quickly cleaned off his blood from the arrowhead with the shirt. No way was the arrowhead sterile. *Desperate times call for desperate measures.* She handed him the arrowhead.

He gave a strange smile. 'You trust me?'

Do I hell! She stopped herself from saying that. Instead, she turned her back to him, then pulled her hair up from the nape of her neck.

Her tone was sharp: 'Just get it out of my body.'

As she stood there, she realized she was at Nev's mercy. If he so chose, he could cut her throat with the arrowhead. Leave her to bleed out on the floor. *But what choice do I have? So, here goes...*She closed her eyes, while telling herself that the pain wouldn't be so bad.

The tip of the blade felt cold when it cut through the skin on the back of her neck.

The pain...

It was awful. Nevertheless, she didn't flinch. She simply held her breath until it was over. And when it was over, Nev quickly tied the other sleeve of his shirt around her neck. She no longer felt blood trickling under her clothes to run down her back. He'd done a good job of stemming the blood flow, too.

Nev showed her the tiny cylinder with its dark cargo of poison inside. It was evidently a kill switch. If one of the Man's lab rats either escaped or broke free of whatever controlled them, then a touch of an icon on a screen would explode the cylinder inside the individual's neck. After that, fast-acting toxins would flood the victim's arteries, ending their life within seconds.

She flung the death cylinder into the dirt at the side of the tunnel. No sooner had she done that than she saw a figure dressed in black hurrying from the gloom toward them. It was a big guy with a black beard, and he wore a helmet with a headcam attached to the front of it.

In a heartbeat, she hissed, 'Nev. Do what I do.'

Kyra shouted out in pain, grabbed her neck, swayed, then tumbled to the floor. There she lay still. Her eyes shut. She heard a body fall next to hers. That must be Nev. After that, she heard the guard's boots on the floor. *Scrunch, scrunch, scrunch...getting closer.*

Then she heard the man's voice. He sounded close to panic. 'Red Victor. I've found the Kyra test subject in the East Tunnel, Zone Five. She appears to be dead. Nev, too. I don't know how. Kill switch radio frequency is blocked by granite. Do you copy?'

The only answer was static. Then she heard a flurry of movement – grunts, scuffle sounds of boots on dirt, the thumping sound of fists striking a body. Kyra opened her eyes to find that Nev had attacked the guard. The guard was much stronger than Nev. He was pounding his fists down onto Nev's back. Nev doubled up in pain, his hands over his head, trying to protect himself from the powerful blows.

Kyra moved lighting fast. Before she even realized what she was doing, she'd dragged the baton from her belt – the one that John had taken from the guard earlier. Then *WHACK!* The baton had slammed into the guard's helmet so ferociously that he staggered away from Nev.

Then, the strangest thing...everything seemed so calm...so far away. She didn't even feel like she was using any force. However, she flailed the baton like it was a battleaxe. She struck the guard again and again. This time he fell to the ground. Thereafter, she was able to attack the part of his exposed face which was beneath the goggles he wore. The sound of the baton hitting the man's mouth and nose was a wet sound. Kyra thought the noise was a peculiar one. But the baton did indeed make a loud squelch every time it struck. That might have been because the guard's face had begun to disintegrate. His nose had gone. His lips were torn shreds of scarlet. He was no longer conscious. Yet Kyra pounded the baton into the man's face, over and over again.

She knew he was dead. Yet she could not stop herself from hitting him. The violence felt so good. It felt so right. *This is what I was born to do.*

It only seemed a long time later that she was herself again. She was standing there, the baton in her hand. She was panting. There was so much blood. It dripped from the baton. It covered the guard's face and chest. There were sunburst patterns of red on the dusty floor of the tunnel.

Nev gave a nod of approval. 'That was a good ruse playing dead.'

Kyra stared at the baton, like she was an avenging angel staring at the bloody sword of eternal vengeance in her hand.

She could hardly breathe; she was so knotted up tight with horror. 'What if it's true...all true? Everything.'

Nev looked down at the corpse, then he glanced at Kyra. 'Holy shit. They broke you, didn't they? Broke their precious pottery that they'd sculpted. A little too much heat for too long. The Man did succeed in locking the beast away in here.' He pointed at Kyra's forehead. 'But the beast you've got inside of you, Kyra, is much too strong. Much too nasty. They pushed you that bit too far – they made the beast break out again. And it did this.' He prodded the dead guard with the toe of his boot. Nev didn't appear at all bothered by the mutilation, because he quickly began to search the man's pockets. Nev found a small flashlight, which he passed to Kyra. Automatically, she slipped it into her pocket. Then Nev pulled a water bottle from where it was fixed to the guard's belt. The bottle was smeared with blood. Nev didn't even seem to notice. He pulled the valve with his teeth and took a massive swallow of water.

The horror that Kyra felt was immense. 'I killed him.'

'Self-defense. I'd acquit.'

He offered her the water bottle. Kyra looked at the baton in her hand, as if it was swarming with vile maggots. With a cry of anguish, she flung the baton away.

By this time, her mouth was powder dry. She took the bottle from Nev. Before she drank, however, she whispered, 'I had a memory...when I was giving Amber CPR.' She took a huge swallow of water. It was deliciously cold as it flooded her mouth before running down her throat. 'I...I...smothered a baby...in a hospital.' She took another desperate gulp of water, as if it could flush bad memories away that she had completely forgotten until a moment ago. 'I worked in the maternity ward. I was trying to bring the baby back.... using CPR...not I...but *she*. Do you understand?'

'You mean Sarah?' He regarded her with his brown eyes that seemed so wise now, and so grave.

'I think whatever this Sarah did – if she was real – I think she did it to be seen as a hero...that she saved babies.' Kyra's heart felt as if it was turning to ice. A dreadful feeling. Other memories were rising to the surface. 'The babies that died...I didn't do it on purpose. It was—'

'An accident? Nevertheless, she – or should I say "you"? – still smothered them first. Tomayto, tomahto.'

Nev searched the guard again. He pulled a photo from the breast pocket – it was of a young woman with a child on her lap. Nev shoved the picture back into dead man's pocket.

Kyra, meanwhile, continued to speak. 'But it doesn't feel real. These images flashing inside my head of what Sarah did…it feels fake. Like false memories.'

Nev laughed. 'False memories? You *are* the false memory.'

Kyra stared into the gloom, in the direction of the far end of the tunnel. Suddenly, what frightened her more than anything else in the world was *her*. She was terrified of herself. Of all the brutal people she'd encountered during the last few days…was she the worst one of them all?

A pair of red dots began to emerge from the gloom. They grew brighter and brighter until they blazed. Was she seeing the approach of a savage predator with blood red eyes? There was a whirring sound now. It grew louder, as the pair of things that looked like glaring eyes approached.

'Drone!' Nev grabbed her arm. 'Run!'

Nev had dropped the arrowhead on the ground when he'd pretended to collapse. Swiftly, she grabbed it from the floor, then she followed him, as he raced along the tunnel, away from the approaching drone.

When she glanced back, she saw that the drone had stopped following them. Instead, it hovered about four feet above the guard. Clearly, its controller was studying the fallen man via the drone's camera. Seemingly, the drone's electronic system employed a different type of receiver because the controller's signal was reaching the drone through the rock. Or maybe Nev had been lying to her all along…

Kyra ran alongside Nev as they left the tunnel. The sunlight that engulfed them was blinding after the subterranean gloom. Nev cut off to the right, where he started to climb a steep slope that was covered with rocks and thorn bushes. The drone emerged from the tunnel where it stopped and hovered – possibly, the controller was getting their bearings.

Nev pointed at the opening of what appeared to be a narrow cave in the side of the mountain. 'This way!' he shouted.

A moment later, they plunged into the cave. Ahead of them, it seemed to go on forever – deep into the heart of darkness.

CHAPTER TWENTY-FIVE

The Man sat in his lair. He occupied the nexus of this complex operation that had taken decades to build to this level of excellence. True, he had experienced many failures before attaining this enviable degree of success. It was equally true that most of his failures were buried out in the desert. He looked sleek and professional in his Armani suit as he sat at his desk. The wall full of TV monitors in front of him allowed him to observe all aspects of his experiments from his luxurious swivel chair. On one screen, a line of Protos stood chained to an overhead rail. They gazed into thin air with that thousand league stare of theirs. Blue lights glowed in their blinders, and they'd be hearing soothing white noise. Their minds were coasting in neutral. Neither excited nor angry. They were, in effect, peacefully slumbering, though they were on their feet and their eyes were open. Another screen revealed Daniel Hawkins (AKA John) sitting on his bunk in a prison cell. He had a tray on his lap, and he stared down at a plate of uneaten pasta. He appeared to be struggling to remember. But remember what? Kyra? Who had been such an important part of life for a few short days. If anyone should ask Daniel if he remembered Kyra, he would simply give a sullen shake of his head. He remembered nothing of her. All recent memories of Kyra, Goliath, Amber, and Nev had been suppressed by the Lethe device.

On a split screen in front of him were the heads of a man and a woman, both in their forties. The guy wore a shirt, open at the collar. The tie had been pulled down a little, as if he had been feeling the heat of some controversy and had been worrying the knot of his tie with anxious fingers. The guy looked sweaty. His dark fringe was stuck up – a visible manifestation of what must have been a long day of considerable vexation. The woman, on the other hand, looked cool and glamorous without giving the impression of trying hard. She wore a beautifully tailored black jacket with a coral pink blouse that exactly matched the shade of her pink lipstick. The camera revealed that the room she occupied was equally glamourous, with velvet drapes and an antique vase on a plinth. Everything about the woman exuded wealth and exquisite taste. The Man knew she was a seasoned politician that could charm people with a beautiful smile. A few words, however, from those enchanting lips could viciously assassinate the character of a political opponent. She would be a valuable ally to have. On the other hand, if she chose to be so, she could be a dangerous enemy.

The Man knew this video meeting was a crucial one. He would need to navigate the conversation with great care – he faced a wary guy who was looking for an escape route to safeguard his professional reputation. And he faced a woman who could smile in such a disarming way as she signed a paper that would slaughter his career. Then everything he had worked so hard for...*ffft*...gone in a moment.

In fact, that deeply troubling thought about all his work being thrown away pulled him back in time to a truly horrendous incident ten years ago. The Man had labored ferociously on a project that would transform humanity. This was a project that he was so proud of and which he pursued with all the zeal of one of those Medieval knights, who put on their armor, picked up a sword, then bloodily fought their way across Europe to Jerusalem in search of the Holy Grail. For the Man, this project was far more important than the discovery of the Holy Grail. The work he was doing would, he frequently asserted, ultimately improve the lives of billions of people.

However, remembering the vile things that were said about him by those who doubted his abilities – and who ridiculed his vision – made his heart pound as anger surged through his body.

The Man recalled the toll on his health as he strove to create this extraordinary facility in the desert – one housed in mundane industrial buildings, so as not to attract the attention of anyone who happened to be wandering too close. Of course, the facility was well-guarded; however, the compound's humdrum appearance consummately masked what occurred inside. And what was occurring was nothing less than an entire series of technological miracles, which he had created by applying his intelligence and willpower in order to reveal the mysteries of the human mind.

Then, a decade ago, a politician arrived. He'd been sent by a government committee, to conduct an unannounced check on the program – to evaluate its progress, to collect enough information for the committee to decide whether to continue funding the program or shut it down and bulldoze the facility to rubble, then leave it for the windblown sands of the desert to bury the ruins forever, thereby creating a tomb for the Man's ambitions.

The politician, a red-faced guy of fifty, in a gray business suit and a gold-colored tie, had strode along the corridors like he owned the place. The whites of his eyes were threaded with bright red veins. And his expression was permanently angry. It was like the building he strutted through angered him. The color of its walls appeared to cause him intense displeasure. The staff he met infuriated him. Even the coffee he drank had him glaring at the coffee mug with utter contempt, as if he wished he could furiously smash it to pieces, because it dared to exist in his presence. Without asking permission beforehand, he'd flung open doors to sterile laboratories and workshops, thus risking contamination, and thereby damage, of delicate instruments. He'd barked questions at technicians and scientists. He did, however, introduce himself to everyone he interrogated in his brusque manner. 'My name's Klovelly. That's Klo-Velly. *Klovelly!* Now, tell me your role here. No, I don't need to know your name. Not interested in your name in the slightest. What do you do? How much is it costing the taxpayer?'

Then he had demanded to see the Lethe device in action.

The Man had protested. 'Sir. The Lethe must be prepared. Each time, it needs to be recalibrated.'

'Then it's a temperamental son-of-a-bitch.' Klovelly remained angry. Very angry. The Man believed this politician had been born foul-tempered. No doubt he'd emerged from the womb raging at a world that he'd despised from the second his newborn eyes saw it.

'Mr. Klovelly, development is still in the early stages. Soon, however, it will run from start-up to full operational capacity within seconds. At this point in time, we need five hours, minimum.'

'Well, I'm giving you those fucking five hours. I don't need to drive away from this Godforsaken place until seven o'clock tonight. Okay, chop-chop, get your people busy.'

Five hours later, and the Man stood beside Klovelly in the control room – this was a bleak chamber, with walls of gray cinderblock. Back then, the control room had shared the operational area with the Lethe device. In its center was the gurney where the subject would be strapped down before having their eyelids taped back.

Klovelly, with his trademark expression of fury, glared at the three concentric steel rings from where the light-emitting orb would be lowered.

He snarled, 'So, this is it? The Lethe. It doesn't look like a whole lot of tech, considering its devoured hundreds of millions of dollars.'

The Man tapped at a keyboard while gazing at the computer screen. Geometric shapes flowed across the screen to merge, overlap. Greens melting into blues. Calibration was nearly complete.

'What you are seeing, Mr. Klovelly, is the pinnacle of technological development. It has taken me twelve years to perfect the device. One day, every nation on Earth will be using the Lethe. I chose the name 'Lethe'. I named it after the river from Greek myth that flows through the Underworld, where men and women migrate after they have died. When the dead drink from the River Lethe, it is said that all memories of the life they have lived are washed away. They forget their families, their friends – they forget everything they have done, whether it be good or bad. Therefore, when they enter the afterlife, they enter with clean minds and the blessing of pristine forgetfulness.'

'Are you bullshitting me? Are you telling me this to delay strapping some jailbird to that gurney and zapping their brains?'

'Not at all. I thought you would be interested to know why I chose the name 'Lethe' for the most remarkable machine ever devised by a human being.'

Klovelly, if anything, looked even angrier. The red veins in his eyes became more intensely red, like they were a gauge that measured his fury. He growled ominously, 'You do know, if I'm not impressed by what I see today – and I mean *hugely impressed* – it is within my power to recommend to the committee that they close down your carnival show immediately. Whoosh. Gone. Deleted. Not another cent. All expenditure removed. Your fancy Greek name for that contraption won't save your career, either.'

The Man was spared the effort of finding something diplomatic to say in response to that decidedly shitty little speech of Klovelly's, because a pair of guards brought in a huge guy that was bare chested and wore pale green sweatpants. The giant of a man was the test subject. He had angry eyes all of his own, which matched the ferocity of Klovelly's stare.

The guards spoke matter-of-factly to the giant, using his name, 'Ryan'. Though Ryan could have put up a hell of a fight if he didn't want to be strapped down onto the gurney, he did comply with instructions and lay down on it – he lay on his back, face up, gazing at the three concentric rings with barely a hint of curiosity. He didn't even seem to notice when a guard taped back his eyelids with sticking plaster, thereby making it impossible for him to close his eyes.

Klovelly dropped his voice so Ryan wouldn't hear. 'Ah, Ryan Durker. I remember his face from the news coverage. He killed three police officers with an axe. It took ten cops to hold him down, so they could put him in chains.'

'And now he's been removed from Death Row because he has become a willing volunteer.' The Man took a step toward where Durker lay. The guards had strapped his wrists to the steel frame of the gurney. Durker lay there, clenching and unclenching his fists. However, he remained calm. When the guards were satisfied that Durker's restraints were secure, they withdrew.

'Aren't the guards going to remain here during the procedure?' asked Klovelly.

'Their presence is no longer necessary.'

'Do all your staff come and go as they please? An hour ago, I saw most of them scuttling back to their cars, then bugging out of here like the place was on fire.'

'It's Friday evening. My staff are completely dedicated, but even they need to take time off every now and again, otherwise we start to experience employee burnout.'

'They sound like a gaggle of lightweights to me.'

'They are professionals who deserve the occasional weekend of relaxation. Besides, I don't require the assistance of any team members now. The Lethe, at this stage, is fully automatic. Incidentally, there are only a small number of guards on duty now, and they are in the security bunker. Of course, if they are required, I can summon them.' He decided to drive home the point that the facility was largely devoid of people to the extent that Klovelly couldn't expect preferential treatment. 'Also, I should point out the canteen is closed; therefore, if you'd like another coffee, I respectfully suggest you make it yourself.'

Klovelly glared at the Man. His anger hadn't diminished – in fact, the opposite had occurred. He looked angrier than ever. His tone took on a contemptuous sneer: 'Then I will add another item to my report.' He glanced at his watch. 'From six o'clock on a Friday evening, your complex empties out for the weekend, no doubt leaving a couple of guards who eat pizza, guzzle beer, and watch TV while your staff party at some roadside bar.'

The Man chose not to reply to the disparaging statement. Instead, he spoke to the subject who lay on the gurney. 'Ryan Durker, you still consent to undergoing the procedure?'

Durker continued to stare up at the device (then could he do anything else, considering his eyelids were taped open? Which must have felt like nothing less than barbaric torture). 'I do,' he grunted. 'This has got to be better than sitting in a fucking jail cell, waiting to get fried in the electric chair.'

Klovelly moved forward until he could look directly down at Durker, lying there, strapped to the gurney.

'If the decision was mine,' Klovelly snarled, 'you would still fry in the chair, you fucking cop killer.'

Durker reacted with fury. 'Hey, who is this jerk? Why does he get to insult me? I volunteered for this. Aren't I giving something back to society?'

'What society wants,' hissed Klovelly, 'is to smell your skin burn as you take fifty thousand volts up your ass.'

Durker began to strain against the restraints; thick muscle in his arms bunched, the veins stood out in his forehead as a murderous rage engulfed him. 'Hey...I'll rip your fucking head off and stick it up *your* ass.'

If Klovelly's gloating smirk was anything to go by, he was clearly enjoying his moment of power over the restrained man. Klovelly could say whatever he wanted, and he knew that the prisoner couldn't even lay so much as a finger on him. Without a shadow of doubt, Klovelly was an infuriating shit.

'Durker.' Klovelly's grin was a mean one. 'You are one of life's losers. You are garbage. Your wife will be in another guy's bed now. They'll be laughing at you. Because you-'

Durker howled with rage. He tried to raise his arms so he could grab Klovelly. The straps were made of formidably strong material; they still held. Even so, the metal buckles started to distort, such was the man's strength.

Klovelly prodded Durker's forehead. 'You're so chicken shit scared of Old Sparky you volunteered for this. I wish the families of those police officers you murdered could see you now. Lying there, like a scared little baby!'

'You fucker!'

The Man had been carefully appraising data onscreen. But now Klovelly's goading of the volunteer, despicable though Durker was, had begun to try the Man's patience.

'Please stop antagonizing Mr. Durkur. He has volunteered for this program. What's more, he should be calm, rather than agitated, when the process begins.'

'Durker is excrement. Nothing more.'

The Man handed the politician what appeared to be a pair of sunglasses. Of course, they were much more than that. 'Please put these on. It's important to protect your eyes during the process.'

Durker reacted to these words with alarm. 'This process. Will it hurt?'

The Man smiled. 'You will feel nothing more than a sense of growing calm and of wonderful inner peace.'

Klovelly stared with deep mistrust at the sunglasses in his hand. 'What happens if *I* don't wear these?'

The Man wanted to say: *Your memories from your no doubt dubious life will be so deeply suppressed you will no longer be able to recall them;* however, he merely smiled again and said, 'In the first instance, you'll simply fall asleep. Okay, shall we begin? Eye protectors on, Mr. Klovelly.'

He donned the shades.

The Man did likewise. Then, in calm tones, pretty much like that dispassionate individual who counts down the seconds to the launch of a rocket, he said, 'Programs are running in automatic mode. All systems are functional. Five. Four. Three. Two. One. Lethe activated.'

Durker *was* scared. He was a big guy. A brute of man. A man who would have laughed when he inflicted pain on his victims. And now he was *absolutely* scared. He stared up at the concentric rings above him. He clenched his fists so tightly that nothing less than a vivid tapestry of veins stood out from the skin.

A purple glow began to form around the device suspended from the ceiling above Durker. Meanwhile, the pungent smell of raw electricity, something like the stench of human hair when it is burnt, filled the room – the odor was proof of the huge voltage running through cables to power the Lethe. The purple glow began to assume a shape, and soon what had been a formless light morphed into something that resembled a halo, which floated in the air, encircling the steel rings. A moment later, electric motors hummed softly as the computer initiated the next phase. A metal sphere, the size of a baseball, slowly passed downward through the center of the rings as the device began its descent toward Durker's face. His eyes bulged even more prominently as he stared at the eerie machine. That machine which was a reaper of toxic memory. Gradually, a pulsing tone started. At first, it was quite gentle. Then the intensity grew as the purple light began to ripple and pulsate – the effect was almost like looking at an illuminated liquid that swirled and moved and flowed.

Durker sighed. His body was beginning to relax. Instead of his hands being clenched tight into hard fists, they now slowly opened up, fingers extending. The man's breathing became slower, more regular, like he was starting to fall asleep. Whereas seconds ago, his eyes had been close to bursting out of their sockets, they now gazed drowsily up at the orb, which had descended to within fifteen inches of his face.

The Man loved to imagine what it was like to undergo the Lethe process. It wouldn't be unpleasant. No, far from it. The patient would sink into a blissful coma. There'd be no pain, no anxiety, no fear. Traumatic memories would be soothed away and utterly forgotten. Then the memory implants would be conveyed on waves of high-frequency light into the brain's temporal lobe. The process led to the suppression of the old self. And then, what followed, was the birth of the new self. A better self – one that was kind and good. Admittedly, there were indications that the process was sometimes much harsher than the Man imagined. However, the severity, or otherwise, of the patient's experience was of no importance to him. Besides, the Lethe made the subject forget the process they had undergone anyway; therefore, if they couldn't remember the pain and the distress, how could they complain about any suffering they had experienced?

The eye-protectors hid Klovelly's eyes, though the tone of his voice revealed that he was no less angry than before. 'This is it?' His tone simmered with rage. 'You shine a purple light into the guy's face, then play some stupid whoosh-whoosh sounds? Is that what you spent a billion dollars on?'

'The content of that purple light isn't simple electromagnetic radiation.'

'You're telling me that your disco lights are gonna revolutionize how we deal with criminals?'

'If you will *kindly* shut your mouth and *kindly* listen to my explanation, then you might understand how this device works.'

'How dare you? I call the shots! I can close this program down – like that!' Klovelly raised his hand, then clicked his finger and thumb just two inches from the Man's face. 'So, show me some respect, Doctor Frankenshit.'

Purple saturated the air around them. This was like being in a room full of liquid light – swirling, pulsating, flooding the brain. That's how it felt with the eye-protectors on. Without those, the electronically remastered light would flood in through the open eyes, to flow along the optic nerves into the brain. This was more than light. This was alchemy of the soul.

Klovelly still sneered his contempt for the program. However, the Man began to speak over him with such a tone of authority that even Klovelly, a guy born with a big mouth and a bloated ego to match, fell silent.

'Listen carefully to what I'm about to tell you,' the Man said. 'Medical science has known for decades that different forms of light have the power to affect human beings. Brightly colored lights can stimulate and excite individuals, while strobe lights and flickering lights are known to sometimes trigger seizures in those afflicted with photosensitive epilepsy. Indeed, people who do not suffer from epilepsy can experience nausea and dizziness when exposed to flashing lights. Now, what is important for you to understand is that the Lethe emits light that appears purple in color to the human eye. However, I propel this light into the region of nine hundred trillion hertz, which would not normally be visible to human sight. My process actually renders the light visible. That light's frequency is synchronized with the electrical frequency of the human brain, and it has such a profound and powerful effect on the temporal lobe I can, in effect, manipulate the contents of the subject's mind. Thereafter, I can suppress memories that have corrupted the subject's personality. And I can weave new memories that I have synthesized into their psychological matrix. Those manufactured memories are utterly real to them. I can remove grief and substitute joy. I can eliminate evil instincts and introduce benevolent characteristics. In short, Mr. High and Mighty politician, I can turn bad people into good people.'

'Don't you dare speak to me in such an insulting way.'

'I dare, sir, and I will, because this machine will change the world for the better. Other nations will beg us to sell copies of the Lethe device to them. Consequently, the government's investment in my program will become as profitable as a hundred oil fields.'

Klovelly grasped at anything that might restore his cocksure arrogance. His ego was hurting for sure. He'd been humiliated. 'But...but you have failures. I've seen videos of those poor wretches with those blinder contraptions on their heads. You call those failures Protos. You had to use those blinders to stop the Protos running amok.'

'A small number of failures are only to be expected with such a radical device as this. After all, how many rockets blew up on launch pads before the first satellite successfully orbited the Earth? And the blinder apparatus will be valuable to both the military and the prison system. Once again, I have modulated high energy electromagnetic radiation, which is visible as light, to modify human behavior.'

'So, why not use those blinders as a portable gizmo to edit a human being's memories?'

'The blinders are quite a different instrument of mind control to the Lethe. The blinders can't suppress memories and implant new memories like this machine here. As I have already told you, though you are too intellectually stunted to grasp the information, the Lethe, which is now emitting purple light into Mr. Durker's eyes, is the machine that will deeply suppress toxic memories and insert good memories. It will transmute him from murderer to a gentle human being that would not dream of hurting even a fly.'

'I will be repeating, verbatim, the insults you directed at me when I make my report,' growled Klovelly. 'I will have you fired from the program. Six weeks from now, you will be washing cars to earn enough to keep your sorry ass alive. I'm going to ruin you. I'm going to enjoy watching you take a one-way trip to a life of poverty and misery.'

A single chiming note rang out through the room. The whoosh of white noise quickly faded away, and the purple light suddenly became dim before vanishing completely.

Klovelley chuckled. Evidently, he felt empowered again now that he'd promised to get the Man fired. 'That noise...the equivalent to the ping of a microwave? I guess Durker's brain has been cooked?'

'Something like that. It's safe to remove the eye-protectors now.' Without waiting for a response from Klovelly, he removed the pair he wore. 'It will be several minutes before Mr. Durker wakes up.'

Klovelly pulled the eye-protectors from his own face. 'And he will be a different person? With new memories?'

'Yes. He will believe that he trained for the priesthood. Mr. Durker will have ambitions to undertake charitable work.'

'Speaking nice to me now won't save your miserable skin, you know? I'm still going to get you fired. There are plenty of other scientists who can take over here.'

'If that is what you wish. Oh...this might interest you.'

'What? A baton?'

The Man had picked up a stick from beneath the table on which the computer stood.

'This...' He held it up for Klovelly to see. '...is one of my first inventions. I developed this device after discovering I could modulate light frequencies to override a person's mental function.'

'It looks like a guard's baton to me.'

'It's a deceptively simple weapon. In some cases, this is more effective than a firearm, because its effect is instantaneous.'

'Ah, I get it. You want me to recommend the baton weapon to my committee. That way you earn their praise and keep your job.'

'Governments worldwide will want this weapon, just as much as they will want the Lethe.'

Klovelly shook his head as he laughed. Once again, that note of derision was running thickly through the laughter. 'Don't forget. You signed a contract that confirms the government owns everything you invent here. We don't need your permission to mass-produce your baton – that is, if it's really as good as you say it is.'

'Oh, it is.' The Man spoke in calm, friendly tones. 'It doesn't control a human's actions like the blinders can. Nor does it suppress toxic memories and implant synthesized new memories. It simply emits a blue light that instantly renders a person unconscious. Moments later, they wake, and they haven't suffered any permanent injury.'

Klovelly shrugged. 'Okay. I will take your blue light stick with me. Though you're still gonna get fired.'

The Man circled around the table, getting nearer to Klovelly. 'You should have a demonstration first. You will be impressed by what a flash of this blue light can do.'

'Who are you going to use your flash-stick on? There's nobody else here, other than...' That's when Klovelly's voice died away as he finally understood. 'No...don't you dare!'

The Man swiftly put on the eye-protectors, thumbed the switch, then he smiled as a blue flash drenched the face of that infuriating creature by the name of Prendergast Klovelly.

Klovelly slumped across the gurney, where Durker still slept as new memories, which were as false as false can be, gradually embedded themselves into the pink mush of his brain.

Klovelly would continue to sleep, too. In fact, he was going have a long, long sleep in one of the caves out in the desert. A deep cave where the Man had concealed so many secrets – and regrettable failures – in that forlorn and barren place.

Klovelly had paid that visit ten years ago – and was never seen again. The Man had no choice. The government committee was largely in favor of the Lethe project. It was Klovelly who was dead against it, and it was he who had attempted to persuade the committee to withdraw funding from the Lethe's development and divert that funding to Klovelly's own project, which would have seen the construction of a bridge in his hometown. Rumor had it, that some critics murmured that it would be a bridge to nowhere. Admittedly, they murmured their doubts very quietly as Klovelly wielded huge influence in the higher echelons of government. There was a very real danger that Klovelly would undermine faith in the Lethe's effectiveness to such a degree that the government would order the abandonment of all experiments connected to the project.

With Klovelly out of the way, the Man had a chance of completing his work here. It still wouldn't be an easy ride, but nobody on the committee was a pathological hater like Klovelly was. The Man believed he could persuade the committee to continue funding research here – something that they did subsequently agree to.

And Klovelly? Did anyone miss that poisonous bag of blood and bone? Maybe some of his cronies did, those who benefited from his big-spending follies. Though, in the end, it seems that nobody tried too hard to find out what happened to him. The Man had that hateful politician's car secretly moved to a clifftop overlooking the ocean. Inside the car, the police found an empty bottle of vodka, a seat strewn with tranquilizers, and a note printed from a computer that seemingly revealed Klovelly's inner-turmoil, his despair, his all-consuming regrets in life, and...well, everyone was very quick to guess what happened next.

The Man heard later that Klovelly's political colleagues had gathered to drop a wreath of flowers from the clifftop, near where the car was found. Though later the truth came out: they had, in reality, sent an intern to cast a floral tribute down into the surf.

All that unpleasantness occurred a decade ago. Today, The Man knew that he would have to charm these two politicians and persuade them to continue funding his experimental program. The Lethe was very nearly perfect. However, there was still more work to be undertaken before the Lethe could be mass-produced in a factory. Therefore, the Man spoke to the two individuals onscreen in soft tones that oozed authority: 'As you read in the report, the experiment demonstrates how well the implanted memories hold under stress. In early cycles, we wiped all newly formed memories between tests, so we could see what memories would seep back through – and what would trigger them.'

The wary guy raised a finger. 'They did remember some things...'

The Man smiled as he stirred a dollop of plausible bullshit into the mix. Something he was undeniably adept at accomplishing. 'Just trivial things from the previous test. A very small amount of memory bleed-through is only to be expected, yet so trivial as to be of no consequence.'

The woman nodded. 'As we all saw, even when the Kyra and John test subjects were shown footage of them volunteering for the study, they still didn't remember who they were.'

The wary guy sighed. 'Yes, yes, all very encouraging, but additional funding is not in this year's budget. There's been a deficit.'

The Man decided it was time to deploy the weaponry of concrete-hard statistics. 'It costs ninety thousand dollars a year to incarcerate a person on Death Row. There are currently two thousand nine hundred and seventy-eight people awaiting execution. That's two hundred and sixty-eight million dollars a year. Now, what if instead of that cost, an inmate's identity could be replaced with a memory implant? They are then released, given a minimum wage job. After that, they're now costing the state nothing. Instead, they're paying taxes, and contributing to society.'

The wary guy gave a reluctant nod. 'It's a prison chain-gang. Without the prison. And without the chain.'

The Man rewarded the comment with a warm smile. 'Exactly. And, with a successful rollout, there will be no Death Row. No industrial prison complex. That would please everyone in society: bleeding hearts as well as hardliners. It's a perfect coalition.'

The woman's eyes narrowed. She foresaw difficulties ahead. 'It's still going to be a hard sell. Those inmates were sentenced to die. That's what the victims' families want.'

The Man nodded. 'True. But if a murderer no longer remembers who he or she was...is that person – to all intents and purposes – dead?'

The wary guy seemed more at ease now, and the woman appeared to have heard what she needed to hear, which would allow her to convince others to release more funding. The Man intended to spoon on more vote-winning honey by telling the pair that his technique could be applied to others in society – those individuals that were considered by some to be misfits or slackers, who were a drain on the tax dollar, rather than a contributor to the economy. However, another screen began to flash red as an urgent, must-answer-now call came in. The screen then revealed a gruesome portrait that could have been rendered in bloody gore rather than paint. The pair of original callers couldn't see the image, of course. The Man could. He realized that he was seeing footage from a drone-cam of a guard with a mutilated face – the guard lay still. Evidently dead. A diamond shaped symbol in the corner of the screen flashed insistently. This was a call he must take. And quickly.

Nevertheless, he didn't allow what he'd seen to disturb his aura of professional calm. He smiled at the man and woman on the split screen. In a smooth voice that would have suited a TV commercial for a luxury car, the man said, 'I'll leave you two to discuss the details.'

Swiftly, he clicked the mouse, thereby exiting the video meeting. He clicked the mouse again and he was connected to his head of security. An ex-military guy with a voice like a marine poised for a death or glory mission.

The Man's gaze locked onto the dead face of the guard onscreen as he snapped out the words, 'What happened?'

The urgent voice of the head of security crackled from the speaker, 'Sir, we found the officer dead in the arterial tunnel, Zone Five.'

'Nev did this?'

'Sir, this is the last video recorded by the guard's headcam.'

The image of the dead guard was replaced by footage from the guard's point of view. The camera fixed to his helmet was recording the last thing he saw before he died. The Man prided himself on his emotional detachment; however, this was horrible. For, onscreen, he saw a woman with such an expression of vicious hatred on her face. Her eyes were blazing infernos of utter violence. Her hair flared out around her head as she struck down toward the camera, the baton in her hand momentarily filling the screen as she delivered savage blows. The Man could hear the woman panting. He heard the crunch of breaking face bones. The beating was savage. It was relentless, too. The baton was wet with blood. And even when the guard was no longer a threat, the woman kept thrashing the baton down. Drops of blood flew through the air. They smeared the lens of the guard's headcam.

A moment later, the woman appeared to notice something that spooked her, because she stopped clubbing the fallen man and looked away to her left. After that, she quickly climbed to her feet before darting away from the camera's view, leaving solely the image of the tunnel's ceiling. That's where the gruesome footage ended.

The Man's blood ran cold as he asked a question that disturbed him to his very core. 'Kyra?'

The head of security sounded like a man in need of revenge. 'The bastards removed their kill switch. Nev is helping her. He's on the run, too. A drone revealed them entering the mine. Sir, what are your orders?'

The Man's air of calm professionalism was evaporating. He stood up, ran his fingers through his hair, then he began to pace the room. He'd worked so hard to get this far. He was very, very close to achieving total success. He had the power to change the world – or so he believed, until a moment ago when Kyra reverted to her Sarah persona and killed the guard. Memories of his own came flooding back. When he was a child, standing with his mother in the Florida sunshine, watching a rocket on a launch pad. A rocket with a billion-dollar price tag – and then the rocket exploding into a million very expensive pieces before it even cleared the launch gantry. Was Kyra his billion-dollar rocket that had just detonated on lift-off?

'Sir?' This was the head of security wanting an answer to his earlier question.

The Man suddenly paused. He now understood what he should do to solve this problem. Even before he spoke, he felt a savage triumph flooding his veins. *Yes. Time to go for the nuclear option. Slash and burn.* He spoke loudly, his voice ringing with authority: 'Unleash the prototypes into the mine.'

'The Protos? My God...all of them?'

'All of them.'

The head of security's tone became one of actual fear. 'The rock will retard all our signals. We won't be able to control them in the mines. Sir, you know what the Protos are like. You know what they are capable of...'

'There is no need to control the Protos. Default set the blinders to red. No restraints. They'll flush Kyra and Nev out of the tunnels. Or they'll eliminate the problem.'

'Order received and understood.'

The Man felt a sudden flush of excitement heating his blood. He'd never fully unleashed the Protos before. His warrior beast-men were the consummate exterminators. So, let them go forth. And conquer...

He smiled as he said, 'And tell no one about this. Absolutely no one.'

'Yes, sir.'

The Man returned to his swivel chair where he sat with an expression of self-satisfaction on his face. He was the spider in the center of his web again. He was in control. He was the master of his destiny.

And the destiny – and the fate – of other people, too.

Let battle commence.

CHAPTER TWENTY-SIX

The Protos were lined up in the corridor. Their blinders were set to a neutral yellow glow. Meanwhile, from a nearby speaker attached to the wall came a gentle pulsing drone – relaxing mind music for the damned. All of this revealed a cynical disdain for humanity. The sound was part of the mind control system. Soft pulses of sound were synchronized to the brain patterns of these tragic figure, keeping them in a fugue state. The Protos stood absolutely still, while they gazed blankly at the wall. They were weapons in human form. Yet, for the present, they were weapons that awaited activation. All that was required was for someone to pull their rage trigger.

And that would be soon...

The Protos were dressed in torn clothes, which revealed wounds in their flesh. Some were covered with dried blood. Some were missing fingernails – lost during past battles.

All of them were connected by chains, which were attached to their body harnesses, to an overhead rail. There, an O-shaped steel ring, fixed to the end of the chain, allowed them to move along the corridor, even though they were still shackled, much in the same way as a drape, attached to drape rings, can be pulled along a rail to cover a window. One of the Protos was a young female with clear blue eyes, and with a wound inexpertly stitched shut on her right cheek. Grief for a dead lover that she could no longer remember still forced itself to the surface of her mind, causing her to sob softly. Her eyes were wet with tears. Misery caused her entire body to tremble.

Most of the Protos had flesh wounds that had been sutured in a carelessly inept way. If a patient in a hospital had been treated in such a cack-handed manner, they'd have one hell of a meaty compensation payout from a lawsuit. Whoever administered care to this group of men and women was either a sadist or grossly incompetent – or both.

A pair of guards, dressed in black, wearing black helmets and with visors that concealed the upper half of their faces, entered the corridor. One of the guards viciously prodded the young woman with his baton, prompting her to move forward, as if she was a cow being driven toward the killing floor in a slaughterhouse. The second guard began to roughly push the other Protos, to encourage them to start walking to a pair of large doors at the end of the corridor. The lights in the blinders turned blue, while the sound from the speaker became a *shushing* sound, like ocean waves, so gentle on the ear. Both the blue light and the electronically manipulated sounds turned the Protos into something like sleepwalkers. Allowing them to move their legs, yet damping down emotions and thought to the point that they were psychologically inert...that is, as inert as a hand grenade until the pin is pulled.

The doors swung open, thereby allowing sunlight to come blasting into the corridor. That's when the guards unclipped the chains, and the Protos silently filed out into the sunlit desert.

Voices from the control center started to murmur commands through the headsets. Which direction they should take...to hold formation...so they could attack as a squad, rather than individually.

The Protos began to lope through the desert. They were as menacing as a pack of wolves hunting for a vulnerable animal to slaughter. Ahead of them was an opening in a cliff – the opening was vast, revealing a dark cavern that pierced the mountain.

That's when the color of the blinders changed.

They began to glow red.

Blood red.

Rage red.

Red for murder.

CHAPTER TWENTY-SEVEN

Kyra walked deeper into the mountain. The mine workings were an underground maze. Dangerously, every so often she'd find herself almost walking into an opening in the floor. When she shone the flashlight down, it revealed a shaft that went down a hundred feet or so to another level below. If she failed to notice such a shaft, and fell into it, that would be the end of her. Nobody could survive a fall of that distance.

Beside her, Nev was glancing this way and that. He was trying to make sense of the confusing labyrinth of tunnels, side passageways, shafts that led downward, inclines that led upward. Everywhere, there were the remains of timber supports that were so rotted they were emitting powerful fungal odors. The walls of the tunnels had been roughly hacked; they were gouged and scarred by excavation tools. Mining machinery had been abandoned here long ago. They formed carcasses of dead metal, which resembled iron creatures that had died long ago and been left here to decay. All that mechanical wreckage was blood red with rust. Water dripped from the ceiling. Kyra felt the pat of cold liquid on her head, which soaked into her hair – a revolting sensation.

She directed the flashlight into a narrow tunnel. There were metal spars protruding from the rock wall. The spars were all bent in the same direction, probably as a result of a massive explosion that deformed a steel structure within the mine. The spars now resembled fangs that were fully five feet long. Corrosion had eaten away at the ends of the protruding spars, so that they became dangerously sharp. If someone was to blunder into those in the dark? She shuddered.

Yet there was something about those spars – the way they protruded. How they looked like sharp teeth.

Kyra murmured, 'I think I've been here before.' She touched one of the cold 'teeth.' 'I can remember these.' She shuddered again as she began to understand a disturbing truth. 'That means we're right back where we escaped from.'

Nev wasn't convinced. 'Maybe not. This is an old mine. Probably abandoned decades ago...they might be using it. Tying into it. But the mine was here way before them. This could be a different tunnel than you were in before. They all look the same to me, anyway.'

From one of the spars, a small electric lamp was hanging by a strap. Nev pulled the lamp from the spar, thumbed the switch – a light sprang from the bulb. As soon as the light flooded out onto the floor, which was littered with stones, she noticed a tiny object that was bright red. She shone her own flashlight onto what was clearly a piece of red candy.

The ghost of a memory started to glide forwards into her mind. A piece of red candy? She'd seen something like that before. Quickly, she aimed the light along the tunnel. And there, carefully placed on stones, were more pieces of candy. Candy that formed a line that ran into the gloom.

'Nev. This way.'

Kyra began to follow the candy trail, deep into that tomb-like place, which grew colder and colder the further she moved from the outside world.

Protos surged into the cavern. Soon they left all trace of sunlight behind as they moved into the darkness of the mine workings. Blinders cast a red glare into their faces, and soon their faces were the brightest things in the tunnel. The glow provided just enough ambient light to discern the way ahead. Not that the Protos felt fear. Rage surged through their bodies now. Sheer, bloody, murderous rage.

As they moved deeper into the tunnel, they paused to grab rocks from the floor – rocks that could be used as weapons to shatter skulls, to break bones. Some of the Protos wrenched hunks of metal from rusted machinery. Those pieces of metal would, in their powerful hands, become blades or clubs. Objects that could be used to stab, to bludgeon, to kill.

The Protos began to run. They had become a pack of ferocious animals. Now, they were in search of their prey.

Kyra followed the candy trail along the tunnel. She walked just ahead of Nev who constantly shot nervous glances back the way they came. Evidently, he believed that it wouldn't be long before people came in search of them. After all, the drone must have broadcast footage of them entering the mine back to its operator. She entered a recess in the rock where groceries, plates, and spoons and forks had been laid out on a block of stone that was the size of a kitchen table. There was a plastic bag containing sandwiches. She picked up the bag, looked inside, then recoiled from the stench of moldy bread that was turning green. Even so, her nostrils detected something else.

'PBJ,' she whispered to herself.

'What's that?' Nev was jumpy; his eyes flashed with anxiety. The guy was scared.

'PBJ. Peanut butter and jelly. You know something? I have been here before. I remember...well, kinda remember. I'm sure Amber was here.'

She shone the light around the section of tunnel. Straight away, she noticed white letters painted across a boulder. The letters spelt out: *RMEMBR. U KNOW JOHN.*

Kyra ran her finger over the name. As if the process of touching the letters would release vital memories.

Nev stared at her. 'How did that get here?'

She glanced at her bandaged arm, where she'd etched words into flesh with a blade, then back at the white letters on dark stone. 'I think I did it...in a past test.'

'Shit. Then we are close to the bad guys. We need to find another way out. A way they don't expect.'

Kyra felt cold inside as she recalled the man who had saved her life more than once. 'What did they do to him...to John?'

'That John doesn't exist anymore. They will have used the machine to wipe his mind clean of all recent memories.'

'What an evil thing to do. Erasing a person's memories is tantamount to killing them.'

'You want a John? They can pop anyone under that damn machine of theirs and give you as many Johns as you want. Ten, fifty, a thousand. They'll all be John. They'll all have identical memories. And, believe me, Kyra, that's exactly what they're gonna do. The 'I am John' fix? That's got to be a five-star memory implant now. But yours – the Kyra memory implant – that rating is TBD. After what you did to the guard, your memory implant is probably destined for the laboratory trashcan.'

Kyra gulped. Tears made her eyes prickle. 'John and me, we went through so much together. I'd begun to invest in him emotionally. Do you understand?'

'Hell, no.' Nev gave a cruel laugh.

'I'd begun to invest emotionally in John, because I thought there'd be some kind of future for us. Now those bastards have taken John away, the investment is wasted. I feel cheated.'

'Careful,' he sneered. 'You're beginning to sound as nuts as Amber.'

For a moment they stood there in silence. A silence that seemed so oppressive.

Nev began to twitch, clearly getting edgy. 'Look, the tunnel ahead branches into two. What I suggest is this: you go left, I go right. Walk for one hundred paces, then take a real good look at what's there – make a judgement whether it's likely to lead to an exit. Then we meet back here and decide which is the best route out of here. Okay?' Nev must have decided that she looked at him suspiciously, like she was thinking he might betray her in some way. He threw up his hands in exasperation. 'Unless you have a better plan?'

'Alright. We'll do it. I go left, you go right. Then we meet back here in five minutes.'

He gave a grim nod. 'We gotta start trusting each other, you know? Our lives depend on it.'

Without waiting for a response from her, he jogged away into the tunnel. Soon all she could see was a ball of radiance from his flashlight, moving away through darkness.

Kyra took a deep breath as she tightened her grip on her flashlight. After that, she moved with grim determination into the evil-looking gloom.

CHAPTER TWENTY-EIGHT

Kyra hurried through the tunnel. It resembled a stone gut that took her down into the belly of the mountain. Millions of tons of rock lay above her. She almost cowered beneath the huge weight that seemed to press down through the frigid air and onto her head. Yes, that was her imagination turning rogue again. Even her own thoughts were becoming sadistically oppressive.

'One. Two. Three...' She counted up toward the one hundred steps that she was supposed to take on this reconnaissance mission. In his tunnel, Nev would be doing the same. She wondered if she'd ever see him again, because this place felt like a lair of monsters. She continued the methodical count as she moved along the passageway, its floor covered with loose stones that rolled beneath her feet. When she stopped to listen, in case there was a lurking figure in front of her – or even one following her – she could hear the *thud-thud* of her heart.

As she walked, with the flashlight in her hand, she realized all too powerfully that its radiance, which surrounded her, was a beacon. The light could be seen half a mile away along these tunnels. The light would betray her.

Kyra took a deep breath. Although what she planned to do in the next five seconds was so frightening, she knew it might save her life.

Kyra switched off the light.

Darkness engulfed her. It was more than darkness down here, deep underground. This darkness was like a liquid. Though it was a notion bordering on insanity, she couldn't escape the dreadful sensation that the darkness flooded into her eyes, her mouth, her brain, her throat. When she pictured that inrush of sheer darkness into her lungs, she found she couldn't breathe.

Darkness can't drown you, she told herself. *But panic can destroy you. Control your thoughts. If you have self-control, you can do anything.*

Kyra clenched her right hand so tightly that her fingernails dug into her skin. She felt them cutting painfully into the tender flesh of her palm. However, it was a good pain. It helped her regain her focus. Then, gripping the unlit flashlight in the other hand, she forced herself to walk forwards through the darkness.

Move through the tunnel, she thought. *Keep counting your steps. When you reach one hundred, stop. Darkness can't hurt you...darkness had no solid form.*

Kyra walked through a void that lacked even a glimmer of light. This was a darkness as absolute as death itself. She wanted to draw her arms and legs tight against her body. To pull back from the terrifying black fog that surrounded her. When a wet thing touched her – a thing that felt like it could have been the wing of a bat – she wanted to scream in absolute terror. But if she allowed herself to scream, she knew she would have screamed and screamed until her throat bled. To reassure herself that that the wet membrane hadn't been a bat that hung down from the roof, she forced herself to reach up and touch it. Her fingers felt something that was soft, slimy, and dripping wet. Her fingertips detected the roughness of woven threads...and she realized that it was a scrap of cloth hanging down from a roof beam. She almost wept with relief.

Despite all this, she continued counting the steps she took.

She still counted when her knee thumped hard into an obstacle. The pain made her eyes water. She grunted as she clutched her knee, and waited for a moment, fully expecting her fingers to turn slippery as blood flowed from a wound. But...no blood. So, the blow hadn't been hard enough to tear open her skin.

She continued walking, 'Seventy-eight. Seventy-nine. Eighty.'

The sound of her footsteps changed. The echo took longer to reach her ears. Therefore, she must be entering a bigger space – a cavern, perhaps, with high ceilings. She could hear the shimmering sound of water falling into a pool. There was a mushroom smell. Everything was sopping wet here. Her feet squelched in mud.

If anything, this place seemed even more dangerous. Her enemies could strike at her from every direction. The tension was so great that her muscles cramped up in her belly. Her neck ached. A pain flared behind her eyes as sheer stress tightened muscles to the point that she wanted to shriek out in total fucking agony.

Bang!

She'd blundered into something that swung away from her in the darkness. A person? A potential attacker that was getting ready to pounce on her?

Kyra couldn't tolerate this anymore. Her thumb darted to the flashlight's switch. A dazzling light exploded into her face. She couldn't see her surroundings. The brightness was too intense after staring into the dark.

Bang!

The sound had come again. Now, she was blinking so hard that tears were pouring down her face. At last, her eyes began to adjust to the glare. And she got ready to fight for her life. She was convinced that someone had reached out and touched her.

However, she saw that she'd walked into a chain that hung down from a roof beam to the height of her waist. What she saw, also, right there in front of her, made her cry out with shock.

Just two paces in front of her, a hole in the floor. The opening was square-shaped; its dimensions were perhaps ten feet by ten feet, and the hole spanned the floor between two boulders that were the size of trucks, meaning that there was no safe way to walk past it – there was no ledge or bridge. The chain was still swinging. She realized that the end of the chain had struck a section of iron pipe when she'd walked into it. This is what had caused the metallic clang she'd heard.

Thank goodness, I did walk into the chain. If I'd missed it… well…

She shone the light into the hole in front of her. The shaft plunged downward a long, long way. The light barely reached the bottom, which was perhaps eighty feet below this level. She could just make out-jagged looking remnants of machinery at the bottom of the shaft. The pieces stuck up, as if a bunch of sword blades had been set into the floor.

Kyra realized that if she climbed over a mound of rubble to her right, she could bypass the pit that obstructed her progress. Then she could continue along the tunnel. That would take time, though. Besides, she'd already reached the ninety mark of the hundred paces she'd been aiming for. Close enough.

For a moment, she paused. The air felt a little fresher here, so perhaps there was an exit somewhere further along. True, she couldn't see any daylight. Nevertheless, her instinct told her that onward was the route they should take.

This time, Kyra left the flashlight switched on as she hurried back to where she hoped she'd be reunited with Nev, near the makeshift subterranean kitchen. She couldn't help but wonder if he had waited for her – or whether he'd gone on without her. Thereby leaving her to her fate.

CHAPTER TWENTY-NINE

Kyra moved along the tunnel. As she did so, she pulled the arrow from her belt. Tightly, she gripped the arrow in one hand, while she held the flashlight in the other. Dripping water made an echoey sound – a kind of maddening music that would truly send you mad if you were to spend hours alone in the tunnel. The return journey seemed a surprisingly long one. Her very real suspicion that Nev had failed to wait for her had begun to prey on her nerves. Her heart pounded. The light she carried revealed wet walls, mounds of stones, timber supports that were rotting dangerously to the point that they would soon become so weak that they could no longer support the roof. If that came crashing down at this very moment…? Millions of tons of rock would crush her flat in a heartbeat.

The tunnel closed in, forcing her to lower her head to prevent it clunking against the wooden beams. Meanwhile, the way became narrower, so that both of her shoulders were brushing against wet stone at either side of her. The damp air smelt of fungus. She tried to breathe through her mouth to minimize the stench; however, she found she could taste the fungus because its odors permeated the air so thickly.

She reached the rendezvous point at the makeshift kitchen where the PBJ sandwiches were going moldy in the plastic bag.

She whispered, 'Nev?'

There was no sign of him. He had left without her! The rat!

Then a scuff of a boot against rock. She whirled round, ready to plunge the arrowhead into the attacker.

Nev grinned at her from a gloomy recess in the wall. 'Kyra, you should learn to trust me. I told you I'd be back.'

She recovered her composure. The last thing she wanted was for him to derive any kind of satisfaction from seeing fear in her eyes. She'd dated men like that before – the ones who tried to detect any indication that they frightened you. She knew what men like that could do.

She took a deep breath then spoke firmly. 'The tunnel you followed – any sign of a way out?'

'I felt a breeze in my face, and there's a stream. I reckon the water's flowing toward an exit point.'

Kyra nodded as she slipped the arrow back into her belt. 'Okay. We go your way.'

'What about yours?'

'There's a shaft in the floor, going way down. It's passable if you're prepared to do some scrambling over a heap of rubble that almost touches the ceiling.'

'Sound like my way is the easiest route to sweet, sweet freedom.' He grinned again. Did she detect a devilish glee in that smile? Or was that curl of his lip due to pure relief that they had a chance of escape from this nightmare.

Nev directed his flashlight along one of the tunnels. 'Very well. I'll go first, you follow. Keep listening hard. We don't want any surprise visits from the guards.'

They began walking. The tunnel was wetter here and quite narrow. Little puddles of water on the floor soon connected together to become a flowing stream. Often, they had to use boulders as steppingstones as the water became deeper and deeper.

They walked past more mining equipment that lay corroding in the shadows. Chains hung down from the ceiling. There were scorch marks on the walls from explosions, possibly from decades ago, which would have blasted the rock into manageable chunks that could be put into carts before being wheeled to the surface.

They entered a section of tunnel where crystals in the rock glittered, bright as a million diamonds.

Nev patted the wall with his left hand. 'You remember any of this? Any buried memory from a past test?'

Kyra stared at the walls that glittered so brightly.

She gave a shake of her head. 'No...I'm sure I would have remembered something like this, though.'

'Good. Maybe we're on the right path.'

They left the tunnel to walk into a massive chamber. The roof was perhaps fifty feet above their heads. There was a huge iron cylinder with pipes that ran from it. That behemoth of a thing reminded Kyra of a steam locomotive she'd once seen running along a heritage railroad. Perhaps the machine was a steam-powered pump that prevented the lower levels of the mine from flooding. Here, the surface of the rock floor was pockmarked with craters the size of dinner plates. This looked like the surface of the moon in miniature. Everywhere, water dripped from the roof into large subterranean pools that were as black as midnight.

Nev shone the light into one of the pools. An object zipped through the water, producing ripples.

Kyra pointed. 'That fish. It had to get in here somehow.'

'You're right. Then we best keep following the stream.'

The man's expression was unreadable. Once more, Kyra was nagged by the awful suspicion that he might be getting ready to betray her. Perhaps he was leading her toward guards who lay in wait. She'd beaten one of their own to death, which meant the dead man's buddies would be eager for revenge. They'd crave to break her bones with their batons and kicks. She doubted if they'd take her back into custody alive.

She put a little more space between herself and Nev in case she had to make a run for it. After all, he'd attempt to grab hold of her if he was going to sell her out to the guards. Kyra decided to make conversation with Nev. If he was talking, then he might not pick up on the fact that she was becoming increasingly wary of him. Of course, he might not be leading her into a trap; maybe that was paranoia on her part? But how could she be certain he was trust-worthy? So, she encouraged him to talk.

'Nev. What did you do...to get on Death Row?'

'Does it matter?' He glanced back at her, then shrugged. 'Just a fight with some guys messin' with my sister. Got out of hand. I fired some shots. They died. They would have just as likely killed me, but I pulled out my shooting iron first.' He smiled as if making light of what he'd just told her. 'That wouldn't have got me death in Sparky or the gas chamber. Nah, it was that lady, far away in the back, who took one of my bullets. Pure accident, of course. But the judge didn't see it that way.'

Nev laughed at his 'funny because it's true' anecdote as he sloshed through water that came up to his knees. Kyra didn't find it funny in the slightest. She'd seen so much violent death in the last few hours that she'd never make a joke about bloody mayhem.

They walked out of the water and onto a bank of shingle. Both were panting now, their breath blowing out clouds of white.

Then, ever so faintly...*clink*.

The sound of a chain ...

CHAPTER THIRTY

Kyra froze. Nev froze, too – he was staring at her in horror. The savage glare from the flashlight in his hand made his face hideous. Like a human skull of cold white bone.

Kyra held her breath as she tried to gauge where the sound came from, but the rock walls of the tunnel bounced sounds back from all different directions. The clink of the chain came again. Then the sound of many chains. After that, there was the clatter of footsteps. Then, most frighteningly of all, there was snarling. Like the snarls of a wild animal.

A tremendous crash reached them, as if someone had thrown a boulder at a steel door. The sound swept over them like an avalanche, and with such power that they both rocked back on their feet, almost losing their balance. The sound went echoing away through the tunnels where it became distorted into a strange, mutant thunder...which slowly faded away in the depths of this tomb of a place, and finally died.

The sound of running feet, the savage growls, and the rattling of chains grew louder.

Nev gasped in shock. 'Protos...they sent fucking Protos to kill us.'

'Which way are they coming from?'

'I can't tell. The echoes are coming at us from every direction.' Then, with a grimace, he seemed to pluck a decision out of the air. 'This way!'

They began to run in the direction the stream flowed. Fish skittered away just under the water's surface. Running with a flashlight wasn't easy. Kyra's arms were swinging wildly as she ran, which made the light go fucking crazy. It swung right, left, up, down. They accidentally shone the lights into one another's faces, dazzling each other so much that sometimes they'd lose their balance completely. Kyra tripped over a piece of wood and fell face down with such force into the wet muck that she screamed in pain. Nev immediately stopped and helped her to feet.

'We're a team now, me and you,' he panted. 'We stick together.'

His face was so solemn and so compassionate that her heart went out to him. She wondered if the time had come to trust him. Maybe he truly wanted to escape this place as much as she did.

A moment later, they were running along the tunnel again. The sound of chains clattering and the beast-like snarls filling the air. The rock walls distorted the sound until it became a symphony for the devil. The cacophony filled her head. The swirl of echoes made her dizzy. And when they ran with the lights down, to prevent themselves from being dazzled, the darkness would rush in. Kyra felt the weight of that oppressive darkness. It was pressing down on her, trying to crush the air from her lungs.

Then she saw a glow ahead. The red glow of sunset she hoped. Daylight must be filtering from an exit ahead.

No such luck...

Nev shouted, 'Oh, shit...here they come!'

And here they did come. A snarling pack was running along the tunnel towards them.

The Protos lurched from the darkness. They, themselves, were barely visible in the gloom – only their faces were revealed by the red lights in the blinders. That light was definitely 'red for danger.'

Kyra dashed into a side tunnel followed by Nev. Straight away, a Proto – a giant of a guy with tattooed fists – burst from the gloom with the suddenness of an explosion. He swung those huge fists at Kyra's head.

Just in time, she ducked. A second later, she and Nev were running back the way they came. Though that direction would take them back into the violent hands of the other Protos.

With moments to spare, before the end of the tunnel was cut off by their attackers, they made a sharp turn. After that, they were running back to where they'd come from, back to the improvised kitchen.

Kyra shouted, 'Nev, we'll follow the route I took. The one with the shaft. I'm sure I could feel a fresh draught on my face...there must be a way out.'

The air all but screamed through Kyra's throat as she fought to suck enough oxygen into her lungs to keep moving. Her ribs hurt from the fall back there. She hoped she hadn't broken any bones – her chest hurt like fucking hell fury. And now a stitch drove its fiercely painful spike into her side.

They turned a corner and ran into a Proto. Nev actually collided with the guy. This Proto had dreads that poured down the back of his coverall. His hands were covered with dried blood. He punched into thin air like he was battling an invisible demon.

Nev staggered back after his collision with the guy, groaning with despair as he did so. 'He'll kill us for sure.' Nev looked close to tears now – panic was clearly beginning to overwhelm him.

The Proto threw punches at the wall. One struck the rock – the skin across his knuckles split open, drops of blood flew through the air to spatter the tunnel floor.

Nev cried out, 'I'm going to die here, I know I am.'

Kyra grabbed Nev's arm. 'Look...there's something wrong with his blinders.'

The Proto swayed from side-to-side as he threw punches at the wall. One blinder flashed red; the other was a tranquil blue. The man was clearly disorientated. He began to stagger like he'd guzzled down a bottle of vodka.

Kyra whispered, 'All we need do is get past him.'

Easier said than done. The tunnel was narrow here. Nevertheless, she pressed her back to the wall, then slid along the rough bedrock.

When Nev realized that the big guy didn't even appear to know that they were there, he followed Kyra's route, his back pressed hard to the wall.

At that moment, the Proto turned around. He swung his fists like he was a lumbering drunk. He didn't even appear to target Nev but one of the fists connected with the side of Nev's head. There was a loud clunk of knuckle against skull. Nev fell to the floor with a moan and lay still.

Kyra returned to the pair, ducking down below the swinging fists of the Proto as she did so. She grabbed hold of Nev's hands then dragged him across the loose scree of stones. He was only part conscious and groaning loudly.

That was when the malfunctioning blinders automatically reset themselves. The blue light in one half, and the red light in the other half, both turned white. Just for a second. Then the lights went out completely. When they came back on again, both lights were an uncompromising, murderous red.

Instantly, the Proto realized that his prey was just yards away. The guy locked his ferocious gaze onto Kyra. He began to follow her, his feet moving faster and faster as he picked up speed.

Kyra dragged Nev while yelling at him. 'Get to your feet! Run! Or we're both dead!'

Her voice was powerful enough to cut through the fug in his brain. Groggily, he scrambled to his feet.

'Thank you,' he muttered to her as he began to run.

Kyra raced along the tunnel with Nev just behind her. And behind Nev, came the Proto, dragging his chains behind him, which were connected to a leather harness that he wore around his chest. He was like a furious bull. He was roaring. He held out his hands in front of him. His fingers were opening and shutting, like he was practicing snapping their necks. The blinders flooded his face with a blood red glow. The guy had been programmed to kill. To utterly destroy.

Kyra knew that the instant he caught up with them that's what he would do.

The Proto was just ten paces behind them. Running fast. Gaining. Getting closer.

Ahead of them were those fangs of metal that directed their points in her and Nev's direction.

Kyra shouted, 'Nev! Switch off your light!'

'What?'

'Do it!'

Nev obeyed.

She put her thumb on the switch of her own flashlight. 'When I kill my light, duck to your right, into that recess.

His eyes bulged with terror as he ran. Nevertheless, he nodded. 'Okay. My life's in your hands.'

She switched off the flashlight. 'Now, go right!'

They fell over each other in the darkness. Yet, somehow, they landed in the recess – they were bruised and winded but at least now they had a chance.

The Proto that chased them had been relying on their light for illumination. Meanwhile, the glow of his blinders poured its radiance into his eyes, somewhat dazzling him, thereby reducing his ability to see anything much in the gloom. Even so, he kept running.

Kyra did manage to see what happened next. Her eyes had adjusted enough to make the most of the red glow coming from the guy's headset.

The Proto ran headlong into the metal struts that protruded out from the rock. The sharp points tore through his body in a dozen different places. One spar ripped open his stomach from ribs to naval. Another spar had punched right through the front of his skull. The piece of metal was so deeply embedded that he hung there for five seconds. His entire body convulsing with agony. Nevertheless, he managed to push back and free himself.

But the damage had been done.

Blood squirted out from wounds in thick jets of red. He staggered backwards, roaring like a wounded bull. Then he dragged the blinders from his head. For a while, he stared at them in disbelief, like he was waking from a nightmare.

The nightmare was over for him. So was his life. He toppled forwards to the floor so hard that Kyra heard the loud *crack* as his jaw broke on impact.

When the echoes from the man's roars of agony faded into the darkness, that's when they heard the rattle of chains. That and the sound of running feet.

The Protos were getting closer.

Nev switched on his flashlight. 'We gotta keep moving.'

Kyra headed into a side passage. Its direction suggested it might – just might –

connect with the tunnel that she'd followed before. The one that led to the shaft that pierced the floor and plunged downward, deep underground.

The other Protos were getting closer. What's more, Kyra realized that she and Nev were tiring. Soon they wouldn't be able to run any further.

They were panting hard as they sprinted along the tunnel. Soon, Kyra began to recognize pieces of mining machinery; therefore, they were on the right track. They were heading toward the pit in the tunnel that she'd seen before. She'd felt fresh air blowing into her face, indicating that there might be an exit to the outside world close by. Their lights revealed support beams that were grotesquely budded with cream-colored fungus, which resembled human faces with bulging noses and narrow lips. Old power cables hung down from the ceiling – snake-like things, sheathed in black rubber, they were wet and left smears of water on her face when she brushed against them.

Nev abruptly darted away into a side tunnel.

Kyra shouted, 'No. Not that way! Stick to the main tunnel.'

Nev didn't stop. His light resembled a ball of fire as he continued running. He yelled back, 'I can hear running water. If there's another stream, it will guide us out of this fucking maze!'

She glanced back over her shoulder. Far away, along the tunnel, there were bobbing flashes of red. The Protos were coming this way. They were perhaps thirty seconds from reaching this part of the tunnel where it forked.

She shouted after Nev again, 'We don't know if this tunnel leads outside! If it doesn't, we'll be trapped! They'll slaughter us!'

Nev didn't answer – he kept on running.

Kyra let out a yell of exasperation. Nevertheless, she followed him, while hoping there would be an exit from this bleak thoroughfare that wormed its way through green-colored rock. Painted on raw stone walls were phrases like: *TRIAGE STATION C* and *TEST BED 83F*. Another sign, painted in stark red letters, declared: *NAPALM TRIGGER POINT*. The remains of a metal control panel hung from a wall. There was a red button in the center of the panel that was labelled with a single menacing word: *DETONATOR!* The walls and ceiling were scorched here. Burn marks painted black lines that ran back along the tunnel. There was a smell of burning. Horribly, there was something lying against the wall – a mound of clothes that had been partially incinerated. The odor of burnt fabric stabbed into her nostrils. It was an old smell, but still potent. As she ran past, she glimpsed the white claw of a skeleton's hand poking out from the remains of a denim jacket.

That's when Kyra heard Nev hollering back at her. The ball of light that blasted from Nev's flashlight was now coming back toward her. His voice was so distorted by echoes she couldn't make out what he was saying. Though his tone chilled her to the roots of her bones.

'What is it?' she shouted. 'What's wrong?'

Nev raced toward her. He was wild-eyed with terror. Panic had distorted his face into a mask of sheer fright.

'It's a dead end,' he panted. 'Gotta go back.'

'You idiot. I warned you! The Protos will have reached the end of the tunnel – that's the point where we entered this section. We'll be trapped now! You've as good as killed us!'

'There are other side tunnels – just back there – didn't you notice them?'

Terror accelerated his movements. He ran back the way they came for ten paces, then darted into another passage that led off to the right. Kyra followed while cursing Nev's stupidity. If only they'd stuck to the main tunnel, they could have found a way around the mouth of the shaft, then—

'Fuck!' Nev screamed.

She looked past Nev. A huge Proto, with a scarred Frankenstein's monster face, was barreling through the narrow passageway toward them. The chains he dragged behind him clattered and rattled. When the steel links struck the floor, sparks flashed from them. Blue, silver, orange. The sparks were bright enough to cast his monstrous shadow against the tunnel wall.

'Back this way!' Kyra yelled. 'This time, you follow me! Got it?'

Without waiting for a reply, Kyra ran back toward the main tunnel that they should have followed before Nev foolishly deviated from the route. At the end of the tunnel, at the junction where they needed to be, a cluster of red lights illuminated the faces of the beast people. The Protos were there. They'd gathered at the entrance to the side tunnel. Now they waited for Kyra and Nev to go to them. They no longer needed to chase the pair of runaways.

Meanwhile, the Frankenstein Proto was galumphing along the rat-run from the other end of the tunnel.

They were trapped.

Kyra's hand found the arrow, which was tucked into her belt. That was her only weapon. Had the time come to fight their way to freedom?

Nev was gasping for air. He didn't look as if he had the energy to fight a fucking butterfly now, let alone a dozen rage-crazy men and women.

Kyra took her hand away from the arrow in her belt because her heart suddenly fluttered with hope. She'd seen a narrow horizontal slit in the rock beside her. It was on the same level with her chin. She shone the light through and saw a passageway running parallel to the one they were in. Just three feet away, on the other side of a curtain of rock.

A visceral impulse snapped along her nerves, which prompted a sudden revelation.

'The main tunnel runs alongside this one,' she panted. 'All we need do is climb through that gap.'

Nev was on point this time. Suddenly, his game face switched on. He gripped the wrist strap of his flashlight between his teeth. That done, he laced the fingers of both his hands together to form a flesh and bone stirrup.

Kyra understood. Quickly, she put her foot into his hands. That done, he hoisted her up so she could squirm through the gap. A moment later, she wormed herself into the tunnel that she'd followed before. Nev instantly scrambled after her. Only just in time, too, because the hands of Frankenstein Proto burst through the gap. He was snarling viciously as he tried to grab hold of them.

The Proto was too late, though. They were already running toward the section of tunnel where a shaft punched down through solid bedrock.

CHAPTER THIRTY-ONE

They ran along the tunnel. The Protos, meanwhile, weren't slow to follow them. The Frankenstein Proto, with the face that must have been hideously mutilated before being stitched back together again, had somehow forced his massive body through the gap in the rock that Kyra and John had just squeezed through. He had a head start on the other Protos that were perhaps a couple of minutes behind him.

Kyra all too clearly heard their terror-inducing snarls, and the rattle of chains that they dragged, as they closed the gap toward them.

'C'mon!' panted Nev. 'Gotta run faster! Don't let them catch you, they'll rip you to fuck!'

As they ran, they couldn't keep the flashlights at all stable in their hands, so they either reflected explosions of light from the surrounding rock, or the lights went down by their sides; therefore, they found themselves in darkness for a second or two before the flashlights swung up again, as their arms desperately pumped up and down as they ran for their lives.

Frankenstein Proto was just fifty paces behind them. He was snarling, his huge hand thrusting out toward them, fingers clutching at thin air – for now, that is.

'Watch out for the hole in the floor,' she panted. 'S' deep...very deep.'

Nev shone the light ahead. The tunnel formed something like a massive V shape at this point. There were two steeply sloping mounds of rubble at the left-side and the right-hand side. At the bottom, where the downward point of the V would be, was the opening of the shaft – that yawning aperture must have measured ten feet by ten feet. Above the hole was a wooden support beam from which a six-foot-long chain dangled. The steep sides of the rubble mounds came right up to the edge of the shaft. There was no gap that they could use to safely edge their way past the hole without falling in.

Nev called out, 'Where now? There's no way I can jump across that.'

'Climb up the mound of rubble. There's a space at the top where you can wriggle through, then slide down the mound when you're well clear of the shaft. You don't want to fall into that – it's a one-way journey to oblivion.'

'You've got a way with words, Kyra, I'll give you that.'

Grim-faced, he began to climb the slope. In doing so, he inadvertently dislodged a stone from the heap. It rolled down the incline, then fell into the mouth of the pit. There was silence for a long, long time. Then – *bang!* The stone hit the bottom of the shaft. Kyra thought: *Falling all that way is going to be a bone-breaker for sure.*

Nev scrambled up the mound. He was kicking the toes of his boots into the stones to get a grip – all the time he was shouting back at her, 'C'mon, follow me, hurry. Hurry!'

She had to give him time to get clear of her, otherwise he'd accidentally kick her in the face with his heels as he climbed the mound. Meanwhile, the sounds of chains, and snarling, and feet on rock, got louder and louder.

Protos are coming. They're approaching fast.

Frankenstein Proto would reach her before the others. She had to start climbing now, or he'd catch her. She began to scramble up the steep incline. Nev's feet lashed close to her head. That created a problem – his feet were so dangerously close it slowed her down. Slowed her down to the point that disaster struck.

She screamed. A hand had gripped her ankle. *Goliath! This had happened before!*

This time, the monster wasn't Goliath. However, the Proto bellowed with savage pleasure. He began to drag her down the slope. She glanced back into his face that glowed blood red in the evil gleam of the blinders. His rage-filled eyes burned into her. He was going to kill her. And he was going to enjoy every moment of her terror.

He pulled hard.

Kyra thrust her hands deep into the rubble as she tried to anchor herself there. Then she tried to wriggle up the slope. Her body was thrashing about like a demented seal. She tried her hardest to squirm upward on her belly. Loose stones rolled under her chest and stomach. Her hands became claws as they hooked into the decidedly unstable scree. Frankenstein Proto tugged at her. She felt her fingernails giving way – ripping – separating from the nailbeds as she tried to hang on. She howled in agony, producing a raw sound that bounced from the walls. The sound of her screams mated with the roar of Frankenstein Proto, and the snarls from the other Protos as they got closer. The sounds echoed until they mutated into something like a jet engine scream.

Frankenstein Proto yanked her leg so hard that her fingers lost their grip. She was dragged down the slope where she landed on one knee on the rock floor. The pain was so intense she nearly blacked out. However, she managed to kick herself free of his grasp. She tried to climb to her feet. The pain in her knee was so savage that she staggered. *Run?* She couldn't even walk.

The other Protos were only twenty seconds away.

Frankenstein Proto was taking a deep breath as he got ready to lunge at her.

Nev had reached the top of the mound. She saw him crouching there, up near the ceiling. His eyes had become bright globes of yellow in the flashlight's glare. And those eyes of his blazed with fear for her. He was shouting. But the sounds of her own yells, and Proto snarls, were so loud, so distorted, she couldn't hear what he was endeavoring to communicate to her.

Her head swung to the right. She saw the shaft, which was a yawning pit of darkness. She knew she'd somehow have to jump across to the other side. Or be murdered by the Proto. She took a step toward the edge of the shaft as she psyched herself up to make the leap. Her knee hurt so much she could barely walk, never mind run fast enough to jump that lethal distance.

The chain...

Her gaze devoured those rusty links. Suddenly, an idea – a crazy, impossible idea – exploded inside her head. Her heart pounded, her blood roared through the arteries of her neck into her brain, feeding intelligence, giving her the power to visualize her escape route.

Do it!

Frankenstein Proto lunged at her, hands stretching out. The monster was savagely eager to snap her neck.

Kyra jumped into the pit. Then she was falling into darkness. Cold, damp air blasted up into her face. Then – *clunk!*

She'd grabbed the chain. All she need do was somehow manage to perform a pendulum swing to the other side. The Protos couldn't jump that far, she was sure of it. They'd have to clamber laboriously, and slowly, up the rubble mounds. That was the only way forwards in pursuit of their prey.

Damn...she hadn't jumped hard enough. Instead of her swinging right across the mouth of the pit to the other side, she only dangled there. She was completely helpless. Like a fish hanging from a fisherman's hook.

The Proto began to lean forwards, clearly intending to grab her. Though as his massive torso loomed toward her, she realized she could use that muscular chest of his, which must be as solid as concrete. She lifted both feet and kicked the heels of her boots into his chest. She used him as a launchpad to push herself across the mouth of the pit. The double-footed kick was a hard one. True, her injured knee felt as if the joint had ignited inside her flesh – the pain was unbelievably intense.

But she'd done it. The chain links creaked (*hope they hold!*), rust flaked from the links to fall onto her face and into her eyes.

Yet her plan worked.

She swung like a pendulum. And she was carried out across the shaft. The void beneath her dangling feet was as dark as death.

Frankenstein Proto howled with fury at being cheated of his

prize. The face blazed in the light from the blinders. His eyes were fixed on her with sheer bloodlust. That's when he lunged at her.

By this time, she was beyond the reach of his hands. He still reached out though – further, further.

Then he leaned forward to the point where his center of balance fatally shifted. Kyra watched as he tumbled forwards. His hands clawed at the air, as if he believed that he could hold onto those atoms of oxygen and nitrogen and somehow stop himself from falling.

Gravity was his executioner.

Frankenstein Proto plunged down through the pit in the tunnel floor. She saw his body turning end over end as he fell. He was turning so fast the light from the blinders became a flashing strobe. By this time, her journey across the pit was over…she didn't see him strike the bottom. However, there was a thud. A loud one.

As she dropped down onto the far side of the shaft's opening, she let go of the chain. That's when a hand lunged out of the gloom to grab hold of her arm.

Proto!

Instead, a familiar face grinned at her from the shadows.

Nev's eyes sparkled as he gazed at her. 'Time to leave Nightmare Central. Think you can walk?'

'I'll get out of here. On my hands and knees if I must.'

Thankfully, her knee wasn't so very painful now.

Behind them, the other Protos had slowed to a walk. Perhaps they were figuring out how to get past the shaft? Or maybe they didn't have any gas left in the tank? *Pray God, they have exhausted themselves.*

Kyra had lost her flashlight during the battle with Frankenstein Proto. Nev still had his light, however, and he shone it ahead of them as they jogged along the tunnel. Water dripped from the ceiling to form pools on the bedrock. The pools once again began to form themselves into a stream that flowed away ahead of them. Meanwhile, the stale odors of the captive atmosphere below ground were vanishing, and with every step they took the air became fresher.

Kyra glanced at Nev. He glanced back at her. She knew that their eyes were becoming brighter as they dared to hope.

Just thirty seconds later, a second light appeared – this one perhaps a hundred yards further along the passageway. The light didn't move. It was steady. No fluctuation.

Nev whispered, 'Daylight?'

They paused for a moment. Kyra looked back along the tunnel that was, once more, drowned in absolute darkness. She could hear nothing. No rattle of chains, no beast-like grunts. She couldn't see even so much as a glimmer of red from the blinders.

When she spoke, it was in a soft tone. 'You know, I think they've stopped following us.'

He nodded. 'We beat them. They've given up.'

Kyra hoped he was right.

The pain in her knee faded as her excitement grew as they walked toward the daylight. Before long, the radiance flooding in from the entrance ahead of them was so bright that Nev didn't need the flashlight anymore. He switched it off.

As they moved toward the sunlit opening, Kyra felt a surge of optimism. This felt like being born again. She realized she could put the horrors of the past few hours behind her, because she had a new life to live.

Kyra walked out of the tunnel into sunlight that was so intensely bright after the darkness she couldn't see for a moment. She shielded her eyes. Nev was doing the same. When, at last, they moved away from the entrance, out onto a vast expanse of desert sand that was dotted with shrubs and Joshua trees, Nev paused and looked back. For a moment, he stared at the cliff face behind him with nothing less than awe.

Then he let out a lungful of air. 'We're on the other side of the mountain.'

Kyra's eyes had adjusted to the sun's glare. She scanned her surroundings – there were desert plants, sand, rocks, the Johsua trees and, in the distance, thousands of wind turbines. The blades were slowly turning in the desert breeze, creating a low humming sound.

Nev rested his hand on her shoulder. A gesture that clearly indicated he felt close to her, emotionally. He looked into her eyes. 'If we're lucky,' he said, 'they won't think to look for us here.'

Kyra nodded. She then began to run up a steep slope, between massive rock formations that resembled the sharp horns of some mythological beast from long ago. Nev followed.

The way forward was hard. Sometimes, the soft dust beneath their feet made progress excruciatingly difficult. After the dust, they had to run up a loose scree that rolled beneath their feet, which caused them to slip and stumble. The incline became even steeper, making Nev pant for breath.

Finally, he waved at her as exhaustion stopped him dead. 'Kyra. I need a break.' He sat down on boulder.

She said, 'We can't stop.'

He stared at her in amazement. 'How can you keep going? Why do you even care? You're not even real.'

She glared back at him. 'I'm real to me.'

'You know, if you did somehow make it, that means Sarah's dead. She's dead somewhere inside of you.'

Kyra's blood ran cold. It was shocking to visualize the image of her former self lying dead inside of her. As if her skull had become a kind of tomb. Kyra shrugged away the disturbing image. 'If Sarah exists at all, then she's a murderer. She deserves death – even if it's a psychological death.'

He laughed, but there was no humor in the sound. 'You don't give a shit about Sarah, at all do you? Just yourself. Kyra is all that matters now.'

'This is my chance.'

'You want to carry on with fake memories?' He laughed again. 'You're not only fake, but delusional. Don't you understand? Your face is Sarah's. Your fingerprints are Sarah's. Out there...' He pointed at the far horizon. 'Out there, you are Sarah – the murderer.'

'No. I'll be Kyra.'

He shook his head. 'You are something. You're like one of those killer robots from the movies – nothing stops you. You just keep moving.'

'Don't say those things about me.'

He grinned – it was a total Satan of a grin. 'Yeah, just like a robot. You've even been reprogrammed. Sarah Lott is erased. The Kyra software package has been downloaded, and away you go, to your new life in a different city. That's what you're hoping for anyhow.'

They stared at one another. It was like they'd hit a profound obstacle on the road to whatever fledgling relationship they'd been nurturing through adversity. Abruptly, he thrust out his hand toward her.

When he spoke, it was in a friendly way. 'Okay. Come on. You wanted to keep moving.'

She couldn't help but smile at him as she grasped his hand and then pulled him to his feet.

CHAPTER THIRTY-TWO

Kyra ran up the hill to the very top. It was crowned by jagged rocks. Scorpions lurked in the shadows, their tails curling in a way that was clearly aggressive. Glistening beads of venom oozed from their stingers. They weren't accustomed to human intruders here in their barren wilderness.

Nev was panting noisily as he lumbered up the slope to join her at the top of the hill. Here, the desert stretched before them. Predominantly, it was flat with just the occasional outcrop of rock. Growing from the sand was a sparse grove of Joshua trees, while in the distance there was an entire legion of wind turbines, the blades turning steadily, feeding electricity into powerlines that would light thousands of homes in faraway cities.

Kyra saw that access tracks linked the wind turbines with a highway. She could see the blacktop, the white lines running down the center of the road. For the first time, in as long as she could remember, she realized she was seeing welcome traces of civilization. The highway would take her to a town. There'd be stores, diners, beauty parlors, hotels. Buses would carry her safely away to a big city where she would become anonymous. She could vanish into the population of the vast metropolis. She felt a warm glow of satisfaction as she thought: *And that's where I will begin a new life as Kyra.*

Nev was shielding his eyes against the sun's glare as he scanned the blue sky above him. She heard him give a gasp of shock.

'Shit!' He pointed upwards. 'It's another drone. They are searching this area. They'll find us!'

His anxious gaze turned back to Kyra, no doubt expecting her to respond to the danger.

What happened next was something that he clearly wasn't expecting at all. For Kyra slammed the arrow's point into his stomach. Then she put one of her arms around him as if she would bestow upon him a lover's embrace. But no...she pulled him close in order to force the arrow deeper into his body. Then she twisted the arrow, so that that its sharp edges would tear belly flesh, thereby releasing blood, and inflicting terrible damage to arteries and gut.

He made a loud 'Uph' sound as the pain tore through his body. His eyes bulged with shock.

She murmured quite gently, 'Sorry. I need you to buy me some more time.'

Then she did something that was so horrible...so cruel. She yanked the arrow out, inflicting more damage to his belly. It also left an open wound. Blood gushed out over his hands as he clutched at the gash in his stomach.

Nev gasped, 'Why?'

'You killed people. That's why you were on Death Row. You deserve this.'

'You killed babies!'

'Not me,' she whispered. 'Sarah.'

Kyra turned away from him as he stood there, bleeding. Hurting. Tears rolled down his face. She ran toward a line of boulders that were the size of trucks. She calculated she could vanish into the shadows there, meaning the drone would lose sight of her. That's when Nev – poor bleeding Nev – would be the focus of the drone operator's attention.

Moving into deep shadow cast by the first boulder, she paused to look back at Nev. He was clutching his stomach wound. His hands had turned crimson, right up to the wrists. He stared up at the drone, which slowly descended until it was just thirty feet above him, its electronic eye firmly focused on the wounded man.

Blood loss weakened him to the point where he fell to the ground. There he lay on his back. Still defiant to the end, he picked up stones and began throwing them up at the drone. Clearly, he was trying to knock that little whirring aircraft out of the sky.

Kyra watched for a moment. Nev continued to throw rocks. He was softly sobbing now…his escape attempt was over.

Kyra padded deeper into the shadows. Soon she was weaving her way amid the massive boulders. And as for Nev? She could see him no more.

A surveillance camera carried a livestream of Daniel. For a few short hours this man had been John. Now he was Daniel again. Daniel from head to toe. Daniel, with all his memories intact from his old life. He sat at a table in a grey room. They'd dressed him in an orange coverall of the type that inmates in many a jail the world over wore. He lifted his hands and placed them on the tabletop. Chains were fixed to manacles around his wrists. The chains snaked down to the floor, where they were padlocked to a steel loop that was embedded in the concrete beneath his feet.

Daniel stared down at a document on the table. A pen lay beside it. A moment later, he looked up at a figure that stood in a shadowy corner of the room.

Daniel said: 'I sign this. It's over?'

The Man's voice shimmered on the cold air of this grim-looking chamber. 'Yes.'

Daniel stared at the document again. His expression was sullen. He was every inch the victim of a society that did not care. He had a 'life has beaten me down' appearance. That wall-eyed look of someone who has had cruelty inflicted on them for decades. And now the only refuge from the pain was a dull-eyed acceptance that this was the way it was – that he would suffer injustice and abuse and torment every day of his existence until he died.

Daniel moved his hands. Chain links rattled. That terrible sound again. Chains clinking. Chains that took away his right to decide what he did with his life. There were always chains – some were the invisible chains that shackled the human heart to never-ending sadness. This time, the chains that secured him to one restricted part of this melancholy room were all-too visible. He could touch them. He could feel their cold links. He could even smell their metal odor. They held him in place with the same kind of brutal tenacity that nails would, if his jailors had nailed him to a tree.

Daniel took a deep breath. His mind was spinning. He felt dizzy. He tried to rub his eyes, but the chains weren't long enough. They held his hands down below the level of his shoulders. He had to lean forward and lower his head, which reinforced his melancholy posture of defeat. When he lowered his head, he did succeed in reaching his eyes with his fingers. He rubbed them hard, trying to dispel the odd swirling sensation inside his brain.

He muttered, 'I don't remember anything that happened to me during the last few days.'

The Man spoke with professional detachment. He didn't care about Daniel. 'Short term memory loss is a side-effect of the experiment. Sign the paper.'

Daniel gave a submissive nod. He couldn't fight anymore. He picked up the pen then scrawled *Daniel Hawkins* along the dotted line.

'Thank you, Daniel.'

He grunted. 'When are they moving me out of here?'

The Man gave a little sigh. It was only a pretense of regret. 'I'm afraid there has been a slight miscommunication. The fact of the matter is that we can't revoke your sentencing. You will stay on Death Row.'

Daniel stared at the Man in shock. 'No. I signed up. I did what you asked of me. It's supposed to be a life sentence now. We had a deal!'

The Man remained a silhouette in the corner of the room. A disturbing phantom of a figure. 'It's not in our power to modify the sentence. You were found guilty in a court of law and sentenced to death.'

'I'm innocent. That girl was already dead when I found her in the river. I went into the water to save her. I didn't do it.'

The Man called out, 'Guard!'

The burning sense of injustice drove Daniel to try and rise to his feet. However, the chains snapped tight. He could only raise himself from his chair by two or three miserable inches. His shackles anchored him to the concrete floor. He no longer had the ability to even stand upright.

He cried out in absolute misery, 'You can't do this to me!'

A door opened, spilling bright light into the room.

Daniel pulled at the chains. They'd never break. 'You've got the wrong man!'

The Man's voice was as cold as cold can be 'For the sake of the positive data, I certainly hope not.'

With that, he glided from the room. The door slammed shut behind him.

Daniel felt as if his heart was being torn into bloody shreds. 'Come back here! You can't do this! You can't leave me here!'

He yanked at the chains – over and over. But he knew there was no way of breaking those links of hard steel. The chains were impossible to escape from. And though they were fastened to cuffs that encircled his wrists, they might as well have been screwed deep into the bones of his skeleton. The chains were here to stay. Forever.

CHAPTER THIRTY-THREE

Kyra walked with dogged determination across the desert. She was surrounded by shrubs that sprouted dagger-sharp thorns. Her feet raised spurts of pale dust with every step she took. A coyote's skull rested on a large boulder. She looked into the skull's hollow eye sockets, and a scorpion looked back at her from its little cave of bone.

In the distance, there was a barren mountain range of brownish rock. The sun was dropping toward the horizon now. The light the sun threw across the landscape had become a flood that was the color of blood – that's how it looked to her. A tide of crimson flowing over this sterile world.

It wasn't long before she reached a dirt track that would take her to a highway, perhaps a quarter of a mile away. To her left, there was a huge sign behind a fence of razor wire. The sign bore a stark warning:

PRISON AREA
DO NOT PICK UP HITCHHIKERS

Kyra maintained a steady pace as she walked along the narrow track that ran in a dead straight line toward the highway. The wind was blowing colder now. It was getting darker, too.

A moment later, she heard a thin-sounding whine that cut through the breathy sigh of the desert breeze. The whine triggered a note of alarm in her head. Her heartbeat quickened as she spun around to stare back into the deepening gloom.

For a moment, there was nothing other than Joshua trees, clumps of grass, desert sand. But then she caught sight of a burning point of red that resembled a single eye staring at her. It was perhaps a hundred yards away, and maybe twenty feet above the ground.

Abruptly, the red eye began to move. And it was moving toward her fast. Very fast.

The word exploded from her lips: 'DRONE!'

This drone had a different quality to the others she'd encountered in the last few hours. The whine of its motor turned to a high-pitched scream, something much closer to the sound of a jet engine. The speed it travelled was something else. It accelerated to the point it resembled a missile as it tore through the air towards her.

Run! That was the thought that tore through her mind. *Run. Keep running. Find somewhere to hide.*

Kyra sprinted along the track. Here, the ground was flat, the vegetation sparse; what boulders there were here, scattered across the terrain, weren't big enough to hide behind.

The menacing whine of the drone grew louder and louder. She glanced back to see that it was gaining on her fast. Within seconds, it would reach her.

What can I do? she asked herself as she ran. *There's nowhere to hide. I can't outrun it.* With very few options left to her, she realized that there was one final chance of escape. Desperate words spat through her mind: *Fight it! Destroy the drone. Smash the fucking thing into the ground.*

She stopped running, took a deep breath, and turned to face her pursuer. The drone slowed, then it, too, stopped dead. The thing was just three feet from her face, on the same level as her eyes. The drone was a daemonic-looking machine. Totally sinister. There was something reptilian about its black body-shell. Camera lenses stared out at her from beneath a piece of curving plastic that formed a sullen-looking brow. This was like looking into the face of some freakish lizard. Its propeller blades were rotating so quickly they were just blurry shapes.

As she summoned her strength to lunge at the evil-looking flying machine, the red light on the front of its metal shell suddenly went out. A split-second later, another light burst into life. A light that flickered with nerve-shredding intensity.

A blue light. The blue flash inflicted nothing less than an apocalyptic assault on her brain.

Kyra tried to raise her hands, so that she could grab the machine and smash it into the ground. She couldn't, however. She couldn't move. She couldn't even blink.

The blue light seemed to fill the entire universe. She felt as if she was falling into those silent explosions of blue. After that, there was nothing. No sound. No feeling. No thought.

CHAPTER THIRTY-FOUR

At first, there was nothing but darkness and silence.

Eventually, there came a thin-sounding voice. This particular voice had a distinct mechanical quality, and it appeared to be coming from far, far away. The voice shimmered as if echoing from the cold walls of a tomb.

'Why would you do that?' asked the voice. There was a long pause. After that, the voice returned to repeat the same question. 'Why would you do that?'

Kyra found she could open her eyes. She realized that she sat with her back to a wooden pillar that extended up from a floor of concrete slabs to a bleak-looking ceiling of yet more concrete. The place was starkly illuminated by a dozen bare lightbulbs that hung from cables that wormed through holes in the ceiling. Swiftly, her gaze took in her surroundings. She was in a large room that might belong to a derelict factory. Its brick walls still showed traces of paint that must have covered the walls at some point before time and damp had peeled the emulsion away, leaving raw-looking brick. There were windows. Some were covered with horizontal wooden slats that admitted thin rays of harsh daylight. Other windows offered views of little cell-like rooms, rather than the outdoors. The air inside this bleak vault of a place was cold, and it had the stale odor of dust, which powerfully suggested to her that the outer doors were seldom opened.

And now that the voice had stopped speaking, there was no sound other than the *thud-thud-thud* of her own blood as it coursed through the arteries in her neck.

Kyra realized that her military-style jumpsuit had been replaced with the kind of blue gown that is often provided to patients on arrival at hospital. She was barefoot. The concrete was as cold as ice against her skin. The floor appeared to have been swept, so there was no sharp debris or broken glass that could cause injury to her feet. Around her neck was a bandage. It was tight enough to make its presence felt. She felt the sharp sting from the wound in the back of her neck where Nev had cut out the device that would have killed her with a fast-acting poison if it had been triggered.

Of course, most horrible of all, she saw that she'd been placed in chains again. Both her wrists were manacled to a short chain that was looped around the wooden pillar she leant against. Was the chain untethered?

Kyra pulled at the links. No, her luck had run out. The loop of the chain was padlocked, meaning that she was securely tethered to the post.

Her mouth was as dry as dust. When she licked her lips, she recalled running through the desert. The drone...the blue light. Yes, she remembered perfectly. Even though she knew any attempt at escape would be futile, she ferociously pulled at the chain, hoping that a link might snap, or the padlock hasp might spring free, which in turn would allow her to run from this hellhole of a place. However, the silver links were formed from hardened steel. It would require much greater strength than she possessed to break them. She was back on her leash again. A prisoner in shackles.

A faint buzzing sound attracted her attention. It appeared to be coming from a corroded metal speaker fixed to the wall.

A moment later, the thin-sounding voice returned. A male voice that she knew so well crackled from the speaker. 'Kyra, why would you do that?' The voice had repeated the same question from earlier. However, it then added, 'Why did you bludgeon the guard to death? Why did you stab Nev?'

Am I fuck going to answer him, she thought with absolute ferocity. *He can go to hell!*

That's when she heard the click of a latch, and a door in the corner of the room slowly opened. Light from the corridor beyond the doorway flooded in as a figure stepped into the room.

There he was. Dressed in an expensive business suit, his neatly trimmed beard glinting in the light. He was a prowling figure with bright eyes. A figure that radiated authority. His body language proclaimed, 'Here I am. The Big Man. I'm in control. I have the power to decide who will live and who will die.'

Kyra had seen his face before when it had filled the TV screen in the clinical room that had contained the purple light device, which had the ability to gouge memory from the human mind.

This was the individual she had dubbed 'the Man.' He was in charge of the brainwashing operation that had turned her and John and God knows how many other people into lab rats, which he'd subjected to evil experiments.

Eyes glinting, a cruel smile playing on his face, he moved slowly, like a panther stalking its prey.

He gazed at her – every inch the scientist observing the reaction of his test subject.

His eyes locked onto hers as he murmured in a smooth tone that was almost a purr, 'You can speak freely.'

Kyra kept her lips firmly pressed shut. The last thing she wanted was to engage this sadist in conversation.

The Man continued, 'We're all alone here. Unmonitored. Unobserved. With regard to the gentleman you murdered, and to you skewering Nev from naval to backbone, well...we would not want those unfortunate incidents to reflect poorly on the program.'

The Man moved closer to her. She noticed that he carried a black baton, held down by his side as if he wished to conceal it from her. However, she'd noticed it, alright. And she knew what that pernicious device was capable of.

The Man angled his head to one side as he stepped toward her – a movement which, although slow and measured, was deeply sinister. The predator approaching its victim. Clearly, he hoped that Kyra would say something.

When she did not, he spoke again. 'I know what you did. Your violent behavior is most troubling. You should not be capable of inflicting hurt to such a degree. You should have been more like John.'

At last, Kyra did speak. 'Where is John? I want to see him.'

'You want John? I can place anyone in the machine, and I can create as many Johns as you want...' He gave an ominous little smile. '*As many as I want*. And I intend to do precisely that. The John Implant shows great promise, and the positive results need to be replicated.' He began to circle around her and the column to which she was chained. 'Now...if you want to see John, tell me why you attacked them.'

That menacing, sauntering walk of his took him behind where Kyra sat with her back to the column. She quickly climbed to her feet, while glancing warily at the baton in his hand. Her stomach muscles clenched painfully tight, her heart pounded, because she knew time was running out for her. If she was going to seize the initiative, it would have to be fast, and it would have to be soon.

The man spoke louder. 'It's your last chance. Tell me why you attacked the guard.'

Kyra steeled herself for what she must do. However, she knew she needed to engage the Man in conversation, to lull him into the belief that she could not harm him. Therefore, Kyra smiled. 'The guard? He was going to capture me.'

'And Nev?'

'A drone was coming. I needed a distraction to buy me some time. I had to get away. To survive.'

'Interesting. You do know what you are now, yet you still want to live a life of fake memories.'

'I'll make new memories,' she said. 'My memories.'

The man was clearly interested in her reply. 'No thought for Sarah?'

'If it's true what you tell me, and that until recently I was Sarah, then she's a convicted murderer. Therefore, I reject that old version of me. Sarah no longer exists.' Kyra awarded the Man a shrewd glance. 'You'll learn a lot from me. Isn't that what you want?'

He looked pleased. 'Yes, you do believe you are Kyra.' For a moment, he was smiling...but then the smile died on his face as an unwelcome truth surfaced. 'But you are not the Kyra I worked so hard to create.'

Kyra flinched at the word 'create.' The notion that this evil sadist had 'created' her was nothing less than vile. She imagined Baron Frankenstein gloating over the monstrous creature he had brought to life, and him declaring, 'This is what I worked so hard to *create*.'

I'm not your monster, she told herself. *I am Kyra. I will be in control of my life. I will decide what I do and what I don't do. And you will have no part in my future.* Oh, how she yearned to loop the chain around his neck then twist the links until they crushed his trachea, snapped his hyoid bone, then broke his dirty, rotten neck.

Perhaps the Man saw a hint in her eye that she craved to murder him, because he took two steps back from her, so that even if she did attack him, the chain would pull tight and hold her back.

Nevertheless, he continued to speak as he thoughtfully tapped the end of the baton against his chin. 'What happened to all those implanted passive personality traits? All those happy memories?'

'Happy memories? You put us through hell – again and again. You inflicted torture on us.' Anger blazed within her as she held up the chain. She savagely rattled the links. 'How many times have you put us in chains? How many times have we run through your little maze? You are a sick man!'

When the Man spoke, it was undeniably in response to his own thoughts, not what Kyra had just said. 'Yes, all the tests, all that residual subconscious trauma. That is an unfortunate side effect of the clinical process of suppression. I had to suppress certain traits within your mental structure, yet I was obliged to preserve who you really are. I had to leave the old version of you intact inside your head. Sarah was in there with you, buried deeply within your mind. However, the process I employed meant it was impossible to wipe the slate clean after each test. That's really not my fault. *They* wouldn't allow the total eradication of who you really are. I could only suppress your original personality. That unfortunate restriction on me applied to all my test subjects. That was in case the program failed, and it was suspended. It might surprise you, but even I must answer to my superiors.'

Kyra hissed, 'It did fail. You failed.'

The Man didn't react to her heartfelt judgement. Instead, he paced slowly around her, circling both her and the timber column. He was deep in thought, and when he spoke he was clearly thinking aloud, rather than directing his words at her. She was nothing to him now.

He murmured softly as he worked through the accumulation of data that the test results had given him. 'But John...he was in the same implant batch...had the same latent memories of the tests. And he had positive results. Wonderful results.' He paused as an expression of shock spread across his face. 'However, what if John really is innocent? Perhaps he never did kill that woman. If that's the case, his success as a test subject is meaningless. Because he was never predisposed to commit murder in the first place.'

The expression of worry remained on his face as he worked through the implications of what he'd just said. Kyra could guess what the Man was thinking. *Have I brainwashed an innocent man? If John never possessed an instinctive urge to kill, then it's unlikely he would have attempted to kill Goliath or the guard.*

For a moment, she thought he would throw up his hands in exasperation then storm out of the room. However, his expression began to change. His frown of worry gave way to a steely-eyed glare of determination. He pulled a pair of sunglasses from the breast pocket of his jacket and put them on – carefully, he checked that they completely covered his eyes.

The instant he made sure that his eyes were protected, she understood. She knew what was to come...what he would do to her...

His thumb pushed a switch forward on the baton. Immediately, the end of the device emitted a ghostly blue glow – a glow that grew brighter and brighter. Before it began to flash with that brutal strobe effect, which would shut down her mind, she closed her eyes as tightly as she could.

A massively loud 'No!' vented from her lips.

Kyra pressed her back to the timber post. Using it as guide (now that she could see nothing), she moved around the post in an attempt to avoid the flashing blue light. The chain links *clinked* as she wrapped them around her fists. All that she needed was for him to be close enough. Within striking distance. She could then estimate where her target was. With luck, she could wrap the chain around his neck. As likely as not, he'd have a key to the handcuffs that secured her to the chain. The key would be somewhere in his pockets. She'd find the key quickly enough...after she'd pounded his face to a Godawful fucking mess with the baton.

She heard the Man's calm voice. He had a self-preening tone. He was ever so pleased with himself. 'I must thank you, Kyra. I finally know what I have to do to put everything right.'

Even though her eyes were tightly closed, she could make out the blue flash through her eyelids. Yes, that was a good sign. He must be much closer to her now. In fact, she could feel his breath on her face. She could even detect the aroma of coffee that he'd drunk before stepping into the room.

Kyra kept her backbone firmly against the post as she moved around it. She thought: *Here's hoping that he moves even closer. Then I'll make him suffer for what he's done to me.*

In keeping with her flinching, jittery movements, she pretended to be frightened. 'Get the fuck away from me!'

But she was far from frightened. Her rage was building. This was a vengeful rage that would find its release in the suffering he so richly deserved for inflicting torture on her. And on John. And on all the other poor wretches that had suffered during the Man's savage experiments.

The Man continued to speak in self-satisfied tones. 'I will no longer suppress the test subjects' true identities. I will insist that we eradicate them entirely.'

She ducked down lower, bending her knees until she was almost sitting on the floor as she made a pretense of cringing from him in fear.

He said, 'It will make no difference who the person was before – guilty, innocent – it won't matter. They will be *gone*. Their former selves will be erased. Consequently, there will be no further bleed-through to corrupt the new implants. I am absolutely confident that, from henceforth, the test results will confirm that this is the route to success. And that success will be glorious.'

The light from the baton gleamed brighter through her eyelids. His breath feathered her hair – she could smell the coffee. His face must be just inches from hers. Close enough...

Still with her eyes closed, she sprang upright, lunged at him, and aimed a full-blooded kick where she judged his body would be. Her foot slammed into what she guessed must be one of his legs. She heard him grunt with pain.

She kicked out again. However, her foot lashed through cool air. It didn't strike his body. He must have moved back, trying to reach a safe distance from her. This time, she rushed toward the sound his shoes made on the floor. The chain pulled tight. She was at the full extent of it now. She couldn't go any further. Nevertheless, she kicked out again. A roar of frustration exploded from her lips when her foot didn't connect with human flesh.

Kyra strained forward, trying to snap the chain links. She was like a ferocious, snarling dog that pulled against its leash as it tried to attack the target of its fury.

The man sounded breathless. Her attack had succeeded in shocking him.

'There's no hope for you,' he told her. 'You're just another unstable reject.'

Kyra heard a clicking sound – was that him putting the baton down on the floor?

Opening her eyes to check was not an option. The blue light would rob her of her senses.

She kicked out again. This time she felt his hand grab her ankle, and he maintained his grip on it, holding her foot up from the ground. A moment later, she felt a sharp sting in her thigh.

Panic erupted inside of her. *That was a needle! He's injected me!* Evidently, this is exactly what he had done, because soon she was feeling the narcotic spread up through her leg in a wave of absolute bone-chilling ice. Her bloodstream was carrying the drug through her body, up through her chest, up through her neck toward her brain.

The Man must have been smiling as he purred, 'Your implant is retired.'

Kyra's body began to feel numb. The strength vanished from her legs, leaving her to slide down the timber post to the floor. Using every shred of willpower she possessed, she fought to remain conscious.

'No,' she hissed. 'I don't want to be Sarah.'

The Man chuckled. 'Don't worry. I promise that you will never be Sarah again.' He paused before adding in a decidedly amused tone, 'And you will be with John.'

She felt fingers probe her right eyelid. Even though she tried as hard as she could, she failed to raise her hands to push the fingers away. The drug had a paralyzing effect. All her limbs were drooping limply.

With surprising gentleness, he lifted her eyelid. The end of the baton was just three inches from her open eye.

The light came again. Explosions of blue that smashed her mind into a million pieces. After that, she was sleeping – and dreaming. Oh, what dreams...what frightening dreams...

Kyra floated in darkness. It was as if the darkest of midnights had become a liquid substance through which she drifted. Images began to flow from the dark. First, a nurse wearing surgical scrubs. The nurse had blonde hair that was completely different to Kyra's, yet the nurse's face was identical to Kyra's. In the dream, Kyra thought: *That must be Sarah. I am not Sarah, though. I am Kyra.*

Then another figure emerged from the darkness. This was a lurching figure with eyes that blazed with rage. The figure possessed an aura of danger that made Kyra's heart race with terror.

She saw that the figure was monstrous. Everything about it radiated savagery.

The monster's face was terrifying. And what made it so terrifying was that the monster possessed her face. The monster, which wore a face that was identical to hers, began to roar with fury.

In the dream, Kyra began to weep. She sensed that she was reaching her final destination in life now. Changes were taking place in her mind. Irrevocable changes. *There's no going back from this,* she told herself as tears poured down her face. *This is my destiny...*

This is my fate...

CHAPTER THIRTY-FIVE

The air in the basement was still. And the air was hot. A burning, skin tingling hot. The source of this heat was an industrial furnace, set in the bottom of a brick chimney at the far end of this eerie vault. The basement, itself, measured a hundred feet in length and fifty feet wide. There was no sound. There were no windows that would have permitted a glimpse outside to tell whether it was night or day.

Electric lighting added to the bright yellow glare flooding out through the furnace's open door. It was the kind of furnace (so roomy and so searingly hot), which would be favored by gangsters to dispose of people who threatened to disrupt their business interests.

Most striking of all were thirty concrete columns. Square in shape, they reached up from the floor to the monolithic slab-work of the ceiling. The pale columns formed an enchanted forest in this subterranean vault. The columns could have been tree trunks that featured in a particularly horrific fairy story – that is to say, decidedly uncanny tree trunks which supported a concrete sky. This was 'that' kind of place. A strange, unsettling place that might be a venue for all kinds of atrocities. Did it serve as a torture chamber? The type of underground facility where screams could not be heard beyond its bleak walls. A room to suffer in...and to die.

Then again, it would be the perfect lair for a beast. The kind of beast that prowled human nightmares when the sleeper was in a lonesome place, far from the safety of home.

These wayward thoughts oozed through Murat's head as he lay curled up on the floor behind a stack of metal frames that almost reached the ceiling. It occurred to Murat that this building was once a factory, where steelwork was fabricated for construction projects or for transport infrastructure. And yet this building was much more than a derelict factory. All kinds of freaky shit happened here. Spatters of dried blood on the walls and the floor were evidence of that.

Murat knew all too well the kind of pattern a spray of blood makes on a wall when the victim has their fucking guts hacked out of them. He'd created blood spatters like that many times before when he terminated the activities of rival drug dealers. *Whack with the axe! Into the furnace with them! Let blood bubble and boil! Let eyeballs pop! And skin roast!* Memories of what he'd done made him want to let out a shriek of laughter. To stifle the sound, he pushed his knuckles between his teeth. He bit hard to drive away the urge to laugh with a good healthy dose of pain. After all, he'd been ordered to remain silent. So...time to be as quiet as a mouse.

Murat recalled dispatching his enemies with an efficient sweep of the axe. Also, he recalled his wife and three children, and their loveable puppy. He remembered it all because 'he' allowed him to remember.

After all, Murat had been specially chosen. *I am the Control*, he told himself. *All I have to do is do what I've been told to do. The Man will then have me removed from Death Row.* A pardon had also been promised. That's when he could go back to Bethany and the kids, and the gorgeous, silly little puppy that loved to roll over to have his tummy tickled. That was the life that Murat wanted again. He wanted to leave the jail and the festering boredom of Death Row behind.

Murat took a peek out from behind his little shelter constructed from the stack of metal frames. Okay. Time to focus. He had been given an important assignment. To earn his freedom from jail, he must perform the tasks that he'd been given.

Murat could just make out the figure of a young male with short dark hair. The male was lying on the concrete floor and he appeared to be unconscious. He wore a blue shirt and cream-colored chinos. The shirt was fully unbuttoned, revealing a bare torso. There was a surgical dressing taped to the man's belly.

At that moment, the young man opened his eyes. Immediately, he sat up, even though he was still clearly groggy from the effects of the drug that had rendered him unconscious. The man grimaced with pain. He put his hands on the source of the pain, the part of his stomach that bore the surgical dressing. He appeared surprised to see the dressing there. Clearly, he hadn't realized he'd suffered from a wound of some sort. Pain from the wound must have shoved the stupefying effect of the narcotic clean out of his skull because he was fully awake now, sharp-eyed, focused. He glanced around at his surroundings, taking in the bleak walls, the concrete columns – each one about a foot across, and most definitely resembling bizarre tree trunks that supported the roof.

The man scrambled to his feet.

Murat silently mouthed a name, 'Nev.' He knew he was seeing test subject 'Nev.' Murat also knew that things were about to become extremely interesting. Though the words 'extremely dangerous' might have been more appropriate, considering the situation.

Nev appeared to have only just realized that a leather collar was fixed around his neck. His fingers explored the collar. At the same time, his eye grew wider and wider with astonishment. A moment ago, he'd gazed at this sinister basement, and he must have been thinking, *What the fuck is this place?* Now he was probably asking himself, *What the fuck is this fastened around my neck?*

Maybe he still wasn't thinking clearly, because even though he'd noticed chain links hanging down from the collar, he quickly turned and headed toward a flight of concrete steps, no doubt hoping they led up to the exit. Swiftly, he climbed three steps. On the fourth step, he was stopped with a brutal jolt. Baffled, he looked back, wondering what the hell it was that had stopped him dead. That's when he realized that the chain had pulled taut. The understanding finally sank in that the chain, fastened to the collar around his neck, was also tethered to some anchor point just around the corner of the basement wall.

From where he stood, he couldn't see the anchor point. So, he remained there for a moment, holding onto the chain, while his eyes tracked along the links. He must have been trying to make sense of what appeared to be an increasingly sinister predicament he found himself in.

Nev's expression of confusion was turning to one of outright worry. He must have been thinking: *Why have I been chained up in a cellar? What's going to happen next? Is someone going to hurt me?*

Murat had seen that expression before. He'd seen the way a man's features would twist into a mask of terror, just before Murat had gotten to work with the axe – doing some pruning of the nose with the axe head. Thereafter, cutting off his victim's ears to send to their ma and pa. Oh, yes, Murat knew what it was like to look into his victim's eyes and see terror blazing there. There was no doubt about it. Nev was scared. Totally scared.

Murat felt a hot buzz of excitement in his chest now. Because the most awesome of stuff was yet to come.

Nev was trying to work out what to do for the best. He must have decided to discover where the chain led to – no doubt hoping to find the anchor point. After that, he'd somehow unlock the chain or break one of the links to free himself. With that task accomplished, he'd get the fuck out of Doomsvillle here.

Murat kept silent to ensure that Nev didn't notice there was someone else in the basement.

Nev began to follow the chain toward its anchor point. Wherever that was. He moved slowly. Very slowly. His eyes, however, darted quickly, suggesting that fear might give way to scream-your-damn-guts-out-in-panic at any moment.

Murat felt his muscles tense up. He knew what was coming. He also knew that as the Control in this particular experiment he had a specific role to play.

Nev stopped. His eyes, however, continued to track the chain links as they snaked along the floor before turning around the corner into a passageway and trailing away until they vanished from sight. Nev's expression had changed, because suddenly he'd noticed that a different kind of light had begun to spill from the passageway. The basement lights emitted a harsh white glare. However, the glow spilling from the passageway, or tunnel, or whatever it was, was a sickly green color. Such an odd color for illumination in this subterranean vault. Hence, the change in Nev's expression. This strangely colored light puzzled the guy as much as it worried him.

Nev still couldn't see the other end of the chain, which was connected to the collar he wore. He leaned to his left. No doubt he wanted to locate the chain's anchor point without actually getting any closer. That sickly green glow was deeply disturbing. And Nev was becoming increasingly anxious about what he was seeing down here.

Nev tugged at the collar again. The thought running through his head must have been, *If I can break the collar, I'll be free. I'll be able to walk out of here.*

But the collar was made from thick leather. The padlock that secured it to his neck was toughened steel. Neither the collar nor the padlock would break anytime soon.

Nev took another cautious step forward. His instincts must have been shrieking at him that something dangerous lurked around the corner, just out of sight. Nevertheless, the man had a burning need to locate the end of the chain that shackled him down here.

At that moment, the green glow abruptly vanished. Now, the only illumination came from the furnace's glare and the overhead lights. Even as Nev frowned, wondering what had happened to the green light, another light sprang from the passageway. This light was yellow – as bright a yellow as the yolk of an egg.

Nev took a step backward. He never took his eyes off the mouth of the passageway, while those warning sirens must have been screaming inside his skull.

Nev had every reason to be alarmed because a figure abruptly emerged from the passageway. They had their back to Nev (their face wasn't visible), and they walked sideways. The movements were somehow inhuman. What's more, there was a sense that this was a newly-formed creature that still hadn't become used to walking on two feet.

Nev, by this point, must have realized that the figure he was seeing was that of a woman. She remained standing with her back to him. She wore a grey coverall. Over that, on the upper half of her body, was a harness of leather straps that formed an X-shape across her back.

Nev reacted with shock. Immediately, he backed up several steps, dragging the chain with him.

The woman turned around to face him. Clamped to her head a set of blinders, which bled a yellow glow into her face. They made her wide-open eyes blaze with an unnerving intensity as she stared at Nev.

The woman did not move. She merely stared at Nev who stared back at this strange being in utter shock.

Nev took a deep breath, obviously trying to prevent himself from being overwhelmed by the rising tide of panic that surely had a stranglehold on his clamoring heart.

Nev gripped the chain in both hands as he spoke to the menacing figure. 'Hey. What's going on? How did we get here?'

The woman did not answer his question. She merely stared at him with such a powerful glare it would have made anyone's blood run cold.

Abruptly, the woman took five steps forward into the basement. Just as abruptly, she stopped dead, her body stiffly rigid, her eyes staring. Murat saw how Nev could not take his gaze off the woman. He was evidently noticing other details about her now. She had a bandage around her neck. There was another bandage around one of her forearms. Nev realized, to his horror, that she wore a manacle around her wrist. Attached to that manacle was a chain – a chain like the one that ran from Nev's collar. His gaze followed the silvery links as they snaked out across the floor. A moment later, he realized the truth. His chain was attached to the manacle around the woman's wrist. They were leashed together. She took another single step forwards. This time, Nev saw that the woman was attached to a second chain. This one was fixed to the leather harness that she wore on her torso. The second chain led off across the floor and into the gloom.

The man that Murat knew was called Nev took a nervous intake of breath, then Nev addressed the woman again. 'Can you hear me? I'm John.'

Murat nodded to himself. The conversations between the guards that he'd overheard all made sense now. The guards had whispered secretively amongst themselves about how the Man had built a machine that could erase who you were and then implant an entirely new personality inside your head. Murat understood the shocking truth. The guy called Nev now believed he was someone called John. This 'John' would have had false memories engraved into his brain. *That is brainwashing, isn't it? The Man washes away the old you, then he wickedly transforms you into someone else entirely. That's the kind of stuff you get in miracles. Or in nightmares.*

The guy who was once Nev studied the woman's face with a kind of searching anxiety, like he was hoping that she'd suddenly smile and introduce herself.

Murat grinned to himself. *Is that going to happen?*
Like fuck it is.
Because here it comes...here comes the shitstorm.

A dangerous humming sound abruptly burst from the blinders. The woman tilted her head in response to the hum.

That woman, Murat told herself, *the guards said she was once known as Kyra.*

The name 'Kyra' had been gouged from her brain. The name had been absolutely, totally gouged, along with most of the portions of her mind that had once made her human.

The creature that people had once addressed as 'Kyra' took two savage steps forward. The chain snapped tight, and Murat felt himself being dragged through the stack of metal frames that instantly toppled over with a mighty clatter.

Because the brutal truth was clear and perfectly simple. The chain that ran from Nev's neck was connected to the woman's wrist by a manacle. And the second chain that ran from the woman's leather harness was locked to a steel cuff around Murat's own wrist.

The fact of the matter was this...the three people in the basement were all shackled together. That meant their destinies were conjoined. Where one went, the other two must follow. Without a shadow of doubt, they formed a chain gang of sorts.

Murat remembered what he'd been instructed to say when Nev was confronted by the terrifying woman in the blinders. First of all, he must call the young guy by a different name – not Nev.

Therefore, Murat yelled, '*John!* You gotta kill it!'

Nev clearly believed he was actually someone called John, because he showed no surprise when Murat had yelled 'John! You gotta kill it'. However, for now, Murat decided to mentally refer to the guy as 'Nev.' He sure as fuck wasn't going to scramble his own brain to shit by switching names at this point, during what were becoming very interesting – and very high-stakes – proceedings.

Nev clearly had zero understanding of his predicament. Or any comprehension of the very real danger he faced. Nev took a couples of steps backward, looking this way and that in confusion, maybe hoping someone would arrive to put an end to this bizarre and disturbing stream of events.

Murat remembered the instructions he'd been given. He pulled at the chain as he desperately tried to hold the woman back.

He yelled again, using Nev's new name. 'John! Choke it! Use the chain!'

The woman took three powerful steps toward John. Such was the woman's strength, Murat was dragged to one of the concrete columns. He collided with the structure hard enough for him to let out a grunt of pain. And still the woman moved forward. The chain pulled tight, once again threatening to drag Murat along like he was at the end of a leash. He tried to wrap the chain around the column. That length of reinforced concrete was stronger than his arms. If the concrete could take some of the strain...

Murat shouted, 'Loop the chain around its neck. Strangle the fucker!'

Nev reacted with horror at the suggestion. 'I don't want to hurt her.'

'Her? *It!* That thing is a Proto!'

'Proto? What's a Proto?'

Nev shook his head in confusion. They'd done a damned good job ripping out all the memories the guy possessed of his time here in the facility. All recollection of previous tests had been swept from his mind. He remembered nothing.

When Nev just stood there with a helpless expression, clearly not knowing what to do, Murat realized that he had to prompt him. After all, it was Murat's job to guide him. To egg him on...

Murat yelled as loudly as he could. 'John! Listen to me! That thing is a Proto! You gotta hurt it...if you want to live!'

The lights in the Proto's blinders suddenly blazed red. These lights were nothing less than the fires of hell. The red glare reflected against the Proto's skin. It looked like her face had ignited and was bathed in crimson flame.

The Proto had been strong before. Now her strength became immense. Overwhelming. Like a raging bull.

Nev tried to stumble away from the Proto as she lunged at him. For a moment, however, Murat held her there. She was leaning forward, snarling. She was the essence of fury. She was like one of those brutal pagan goddesses that was hellbent on wreaking bloody vengeance on her human victim.

She strained forward with such force that Murat could no longer hold the chain in place around the column. Chain links began to slip across the concrete surface, sheer force ripping out chunks of concrete. The movement was so violent that sparks flew from the steel links. When the sparks struck Murat's face, they stung like rats were doing their evil best to bite through his skin.

That's when all hell broke loose.

The Proto that had once been Kyra roared with total fury. A siren started — the mechanical wail was so loud it felt to Murat that it shredded his eardrums. Dear God, it was so loud that the light fittings vibrated. This in turn created a violent flickering that made it seem as if a storm had broken out in the basement. A storm that fired lightning bolts through the gloomy vault. Yes, this was purely an effect of the scream of the siren shaking the light bulbs, but the strobing effect almost overwhelmed his senses.

Deafened by the siren and the furious roar of the Proto, Murat found himself being dragged along by the chain as the Proto surged toward John. She was murderous rage in human form. The blinders erupted with a blood red light that was as intense as burning napalm. Strangely, the woman's eyes had the ability to feed on the red light — it seemed to increase her physical strength to levels that couldn't feasibly be human. Her eyes blazed with shocking flashes of crimson and homicidal red.

Murat's skull was aching from the sheer storm of sound. The

flashing lights were so intense they drove spikes of pain through his eyes. And brutally, relentlessly, he was dragged by the Proto as she fiercely lunged toward Nev.

As for Nev, he stood there. Horror had paralyzed him. He could not even raise his hands to defend himself. He simply stared at this hissing, snarling, roaring creature that closed in on him.

Murat crashed into another column. His head whipped forward. It smacked into the hard concrete with such force the bone in his nose snapped. That new surge of agony was, in itself, like a bolt of white-hot lightning that ripped through his brain. Even as he howled, the Proto dragged him away from the column as she targeted Nev. Murat kept his legs straight while he tried to brace his feet against the floor. However, he was dragged along like he was on water skis being hauled by a speedboat. When he crashed into another column, he succeeded in wrapping the chain around it. Metal links snapped tight. Meanwhile, the siren screamed so loudly that Murat could have believed that the sheer power of the sound would split the universe in two. The electric lighting was strobing ever faster now. It sent out bursts of light that ripped every shadow in the vault to fuck.

The Proto then pulled so viciously at the chain he'd looped around the column that the links started to yield. He saw the weld points gradually splitting. The loops of steel began to stretch. It wasn't humanly possible for a person to break a chain like this with their own brute strength. But then the Proto was no longer human, was she? Her strength defied comprehension.

The chain formed a quivering straight line because it was so tight. Links continued to deform as if the steel was becoming soft.

Murat did what he'd been instructed to do. He tried as hard as he could to snap Nev out of the shock that had paralyzed him. Murat was the Control. It was his job to prod Nev's behavior in a certain direction. Murat had been ordered to test Nev's neural programming to destruction.

Murat's arms felt as if, at any moment, they'd be ripped from his shoulders. Nevertheless, he howled the name that had been tightly woven into Nev's brainwashed mind, 'John! Stick your fingers into its eyes! Right into the sockets! *Blind it!'*

Nev stared at his own hands. He must have known he absolutely had to turn his hands into lethal weapons. Yet the programming that transmuted him into a compassionate human being was strong...too strong. He would not inflict hurt. He could not kill.

The Proto lunged forward again, trying to pull Murat away from the column. Thereafter, she could inflict carnage on the man in front of her. Because, to her, Nev was the creature she hated. He was the creature that must be destroyed.

The Proto pulled harder.

Murat felt her incredible strength as she wrenched at the chain in his hands. His fingers gave way, one after another, as they dislocated, finger bones popping out from their joints.

Despite the agony, he screamed, 'Don't you want to live? Kill the Proto!'

The siren's scream had become daggers of pure force that stabbed through Murat's ears. That is when the electric lights began to explode. They couldn't withstand the destructive onslaught of the soundwaves any longer.

And the chain links were still yielding. They were stretching as if they were made from soft rubber. A link suddenly snapped.

The Proto was free.

Nev raised his arms in a futile attempt to protect himself.

The light from the blinders, which shone into the Proto's face was an incandescent red that seared the human soul.

The woman roared with fury – she was roaring with the same raw aggression that had driven her primeval ancestors to slaughter their victims. Back when wars were fought with stone axes and spears. She hurled herself at Nev who flinched back. The timeless act was played out in the same way as it ever was. The predator had its helpless victim in its brutal grip. There would be no compassion.

Then, wasn't it inevitably the case? That the laws of nature would always, eternally, forbid any act of mercy?

Nev's eyes bulged in horror as the Proto's hands grasped his throat.

The onslaught of sound from the siren shattered the last lightbulb.

Darkness engulfed this end of the vault. The glow from the furnace didn't reach this far. And nor was the blinders' red glare sufficient to illuminate the scene, as the light was concentrated on the Proto's face.

Therefore, Murat could not see the violence that the Proto inflicted on the man.

He could hear, though. Despite the fact the siren continued to howl, it wasn't loud enough to drown out the man's screams.

Nev kept screaming and screaming. And Murat prayed for the moment that Nev's heart stopped. And the screaming would end.

Of course, Murat would remember the sounds that Nev made. And the memory would be a fire that would burn forever in his brain.

After all, nobody could take that memory away from him.

Could they?

THE END

If you loved THE PROTOS EXPERIMENT, you'll love the BLOOD CRAZY SERIES. Here are the first four electrifying chapters of Book 1 to whet your appetite!

BLOOD CRAZY

'Blood Crazy changed my life. I saw the world differently after reading this novel.'

EVERYONE OVER THE AGE OF NINETEEN BECOMES MURDEROUSLY INSANE.

THEY BEGIN KILLING – ESPECIALLY THEIR OWN CHILDREN

Saturday. An ordinary day. People out shopping. Going to the movies. Eating fast-food. Just an ordinary Saturday. Right?

Wrong. Twenty-four hours later, civilization has been torn apart. Adults roaming the street in howling mobs. Nobody under the age of nineteen is safe.

Seventeen-year-old Nick Aten must flee thousands of murderous adults and find a place of safety. As he fights for survival, he finds new friends, and a new love in a dangerous world.

THERE IS AN ETERNAL MYSTERY AT THE HEART OF THIS STORY THAT CONTINUES TO INFLUENCE HISTORY.

AND THAT PROFOUND MYSTERY LIVES WITHIN US. IT SHAPES OUR LIVES. AND EACH AND EVERY ONE OF US WILL FEEL ITS IRRESISTIBLE POWER

CHAPTER ONE

THE START OF THE END OF EVERYTHING

'What happened?'

Baz stared at the blood.

Fresh and red and wet, it drenched the paving slabs in a slick that looked big enough to paddle your canoe through.

I elbowed him in the ribs.

'I said, what happened, Baz?'

He looked up at me, his eyes egg-size with shock.

'I've just watched them shovel the poor bastard off the pavement ...Christ. What a mess. That cop there puked all over his car...They've seen nothing like it, Nick. They can't handle it.'

Baz talked like he was firing a machine gun at nightmare monsters. If you ask me, he had a psychological need to tell me what happened.

'They say – they say he'd just walked out of Rothwell's, crossed the street when – slam! slam! Poor bastard never knew what hit him. He was dead before the ambulance got here.'

All around us Saturday morning shoppers stared at the blood. That mess of red had got them by the short and curlies.

On the balls of their feet, cops ran, directing traffic, cordoning off the street with candy-striped tape or repeating that famous lie that no one ever believes: 'Move along. There's nothing to see.'

They sweated in the Spring sunshine. On their faces weren't the usual expressions of our seen-it-all policemen.

'An axe, Nick...A bastard axe...Can you believe that? Laid into him with it right there outside the shop.'

'Who was it?'

'Jimmy...Jimmy somebody. You'll have seen him round town plenty. About seventeen. Went to the art college, had a pony tail. Always swanned round with a green guitar under his arm...Smashed that up, too. Like they wanted to kill both of them...him and his guitar.'

'You saw it happen?'

'No. I got here just as they scraped him off the street. I saw the people who'd seen it happen, though. They were flaked out across those seats over there like they'd been neck-shot. Just flat out from shock. I tell you, Nick, it was like a fucking war or something. Blood on the street. People shaking and throwing up. You know, like you see on the news or...or...'

The charge that fired the words like silver bullets from his lips suddenly exhausted itself. His red face turned white and he said no more.

From a hardware store came two old ladies carrying buckets of water. They poured them onto the blood which was setting to jelly in the warm sun. It took four more buckets before the blood slid off the paving slabs and into the drains where it was swallowed with a greedy sucking sound. There were solid chunks of red in there. Like cuts of raw meat.

Eventually only wet pavement reeking of disinfectant was left. Now there really was nothing left to see. But Baz still stared at the wet slabs.

I said, 'Someone must have really hated the kid to do that to him.'

'They did. Jesus Christ, they did. They unzipped him like a holdall.'

'Do they know who murdered him?'

'Yeah.' Baz looked up. 'It was his mother.'

The day the world went mad I was on my way to McDonald's with two things on my mind.

One. The Big Mac I was going to stuff down my throat. Two. How was I going to hurt that bastard, Tug Slatter?

Normality oozed through the town as thick as toothpaste through its tube. People shopping; little kids in buggies; big kids hunting down the record and game stores, their pocket money red-hot in their hands. Total, utter, complete small-town normality.

That was until I saw the blood on the street. They tell you this at school.

Every so often in history, there will come this colossal event that splits time in two. You know, like the birth of Jesus Christ. Everything before – BC. Everything after – AD.

On my way to McDonald's, it happened again. After two thousand years the old Age, Anno Domini, had died a death.

Naturally, like everyone else at the time I didn't know it. Any more than a passer-by seeing that baby squawking in a manger somewhere in suburban Bethlehem would have known that the world was going to change PDQ.

At that moment, as I left Baz watching five slightly moist paving slabs, life – on the surface – was returning to normal. New shoppers flowed into town, kids in buggies got stuck into ice creams, lovers walked hand in hand. And they saw paving slabs wet with nothing more than water.

So, I showed the wet stretch of street my back and I headed toward the building with the golden arches that formed the magic *M*.

Now I was hungry. All I wanted was that Big Mac, fries and a monster coke rattling with ice.

Of course, I was ignorant as shit. I didn't know the truth. That before long I'd look back and call this:

DAY 1
YEAR 1

CHAPTER TWO

WHO THE HELL'S NICK ATEN?

Before we get any further into this, something about me.

I'm seventeen. The name's Nick Aten (yeah, yeah, it rhymes with Satan).

Mother Nature sprang me on middleclass parents. Father: an investment advisor. Mother: an accountant.

Things changed a bit when I was born one Sunday morning, 3 March. My mother had already given up work when she fell pregnant so the Atens had to shave back on some of life's luxuries. Not that they didn't want a baby. They'd been trying for years. There had been three miscarriages before me. And one son who had lived two weeks before the doctors gave up the fight and let him die. My parents called him Nicholas and cremated him.

In my mother's drawer there's a bundle of cards, the deepest condolences kind with angels and babies sleeping 'safe in the arms of the Lord.'

They are for a dead boy called Nick Aten. People sometimes ask if it feels weird to see your name on these cards. There it is in black and white. Documents to say you're dead. A bit like seeing a video of your own funeral.

I laugh it off.

As a snotty-nosed two-year-old, I would spend my days stalking around the garden carrying a stick. With this stick I'd whack the ground, bushes and Mum's prized bedding plants.

When they asked, 'Why are you hitting the bushes, Nicholas?' I'd reply, 'Nick killing monsters.'

When I was three a rat somehow sneaked into the dining room. There I was, sat on the rug, happy as Larry, playing with my bricks. My new baby brother snug in his layback chair.

Ten minutes later when Mum came into the room, she screamed and sprayed a mugful of coffee across the wallpaper.

Because there I stood, a statuette of Aphrodite in my hand, watching the rat. It lay twitching its legs, with its rat brains looking like pink cottage cheese stuck to the head of the statuette.

Unusually tidily for me, I'd picked out its titchy rat eyes and dropped them into my dad's tankard he'd won in some tennis tournament a million summers before.

That passion for killing monsters is probably my most valuable asset.

Since it happened – that BIG DAY ONE – I've had plenty of time to wonder if that passion – that obsession – to kill monsters was somehow imprinted onto my mind in the womb. That it was my destiny.

Before I sat down with a pile of paper to write this, I looked at manuals to see how you're supposed to write a book. They say it's important to make you understand what I'm like. What makes me tick. So you will understand why I did the things I did.

Here goes.

I've no real lifetime friends. But I had a lifetime enemy. Tug Slatter. We fought one another on our first day at school. The first time he tried to kill me – I mean actually terminate my existence on planet Earth as opposed to merely ruining my face – was when we were fourteen. I'd aerosolled TUG SLATTER IS A SHITHEAD on the wall of the local scout hut. Slatter broke three fingers of my left hand with a fence post.

Broken fingers don't sound life-threatening, but I was using them to protect my skull at the time.

I left school at sixteen. No qualifications. I've had three jobs: glass collector in a night club. Trainee plastics extruder. And, last of all, driving a pick-up for a general dealer.

So. If you'd seen me walking down the street on that Saturday morning what would you have seen?

A seventeen-year-old, dark hair, jeans, trainers, leather jacket. Your first impression would be, 'He's a cocky bastard.' (And I was).

You're thinking now I'm nothing more than a smalltown bad boy.

Maybe. Maybe not.

Mum and Dad watched me grow into what I am with a bemused expression. They knew they could do nothing to change me. My dad's response was, 'Nick'll either end up a millionaire – or in jail.'

Sometimes my antics would wear down Mum's stamina, then she'd grumble, 'Do you know the sacrifices your father and I have had to make for you?' You know the rhythm of it. You'll have heard it all before.

But I was never in serious trouble. I didn't torture cute animals. And probably the only person who knew the way I ticked was my uncle, Jack Aten.

He was a lot like me. Left school with no qualifications and no desire to join the rest of the pen-pushing Atens. Ambition sizzled inside him. He wanted to be a rock guitarist. For fifteen years he toured with one of those bands who although they play honest to goodness rock music never make it as far as a recording contract.

When I was eleven Jack Aten came back. Starved bony thin, he made you think he'd been somehow scorched.

I guess now he'd married himself to heroin. So it was a case of return home, get off it – or die.

Jack used to spend a lot of time at our house. Sometimes we'd play crazy golf (for some reason he loved crazy golf – then he liked crazy things and crazy people). When we went out on these jaunts he'd always carry a can of beer from which he'd take little sips. He'd make one can last two hours. I thought it was great. I was with this rock rebel.

Now I know he was drip-feeding alcohol into his blood. It knocked just enough of the sharp edges off reality to make life bearable.

Now and again, he'd ask in a joke upper-crust accent, 'I say, Nick-Nick.

Am I alive?'

'You're alive, Jack.'

'Thanks, old man. Sometimes I forget.'

Nights he'd play his guitar in his room, so softly you could hardly hear it. Whenever I heard the music my skin would prickle cold. The music reminded me of a documentary I'd seen about whale songs. I'd hear the tones of the electric guitar floating down through the floors and I'd remember the part about the whale with five harpoons through its back and how the whale sang as it died. The dying whale song – Jack Aten's gentle guitar sounds. In my head the two things were one and the same.

When I was fourteen life killed Jack Aten. He was thirty-eight. Cancer of the bollocks.

They say some cancers are a kind of suicide, grown by men and women who can't change their shape to fit into the narrow slot that society inflicts on them.

For twelve months I didn't open doors like you and the Reverend Green. I kicked them open. Ask me a question, I'd snarl you an answer. I was a balloon full of rage stretched tight to rupturing point. All I wanted to do was run to a mountain top. Then roar at the sky to bury me.

I was the little kid who wanted to kill monsters. As the years passed the monsters disappeared.

I grew up to enjoy a night out with the lads, a few beers. Happiness was a Big Mac. Ecstasy two Big Macs.

Now all that's changed.

The monsters have returned.

And I've got the biggest monster of all to kill.

It's not a monster you'd recognise immediately. It doesn't look like the ones you see in kids' books, with leather wings, claws and teeth like steak knives. But it's a monster all the same. And if I don't kill it, it will eat my bones as sure as you shit tomorrow.

In a way, this book is an instruction manual on how to kill that monster. Because remember this.
You, too, have your own monster to kill.

That's why I'm locking myself away in here for a month. I'm just going to sit down and write the bloody thing as it comes, all right? No frills, no poncey literature. But nor am I going to cut corners, or cut the bad things. This is what happened to me. Also it'll help clear my mind for what I've got to do next.

No one's likely to find me here. It's February. It snows like someone's torn a hole in the sky. The house is miles from anywhere. On three sides of it there's thick forest. In front there's a dirty great river that's more than a mile wide.

Sometimes, to clear my head after hours of word crunching, I go down to the shore to skim stones. There are still a lot of things floating in the water. They look like rotting logs, hundreds of them, day and night, going with the flow of the river down to the sea. I'll throw pebbles or snowballs at them. In the same kind of way any other seventeen-year-old would.

The only time it looks bad is when the undertow rolls them over. One end of the rotting log lifts smoothly out of the water. Then you know what it really is. You see the holes where the eyes were.

I shrug it off. Throw more pebbles. Then kick my way back through the snow, turn up the gas fire, get the pen back in my hand and I attack the paper again. I have to get what's in my head down onto paper.

Throughout my life, I've never wondered about the big – and I mean the REALLY BIG – mysteries. And yet over the last eight months I got answers. Answers to those questions that scholars and people just like you have been asking for three thousand years.

I didn't go looking for them. They dropped into my hands like stones from the sky.

It's important you know.

What you do with it is up to you.

CHAPTER THREE

ALL CALM BEFORE THE STORM

'You know where he'll be. We could take him now.'

'Revenge, they say, is a dish best served cold.'

'Yeah, and in the meantime that shit Slatter thinks he's got away with it.' Steve Price kicked a can rattling away down the road. 'He's laughing at us, Nick.'

'Cold, I said. Not stale. We'll pay him back. But we don't rush it. We work out a plan.'

After the burger blowout in McDonald's we'd walked back from town to my house.

Steve Price, blond hair, round-faced, with a passion for football and Oriental girls, was my best friend. We'd knocked around together for the last five years. Now he was itching to take a crack at Slatter.

As we'd sat there behind the plate glass in McDonald's, chewing burgers, we'd seen Tug Slatter parading his ugly, tattooed face through town.

'You know where he'll be going, Nick?'

I knew. Slatter was patrolling his territory. Dressed in his uniform of denim shirt, jeans, brown leather belt and pit boots. Cigarette in the corner of his downturned mouth, shaved head swinging from side to side like a bad-tempered pit-bull looking for someone to bite.

He'd slouch through town from the market to the High Street, trying to catch some kid's eye. When he did it'd be the old routine.

Slatter: 'Oi. What you want?'

Puzzled kid: 'Pardon?'

'Don't come that with me. You know what you did.'

'No. What?'

Slatter, aggressive: 'You were looking at me.'

'I wasn't.'

Slatter moves closer. Eye contact cobra sharp. 'You did. And I didn't like the way you were doing it.'

'I didn't. I—'

'Damned well did. You were looking at me.' Slatter bunches

hands. 'You think you're better than me, eh? Want to make something of it?'

Kid knows what's coming now. Frightened, he sees those tattooed fists coming up with their biting snakes and handpicked letters across the fingers spelling out HATE and KILL.

He doesn't have to try hard to imagine himself lying on the ground spitting out broken teeth while this ugly ape kicks the living shit out of him.

Slatter: 'You don't just walk through town, you know, just staring people out.'

The kid guesses the safest way out. He goes for it. Show this tattooed gorilla he's undisputed boss.

'I'm sorry...Look...I really am. I didn't mean to.'

'Don't look at me like that again. All right?'

'I'm sorry. I didn't mean to.' (The kids stops short of calling Slatter SIR – just.) I was only walking down...I...I mean I—'

'All right. But don't do it again. I don't like it.'

Respect – induced through terror – is meat and drink to Tug Slatter. Kicking stones, we turned into my home street.

'Tomorrow night,' I told Steve. 'We want to pick the right time.'

'What we going to do to him?'

'After what he did – something that really hurts the bastard.'

'But what? He's armour-plated.'

I grinned. 'Give me time.'

Lawn Avenue reeked of normality. A road of Victorian town houses lined with lime trees that look terrific in the Spring. Kids riding bikes, and the sound of someone playing a piano floating through an open window.

I'd lived in Lawn Avenue all my life. It seemed nothing special to me, but Steve thought it posh. 'You know, I've never ever seen dog crap on the pavement round here,' he'd say.

'That's because all our dogs have their backsides sewn up at birth. You know, you can lay in bed at night and hear them in their kennels just bursting like balloons.'

As we walked up the driveway Steve asked, 'Still clean?'

'It better be.'

I checked my pickup. It wasn't one of Ford's most freshly minted vehicles but it was mine, it was paid for. I'd resprayed it myself a flame red then stencilled in white above the radiator grille its name – THE DOG'S BOLLOCKS.

That would have made Jack Aten laugh. Sometimes I'm sure I do half-crazy things to amuse his ghost.

'Clean as a whistle.' I patted the wing.

'Anyway, you don't think he'd be stupid enough to do the same again.'

'I don't see why not, Steve. He's got as much imagination as that worm there. Once he's learnt a good trick he'll repeat it ad nauseam.'

'Ad what?'

'Until we're sick of it, Steve, until we're sick of it.'

'It looks alright now.' Steve ran his fingers across the paint work. 'No scratches.'

'You should have seen it yesterday. Tyres flat – and he'd smeared shit all over it. Paint work, glass, lights.'

'Bastard.'

'It had set like concrete. And I'll tell you another thing.'

Steve raised his eyebrows.

'It wasn't dog shit.'

'You mean...

'I mean it was pure Slatter. I couldn't shift that stink out of my head all day.'

'What now?'

'Now we go inside and decide how we are going to hit back.'

'Hi, Steve. How's your dad keeping?'

My dad pulled himself to a sitting position on the sofa and brushed cake crumbs off his sweatshirt.

'Fine, thanks,' said Steve. 'He's taking a load of stone down south this weekend.'

'So I thought I'd babysit for him,' I said. 'And make sure Stevie doesn't get frightened all alone in that big, dark house.'

The three of us laughed easily.

Steve's mum and dad had divorced years ago. The weekends his dad worked away a few of the gang would stop over at his house and make a party of it. Lately a gang of girls had been promising to stay too. Suddenly weekends were starting to get not just exciting but electrifying.

I told my dad about the murder. He was as horrified as I expected him to be. He kept shaking his head in disbelief. That kind of thing just didn't happen in a small town like Doncaster.

He looked at his watch. 'I take it you two lads have come to interrupt my honest relaxation.' He reached down beside the sofa and came back with a can of beer. He smiled, exposing the gap in his top front teeth through which he could make the loudest whistle I've ever heard. 'It's not one of those video nasties again?'

'Not this week. I taped a concert last night. We thought we'd watch it this afternoon...that is, if you're not watching anything, eh...'

'This old horse opera?' My dad took a deep swallow of beer. 'It's only the one I saw the night I proposed to your mother. But you watch what you want. It's as bad as I remembered the first time around. You know nostalgia ain't what it used to be.'

He stood up. Cake crumbs showered onto the carpet.

'You're living dangerously,' I said. 'Mother will go absolutely, totally insane when she sees the mess.'

My dad pulled a face. 'I'm safe. I'll blame it on you two.'

He crossed the deep carpet that Mum hoovered with religious zeal every day and left the empty beer can on the window sill.

'Hey, Nick-Nick.' My fifteen-year-old brother called from the doorway, swinging a carrier bag in his hand. 'Got any spare cash?'

'Not if you're going to waste it on anything stupid like dictionaries and exercise books.'

'Nah. Robbo's selling me a couple of his CDs.'

'Thank God for that. It's time you started misspending your youth.'

'Don't listen to your brother,' Dad said. 'He'll either end up a millionaire or—'

'IN JAIL.' We chorused the old Aten catch phrase.

'There's some spare cash in my tin. Not the one shaped like a coffin. The one with the naked lady – so cover your eyes when you get it.'

John saluted. 'Thanks, Nick-Nick. You're a hero.'

The image of my brother standing there in the doorway, eyes flashing happily, big freckled face grinning, is nailed permanently to my mind. It was the last time I saw him alive.

He ran upstairs, his feet thumping heavily. I heard my bedroom door open, then footsteps crossing to the bedside table. A pause.

He was counting the money. He'd take not a penny more than he needed. I heard the feet pass back out onto the landing toward his room.

Then nothing more.

'You shouldn't give your hard-earned away like that, Nick.' Dad shook his head, smiling, flashing that gap in his teeth again. 'He gets money of his own.'

'I know, but he fritters it away on history books and junk like that.'

My dad picked up a hammer from the sideboard and pointed it at me playfully. 'I'll find out how much John's paying for them and I'll give you the money back Monday. Now watch that concert, I've got a job that needs doing upstairs.'

Casually swinging the hammer, he walked out of the room. I trawled through the drawer in the video cabinet for the tape. As always, I'd not bothered writing on the memo label so there would be a five-minute interval of swearing and false starts before I found what I was looking for.

As I pulled out the tapes Mum came in with a plateful of sliced cake and tea – all part of the Saturday afternoon ritual. In her track suit, her dark hair short and neat, she looked ten years younger than she was. Within minutes she would get Steve laughing and chatting shyly.

'I keep telling Nick he should get a decent office job like yours, Steve,' she said, smiling brightly.

'Oh, I think he enjoys what he does, Mrs Aten.'

'Judy.'

'Sorry…Judy. He couldn't stand being tied to a desk.'

'I hope the police never look in the back of that truck he drives. There are enough rumours about Mr Karowski to sink a battleship.'

Upstairs my dad had begun his DIY. Thump. Thump. Thump. It sounded like he was tapping nails into solid brick.

My mother chatted happily over the thumping, handing out more cake to Steve who could never bring himself to say no.

'Found it,' I said as pink lasers cut slices out of the TV screen.

'Oh, I'll leave you to it. Anyway, I've got a boatload of ironing to do. If you want anything I'll be in the kitchen.'

She left, singing lightly to herself.

As I stood up I noticed my dad's empty can. Lucky she hadn't seen that otherwise Dad would have been in for an ear-bruising. Crushing the can, I dropped it into the bin.

Upstairs the hammering stopped.

Suddenly something struck me as strange. Never, ever, in my seventeen years on this planet had I seen Dad drink beer of an afternoon.

'Looks as if it's going to be a good concert, Nick.'

It was. I sat down to watch it and forgot the beer can completely.

CHAPTER FOUR

LIFE IS A BASTARD

Steve kicked us out early.

Well, you have to agree, 8.30 is excruciatingly early for a Sunday morning. His dad was due home by midday so he needed to restore the house so it didn't look like a truckful of drunks had crashed through the front door. Which was more or less what had happened.

The girls we hoped would show, didn't. We ended up getting drunker while playfully shoving one another over the furniture.

The three of us hopped over Steve's back garden wall to cut across the fields, leaving Steve to do what he could with the house while repeating for the thirteenth time that morning:

'My dad's going to kill me when he gets home.'

With the morning sun already hot on our necks, we plodded across empty meadows. My mouth tasted as if a toad had died of the blister in there, then been buried beneath my tongue.

The others went their separate ways as we reached the edge of town, leaving me to plough the last mile through the long grass alone. What thoughts I could keep together mainly centred on how I could do the most damage to Tug Slatter.

I saw no one. I heard nothing. It was only a Sunday morning in Spring with nine-tenths of the population enjoying a lie-in.

I climbed the fence into our back garden, scaring the birds up into a blurry cloud. Then, cutting down the passageway into the front garden, I checked my pickup. Still clean. Slatter hadn't chosen to do an encore just yet.

I noticed my dad's car was missing from the drive. Nothing unusual about that. Some Sundays he'd drive into town to pick up the newspapers. My mother would probably still be in bed. My brother certainly would. Saturday nights he'd watch old horror films in his bedroom into the early hours – then sleep until lunchtime.

'HI HONIES, I'M HOME!' It was my customary greeting in a voice guaranteed to sandpaper anyone's nerves.

The usual 'Shut up! I'm trying to sleep!' never came. They were sleeping with the lid on that morning. I headed for the kitchen.

'Pigs!'

I shouted it again as I pushed a pile of hacked bread to one side of the table and clicked the top back on the butter tub.

If that was my dad who'd left the mess he was playing a dangerous game. Mum would go berserk. Not that he'd normally do something like this.

Come to think of it, he'd NEVER do anything like this. After eating his cornflakes he'd wash his dish then stick it back in the cupboard. The only other culprit could be—

'John! You are dead! You'd better clean this lot up before Mum sees it.'

No reply. Jesus...Maybe beneath that home-work-loving line-toeing fifteen-year-old there was a rebel after all.

Five minutes later I dropped my empty bowl in the sink and, still crunching a massive mouthful of cornflakes, I went upstairs.

Upstairs the house was tidy and quiet.

I changed into my slob-around jeans. Then I decided to roust John and mention the fact that if he wanted to live until lunchtime he would have to clean up the mess in the kitchen.

I pushed open the door.

And I saw something that stopped my breath. My brother's bedroom had ceased to exist.

Oh, the four walls and window were still there. But the stuff that made it my brother's bedroom wasn't.

The bed had gone. The wardrobes, furniture and all the posters of Greek temples and Egyptian statues had gone with it. Instead, in the middle of the floor, nearly touching the ceiling light, was a pyramid.

I stood there and actually laughed out loud.

What I saw was impossible. I laughed again. But this time it was forced. I began to feel cold. Like someone was slowly dipping me into a mountain lake.

Someone had been in here, taken the furniture and then smashed all my brother's possessions. Because that pyramid was built out of books, computer games, childhood toys, holiday souvenirs, comics...Everything that John had ever been given, collected, saved for, bought. Every fucking thing.

Jesus Christ.

That bastard...Slatter.

As I stood there I could see things in my mind's eye. Slatter looking through the bedroom window, bluebird tattoos at either side of his eyes, a grin hacking open his ape face. Then climbing in to smash the place to smithereens.

Tug Slatter had done this. I believed that. But what on earth had he done with the bed and furniture? Where was my brother? He'd have been asleep in here.

I saw it. But a big chunk of me did not believe it.

I didn't move. I just looked. My chest aching, my breathing sounding strange in my ears.

The bastard had been thorough. Far, far more thorough than when he'd done the job on my pick-up with the fruit of his own backside.

Books hadn't just been ripped in two. Every page had been torn to pieces the size of postage stamps. John's computer – he'd loved the thing, he actually polished it – had been reduced to bits the size of my thumbnail. Shaking my head, mind-kicked, I began picking through the pyramid.

Examining a fraction of computer game or a shred of one of John's precious history books. There was his video of the first man on the moon. As I touched it, it fell from the pyramid to expose more of John's treasures. His pirate chest money box, more computer games. A torn mask. A model car. A...

My fingers stopped above the mask. John never owned a mask.

But here was a life-size mask. It had partly open eyes. Lifelike hair. A nose...

I pushed my hand into the pyramid to pull at the mask. It wouldn't come. It had been fixed to something solid.

As I pulled somebody shoved the room. It spun so fast around me I could hardly see the walls and window flashing by. Only the mask stayed in focus.

Made from grey rubbery stuff, it was torn from mouth to ear, opening up a cheek like a parcel, exposing a row of teeth messed with red. The eyes reflected the light shining into the room, making it look as if they were alive. Or had been once.

I remember looking at the thing and seeing a mask. But I hear myself shouting:

'John! John! John!'

Then I was in the street. My throat burning like I'd drunk bleach. I was still shouting. This time for help.

It was like a dream – you shout but no one hears.

Lawn Avenue was empty. The trees shifted slightly in the morning breeze – and I stood there and screamed to a world with stone ears that my brother lay dead in his bedroom. His face nearly torn in two.

For more information about the *BLOOD CRAZY SERIES* and our other books, please visit:

Website: dv-publishing.com

Facebook: DarknessVisiblePublishing

Twitter: DV_Publishing

Instagram: dv_publishing